dating
da Vinci

A tale of love, longing,
and *la dolce vita*...

m a l e n a   l o t t

SOURCEBOOKS CASABLANCA™
AN IMPRINT OF SOURCEBOOKS, INC.®
NAPERVILLE, ILLINOIS

Published by Sourcebooks Casablanca, an imprint of Sourcebooks, Inc.
P.O. Box 4410, Naperville, Illinois 60567-4410
(630) 961-3900
Fax: (630) 961-2168
www.sourcebooks.com

Library of Congress Cataloging-in-Publication Data

Lott, Malena.
  Dating da Vinci / by Malena Lott.
     p. cm.
  ISBN 978-1-4022-1393-9
  1. Widows—Fiction. 2. English teachers—Fiction. 3. Teacher-student relationships—Fiction. 4. Austin (Tex.)—Fiction. I. Title.
  PS3612.O7775D38 2008
  813'.6—dc22
                          2008011977

                Printed and bound in The United States of America.
                   CHG 10 9 8 7 6 5 4 3 2 1

In loving memory of my grandparents who raised me
as their own. I miss you every day.

"To enjoy—to love a thing for its own sake and no other."
—*Leonardo da Vinci*

Chapter 1

I NEVER INTENDED TO take home da Vinci.

I don't mean "a da Vinci" as in a reproduction of the man's art, best known for his *Mona Lisa* and *Last Supper* paintings. I mean to say I took home Leonardo da Vinci, the living, breathing man; only not *that* man, the genius from the fifteenth century, but a young Italian immigrant who shared his name in modern day Austin, Texas.

It is far more accurate to say I took home Italian for dinner.

It began innocently enough, with me breaking my rule yet again not to get involved with a student, but I assure you I had never gotten *this* involved before.

My students, all adults ranging in age from their twenties to their sixties, shuffled into the cramped classroom with the wide-eyed wonder of children on the first day of school. I smoothed my blonde hair behind my ear and reviewed the student roster on my clipboard: eight students, five languages. Of the 6,912 known living languages in the world, I had personally encountered more than fifty in my role as an English language instructor to immigrants (including those speaking languages most Americans have never heard of, like Balochi, Dari, Pashto, and Tajik). But it wasn't an unfamiliar language that caused me to catch my breath. It was a name, jumping off the page like a typo or emblazoned in lights on a marquee. The usual: Miguel, Margarita, Jesús—Spanish; Helena—Swahili; Jayesh—Farsi; Pénélope—French. And lastly, the one that caused the hair on the back of my neck to stand: Leonardo da Vinci—Italian.

My best friend says that funny tickle is the breeze of fate telling you your life is about to change, but I'd been walking around in a fog so long I barely noticed.

I surveyed the students—none remotely resembling an Italian. I'd encountered people with famous names before: a homely grade-school friend named Elizabeth Taylor, a high-school boyfriend named Bill Clinton, even a wiry bank teller with the macho moniker of John Wayne, but someone named after perhaps the greatest genius of all time? This I had to see. I imagined he would resemble the only sketch I'd ever seen of the artist da Vinci: a self-portrait he'd made in his old age, with a crazy long beard and deep wrinkles. I wondered if Cecelia, my friend in admissions, was playing some kind of joke on me.

I watched my students take their places, smiles plastered on their faces as they exchanged pleasant nods to their classmates. A smile was the universal hello, even if it wasn't genuine, but it soon would be. I wished Americans could see how well the students got along: people from vastly different areas of the world, from all walks of life, from peasants in remote villages to descendants of royalty. My students shared one distinct characteristic that bonded them for life: they were outsiders desperately wanting in.

I could typically tell who was whom from their appearances. Their skin colors ranged from the very fair, belonging to a lanky French woman to the rich ebony of an African. Their dress was the second cultural marker, though you could tell how quickly they planned to assimilate if they wore American-style clothing.

I passed out the workbooks, noting that da Vinci was still missing, if he existed at all. Getting lost in America was common, something that we concentrated on heavily in the first six weeks—how to get from point A to point B was critical for survival. Each student carried a map with color-coded instructions. My building, the Panchal Cultural Center of Austin, was in orange. I noticed the map was the one item all my students carried in their hands. I waited a few minutes longer for da Vinci to show, but when he didn't, I started my class as I did each semester, with a welcome in my students' languages.

"*Karibu! ¡Hola! Bonjour! Xosh amadid!*" I welcomed them with a smile, my hands clasped together then widening in a warm gesture.

My students replied back in their native tongues, pleased that we had made a verbal connection. I knew the word *welcome* in a hundred languages, but was only fluent in four: German, French, Spanish, and English. As a linguist, I knew enough to get around in dozens of foreign countries though I'd never traveled anywhere outside of the United States, except for Mexico where I went with my husband every year for vacation. My heart paused as I thought of him, but soon resumed its normal rhythm. I'm not certain how long it takes a broken heart to mend, but I hadn't done anything to speed along its recovery.

In fact, my life had become so simple and routine that I began to believe survival mode was the only mode, or at least the only mode for me. My only source of adventure lay before me, the seven students who would hang on my every word, unlike my two sons, who grew more belligerent with each passing year, especially with their father gone. After Joel died, I wanted nothing more than to stop communicating altogether, yet finances forced me to work right through my grief. In the almost two years since Joel's passing, I found myself more comfortable with complete strangers from around the globe than I did with my friends and family.

I liked that each semester began with a blank slate—I did not know them, and they did not know me. They were floundering to make it in America, I was floundering to make it through another day. I had never had so much in common with my students. For the first time in my thirty-six years, I didn't fit in, either.

Our class began with a lot of non-verbal communication—pointing to charts and learning the signs they would encounter—stop signs, restroom signs, road signs, traffic signals—all important things that could keep them alive, fed, clothed, and not run over by a bus.

"Man," I said pointing to the bathroom sign. "Woman."

"Man," an Italian voice boomed from behind me. I turned from the chart and looked to the door, where my eighth student stood beaming with a smile and pointing to his chest, mastering his first spoken word of English in my class. *Man.* My mouth parted in surprise, for the man in front of me, masculine in every sense, was not an old man at all, but a young, gorgeous Italian with chin-length black hair, broad shoulders, and a tall frame. His brown eyes glistened under large black eyebrows, raised in an expression of pride. He wore cargo pants and a fitted long-sleeved T-shirt with a messenger bag slung over his shoulder. His smile, already on the first day, was genuine. I couldn't take my eyes off of him. Even Cecelia couldn't dream this guy up.

"*Benvenuto,*" I stammered shyly, then pointed to his seat, one off to the side so he wouldn't distract me.

"*Ciao, signora,*" he said, pointing to the sign of the woman and then to me. "Woman."

I nodded, feeling myself blush. He was only pointing out the obvious; he hadn't even complimented me, but the way he looked at me made my insides somersault. "*Mi chiamo* Ramona."

He leaned forward in his desk, which seemed too small for his muscular frame, and pointed to his chest again, this time his large hand over his heart. "*Piacere di conoscerla,* Ramona. (Pleased to meet you, Ramona.) *Mi chiamo* Leonardo."

"Da Vinci," I added. The class laughed. I pointed to Leonardo. "This man is Leonardo da Vinci."

The class recognized the famous name and laughed again. "*Sì,*" Leonardo said, twisting his body to face them, a large grin on his face. "This man is Leonardo da Vinci," he repeated after me in broken English.

After our two-hour lesson, I sent them out with a good-bye in their languages, ending with *Arrivederci* for da Vinci. Yet instead of leaving like his fellow classmates, he stood over my desk where I sat gathering my papers and making notes. I glanced up, my head even with his hips. I caught my breath again, his presence unsettling. He had to be at least six foot three. I stood, my five-foot-four frame coming up to his chest, my mind searching for its Italian language files, where I was conversational at best. I spoke to him in Italian. Leonardo replied quickly, and I tried to process as many words as I could. Key words enabled me to decipher the meaning from the context. I shall translate.

"May I help you, Leonardo?"

"*Sì*, Ramona. I need food, rent, sleep, job." Like I said, key words. He looked at me with those pleading dark chocolate eyes, his Roman nose and chiseled features like the ones the real da Vinci had probably carved a dozen times into statues. This modern da Vinci looked more like a Greek god than any mythological interpretation I'd seen. The only Italians I'd ever met were short men with dark mustaches who operated the Italian restaurants in Austin. But then again, I don't get out much.

I checked my watch. Cecelia would be gone by now, and I had to get to the school to pick up my boys for flag football practice. The social services department, which would help Leonardo with these matters, was closed on Mondays since they worked on the weekends. I couldn't very well leave him stranded, could I?

He smiled at me again, and I noticed the dimple in his right cheek and the deeper dimple in his chin. I couldn't say no to that most of all. I'd lived in a shell the last two years, so helping someone, especially a cute someone with a killer-watt smile, might be the remedy I needed for my depression. Prozac, among other things, wasn't cutting it.

"Come with me," I told him, and even as I said it, I wondered what I was doing. Where would I take him, a hotel? Shove the want ads in his large hands and order him a pizza? Panchal's tagline hung above the whiteboard: *One human race.* Panchal believed everyone belonged, and no one should ever be lost, physically or figuratively. So as a faithful employee, I took Panchal's torch and made sure da Vinci found his way. I didn't unlock his door on my black Toyota station wagon until I scooped the fast food bags and candy wrappers and empty drink cups and shoved them into an even larger McDonald's bag.

Junk food had become my therapy; its salty, fatty flavor was far more soothing than a therapist could ever be. Another unfortunate side effect of widowhood wasn't just the mess that my life had become, but the physical piles of grief everywhere I turned. I had become Linus and Pigpen from *Peanuts* all rolled into one, only my security blanket was around my heart. The Pigpen side of me, however, was evident in my car, the kitchen sink, the closets, you name it.

My mother liked to remind me what a neat freak I was Before, but I told her people change. People die and people change. Two of life's certainties. I should've become *more* organized After, yet all the effort left me so exhausted I stopped caring so much, save one thing: I dusted religiously for fear of dust mites. Have you seen those things magnified a thousand times? Creepier than a monster in a horror flick.

True, some Grievers become *better* people After like some of the heroic 9/11 widows who started non-profit foundations and pursued big dreams, but I don't get that. Until today when I'd felt compelled to help da Vinci, the only thing I'd cared about doing was downing double bacon cheeseburger and raising my boys.

Neatness became a part of my past like so many other things: happiness, joy, adventure, love.

"*Grazie,*" da Vinci said to me repeatedly as we drove down the interstate.

He made himself at home even in my car, fiddling with the mirror and changing the stations on the stereo.

"Rock and roll," he said, nodding his head to the beat of an old Beatles song.

"You like rock and roll?" I asked him in Italian. I wanted more than small talk. I wanted to know everything there was to know about this man in my passenger seat on day one. I told myself it was for insurance purposes; I shouldn't be driving around a complete stranger if he could be dangerous, though I doubted he could be. Even for his size, he looked like a gentle man—maybe it was the kind eyes or the fluidity of his movement. He moved like a dancer in the body of a linebacker.

Talking wasn't a problem for da Vinci. I understood enough to know that I liked him. He spoke lovingly of his homeland, his poor farming community outside of Milan, his four sisters, and he claimed to know a lot about women. I hadn't doubted that a bit. He was twenty-five, never been married, "because there aren't pretty girls like you." If that alone didn't turn me to putty, his next statement did: he missed his mother. (Okay, his mother's cooking, but *still*.)

Like many of my students, he was in America at the University of Texas on a student visa. *Lucky college girls*, I thought. He'd have them lined up for nude portraits in no time, even if he didn't sketch.

Most of my students were poor, scraping together whatever savings they had in their homeland to travel to America to live a better life. I wasn't surprised that da Vinci only had enough money for one month's rent and even then it would be at a cockroach-infested motel. I couldn't see a man this beautiful at an embarrassing excuse for American real estate.

"$200 for rent? I know the perfect place," I told him, my body feeling as light as air. "My studio apartment in the backyard of my house."

Da Vinci seemed very pleased, and because it had been a very long time since I'd pleased a man, I felt pleased myself.

Understand that I have never offered my garage studio to a student before, but then I had never met a student like da Vinci, either. I hadn't touched Joel's private workspace in two years, leaving everything as it had been the day he died. It belonged to Joel, and I felt in some ways that the space would never be anyone's but his. I had wondered if I would just turn it into a museum, my place where time stood still. But it was, by all accounts, time for the hands to start moving again. But how?

During our ride I gathered that da Vinci was not only *not* an ax murderer, but that he was honest, sincere, hardworking, and something I couldn't quite put my finger on, but it was something I'd lost and didn't believe I would ever find again. As I pulled into the elementary school's circle drive, it came to me.

La vita allegra. Joyful living. His eyes danced with excitement and awe and insatiable curiosity. Not just for America. For *life.* I ached to feel that again. This is why I gave him a ride. This is why I rented my late husband's studio for scraps. I hoped some of da Vinci's joy would rub off on me. Although I had meant it more in the metaphysical sense than the physical, that wouldn't be entirely bad, either.

I couldn't understand half of what da Vinci said, but who cared? It was nice to listen to a voice again. A nice baritone voice so different than the calming tone of my father or the tinny voice of my mother or, let's be honest, the whiny voices of my sons. Da Vinci was refreshing. Some women wish for Calgon to take them away; I wished for da Vinci to never stop talking. Or looking at me. Looking at me *and* talking. Especially the part where he'd said I was pretty.

"You'll have no problem making friends," I said as I pulled my station wagon behind a white Escalade. "I'll hook you up."

"Hook up?" he repeated. "Hook up Leonardo with Jessica Simpson?"

I laughed. "No, not *that* kind of hook up. I meant, I'll help you." So he liked blondes with big boobs and big shiny teeth. I checked my dishwater blonde hair in the rearview mirror, six months overdue for a coloring. The rugged gray strands in the middle stood like little Confederate soldiers, ready to shoot down any approach from a male suitor.

Even my teeth, one of my best assets, had coffee stains. What had gotten me out of bed the last two years besides my boys and caffeine? As for the rest, my sister got the boobs in the family and she'd had to pay for them. He probably thought I was old, that people in their thirties were boring has-beens, too settled down with jobs and kids for any adventure. That's what I'd thought when I was his age.

As we wheeled around the school pick-up line at a whopping two miles per hour, I thought about the last time I'd truly had an adventure. Not since Joel had passed, but before then? Six Flags? All that waiting in line and I didn't even ride the roller coasters. Not even one pseudo-adventure. Settled down was putting it nicely—like most families with young children, our lives were wrapped up in homework and after-school activities and playdates and just getting by. Now even that was hard to do.

Getting out of bed each day for the last two years, followed by the tasks most Normals do with ease—showering, fixing breakfast, going to the grocery store—had been difficult. Each menial task felt impossible, yet I did them, each day adding onto the other until the calendar and the change of seasons told me that the second anniversary of my husband's passing was fast approaching. The life insurance settlement that had kept us going was likewise dwindling to nothing. Who needs a big life insurance package before you hit 40? (Answer: *everyone*.)

It felt like slowly being strangled—the closer I got to the date, the more difficult I found it to breathe. The progress I'd made in becoming a functional human being again was slipping from my grasp. So I supposed da Vinci was a nice diversion, a bodyguard against my grief.

I knew it was time to buck up, to prove myself, to regain my place in the world, but the thought scared the hell out of me.

My car had reached tenth in line when I began noticing the stares. Moms who rarely waved to me took notice. Da Vinci was like a neon sign blinking *Ramona Got Her Groove Back*. What must they think? I waved back, both embarrassed and a little proud to be seen with someone who looked like him. I had replaced my *New York Times* crossword puzzle with da Vinci and I wasn't the trading-up kind of girl.

It was a welcome change from the pitying stares I, the poor, young widow, was used to getting—the awkward conversation and the polite invitations to dinner parties I would never attend without Joel by my side. Even worse had been the transition from the hushed conversation about me behind my back to the swelling tide of the world trying to hook me up. As in the Jessica Simpson-type of hook-up.

You see, the world is divided into two types of people: Grievers and Normals. Grievers want desperately to be Normal again, but the journey back seems impossible, and Normals don't understand why Grievers can't "move on" and "get over it." After all, death is just a part of life, right? *Life goes on.* As if.

For those who have never grieved, grief has an expiration date, and mine was imminent. They falsely assumed that time healed, and I didn't have the heart to tell them that I didn't *want* to grieve forever, but it was more accurate to expect more than two measly years. Grievers don't want Normals to know that if Normals lost *their* spouses they would likely never recover. Not fully, anyway. We can't be treated like an alcoholic or drug addict, but the wanting is there all the same. Unlike an alcoholic who could give in to temptation, our yearning can never be met. Even crazier is the idea that a lost love can be replaced with a new love, as if all love were equal. It wasn't that I didn't want to love again, either. It just seemed as plausible as Glinda the Good Witch in *The Wizard of Oz* granting me a wish in *her* tinny voice. But then if you had told me yesterday that I would have a gorgeous guy in my passenger seat, I would have denied that possibility, too.

The school bell rang, sending children pouring out of the school in a mob of multi-colored energy. I scanned the crowd, my eyes settling on a tall woman wearing a red suit—a suit I would not only not fit into but would look ridiculous in because one had to carry herself a certain way to pull off a cardinal-colored suit like that, and this woman, a dark-haired beauty, had what it took. When she spun around, my heart paused again for the second time that day. *Monica.* My cheeks flushed. I wanted to look away—*Just look away, Ramona,* I told myself—but she was like an accident at the side of the road and I falsely believed that if I stared long enough, I would understand what had happened.

My mom-in-law Judith had told me Monica's daughter was attending Lone Star Elementary now—a cute kindergartner by the looks of it, but I hadn't thought I would run into her. It's a big school, and I don't recreate with the PTA. I hadn't seen her since Joel's funeral when I'd wanted nothing more than to run up to her and shake her and demand answers. Wouldn't the world have thought I'd gone insane? Yet if they knew what I knew, or what I *thought* I knew, they wouldn't blame me a bit. But then I didn't know much, which is a part of the reason I couldn't take my eyes off of her until the rustle of my boys demanded my attention.

Bradley's mouth hung upon when he saw Leonardo in the front seat. "Are you a football player?" he asked, his blonde hair falling in front of his blue eyes. "Mom, is he my new private coach?"

"Right," I said, looking at my son in the rear view. "As if we can afford a private coach. Boys, this is Leonardo da Vinci, from Italy."

His little brother William, my dark-haired, dark-eyed version of Joel, viewed me skeptically through his wire-framed glasses. "Is this some kind of living history lesson?"

I had been known to drag my boys to cultural events now and then to encourage them to learn about the world outside of our Austin bubble. *There*, that had to account for adventure, hadn't it? We'd gone to museums and dance recitals and traveling exhibits. We tried new restaurants—Greek, Japanese, Thai. I was determined not to have my boys grow up on Chicken McNuggets and hamburgers alone, though the empty bag stuffed with trash proved even I couldn't resist the addictive junk.

"Can we go to Mickey Dee's before practice?" Bradley asked.

"McDonalds!" da Vinci said, recognizing the global franchise. I'd read that the golden arches were more recognized than Jesus Christ or the President of the United States. A large fries and chocolate shake wouldn't hurt. I hadn't had one in what, 24 hours?

My car perpetually smelled of French fries, the perfume of greasy Heaven. How could I blame them? I checked my watch again. "Fine. But when you're done with practice, we're going to sit down and have a real meal together. Something Italian, perhaps."

William nodded his head enthusiastically. "Does this mean we get to learn to speak Italian, Mom?"

Bradley groaned. He had enough problems mastering the English language.

I glanced over at da Vinci, again messing with the controls on my stereo, something I had always slapped Joel's hand for. I had to admit it was nice having someone fiddle with my knobs again.

"*Sì, è certo,*" I winked at William. "Yes, it does."

Chapter 2

I COULDN'T MOVE THE peanut butter. It wasn't just any peanut butter, but the kind my husband had eaten nearly every day of his life. His mother had said once he got a taste of it, everything else lost its flavor. His father, not knowing at the time that peanut butter was bad for babies, had put a scoop on his finger and given it to his then eight-month-old son. Joel had bitten down so hard on his father's finger with his only tooth that he'd drawn blood.

I'd made the mistake of trying to switch things up over the years, like the time we were in a money crunch and I bought a lower-priced brand (*I only eat Peter Pan*, he'd said to me as if I'd betrayed him), and the time I bought the peanut butter/jelly swirl to save time (*How could you?* he'd asked, only half-joking), so I learned never to veer from the sacred Peter Pan smooth (*never crunchy, honey*) peanut butter.

Joel's ritual was a peanut butter and jelly sandwich on wheat bread for lunch, peanut-butter honey on toast snacks at 3 p.m. while sitting at his architectural drawing board in the studio, and peanut butter vanilla smoothies every Saturday afternoon after his basketball game at the neighborhood park. The jar was nearly empty, the last remnants used to surprise Joel with the smoothie he never got to drink. And yet.

The cupboard would be empty without the peanut butter. The pantry, stocked full to feed two growing boys, would no doubt feel bare without it. The cruel twist of fate was that our boys preferred turkey sandwiches, something for which Joel blamed my DNA contributions.

"I can't believe it's been two years," Anh said as we cleaned out the cupboard, as if I weren't keenly aware of every day without him. She knew sympathy stares were off-limits. I needed to not feel like a widow on exhibit around *someone*, and for me that person was Anh Ly, aptly named for "intellectual brightness" and "lion," my best friend even when I was the last person on earth anyone would want to be friends with. "It's okay to get rid of the peanut butter."

I felt the familiar squeeze in my chest that told me it would not be okay, that throwing away the peanut butter would be throwing away his memory. It's the small things that become giant calling cards of grief after someone you love dies. For me, it was peanut butter and a hundred everyday items and the larger ones, too: the hand-me-down sofa and our marital bed, which we'd named Lumpy with good reason. I shook my head vigorously and bit my bottom lip. I took the jar from her hand and curled it into me protectively. The thing is, when I lost Joel, my life lost its flavor, too.

I wondered if Monica had made Joel peanut butter smoothies when they had been together. She didn't seem like the nurturing type, though I have no proof to base this on other than that she hurt my husband; Judith believed the red Monica so bravely wore stood for she-devil, end of story. I wished Judith were more of a gossip, like my mother, because she was mum when it came to Monica. "Swore never to speak that woman's name again," she said right after she told me that I could be running into her at the school. Why even mention her at all unless there was something I should know? Whatever had happened between them, time hadn't healed. Judith, for so much as preaching how God forgiveth, apparently could not forgive Monica for the transgressions against her only begotten son.

Seeing Monica that day in the parking lot made me realize I couldn't move on until I knew the truth about what happened with Monica and Joel before he died. I wanted to tell Anh this, too, because she was famously good at helping me wade through the muck of emotions that pulled me down like quicksand.

"Fine, we'll leave the peanut butter," Anh said, moving on to the stale chips (trash) and canned food (charity). "But we know it's about more than peanut butter, Ramona. I want you to start considering having a little fun again."

"It's *only* been two years," I told her, switching the emphasis to make it apparent I thought this was a very short time to be without your soul mate, even though every day had dragged on as if it had been years since I'd last seen him, last touched him. I'd been dreading the cooler days, the green draining from the leaves and falling to the ground like nature's countdown to the anniversary of his death.

"This is not a 'moving on' speech. This is one best friend to another throwing out the idea of a little fun. Not a *lot* of fun, just a little something to stir your spirit," Anh spoke with authority, and it wasn't just because she was the CEO of a big accounting firm or because she was voted the Vietnamese Business Woman of the Year. Not a local award or even a national award, mind you, but an *international* award. This much I knew: I was absolutely no fun, though people tell me I used to be.

Fun. If some believe grief has an expiration date, does fun have a start date after losing a soul mate? Or does it just creep up on you when you least expect it? I knew my double-PhD girlfriend was not referring to frivolous fun, like a carnival ride or even a spa retreat.

She meant what da Vinci had: *la vita allegra.* Of course I wanted it, but my joy jar was as empty as the peanut butter. She understood how hard it was to step out in to the world of the living where I believed Normals take everything for granted: their relationships, their health, their marriages. Most people did not find joy in the mundane, and *they* had their families intact. So how could I? I'd gone to bed hoping for an answer, but I'd woken up in the same empty-bed feeling, the thud of loneliness that rose as ritually as the sun.

"At least you've got your class. Anyone interesting this semester?" she said, throwing a bag of old flour in the dumpster.

This would be a great time to tell her that I had done something insanely spur-of-the-moment, acting on impulse, letting fate be my guide—all those things Joel had been known for. He was the spontaneous one who pulled me along for the ride—since then I was as useless as a deserted red Radio Flyer with no one to take me away.

"Well, there is this one guy," I started.

Anh held a loaf of moldy bread in her hands. I wish I could've blamed that on one of William's self-made science projects, but it was my own negligence. When Joel was around, the bread had never lasted long enough to grow mold. "A guy-guy? Not just—there-is-this-man-from-Timbuktu guy, but a *guy-with-dating-potential* guy?"

Dating belonged with fun—two words that could not be found in my personal dictionary. Most people had been patient with me, broaching the subject of "getting back out there" casually as if I didn't feel it like a sledgehammer. But when she said the word "dating," it didn't feel like a blow. It sounded like a normal word, like "broccoli" or "sidewalk" or "orange." Perhaps it was because she said it after she'd asked if there was anyone interesting and my brain had conjured the image of da Vinci and though he was very much foreign, the idea of him in a romantic sense was not foreign to me. But I hadn't thought of da Vinci as dating material *for me*—for the hot, under-thirty set, sure—but not for *me*, the over-thirty, widowy-type. "Hold up. I just said interesting. All of twenty-five, gorgeous, full of life, and happens to be named Leonardo da Vinci."

Anh slapped my arm. "*Hoan hô! Hoan hô!*," she cheered, laughing. "Maybe that's just the spice you need in your life. Someone carefree and void of sticky emotional baggage. Take advantage now before he meets too many people."

"What are you saying?" I said defensively. "That he would only be interested in me until something better comes along?"

Anh gave me the once-over, from my hair in the '80s scrunchie to the worn-down Birkenstocks on my feet. What lay between wasn't any better: an oversized hooded UT sweatshirt of Joel's and black sweatpants (faded to gray) with holes in the knees. Anh may not wear makeup tested on animals and use only organic hairspray and eschew leather, but she was stylish and put together. Anh, who was the first person I'd known to ever wear Birks, didn't even wear them anymore. "Well ..."

"Just come out and say what you're thinking. I can see the motor turning."

"Fine," she said, putting one hand on her slender hip and the other hand on my shoulder. "Let's just say you and your bread have something in common."

"I'm moldy?" I asked.

"No, Ramona. *Stale.* And the thing is, I know that you know this. You're just refusing to do anything about it, because that would mean you have to wake up and breathe again and shed that coat of protection you've been wearing. You don't want men to find you attractive anymore because lo and behold, if they do, you'll have to do something about it. Like kiss them, or have sex, or have a man-woman relationship again. And I'm not saying that you *should* do that—definitely not until you're ready and only you know when that is. And the only person women should try to look good for is them-selves, and you don't even want to do that. That's all I'm saying. With love, from Anh."

I rolled my eyes, something I often did when the other person was right and I, the linguist, couldn't find the words for a decent refute. "I've *been* making an effort. I started wearing mascara again a month ago. Have you not noticed?"

She leaned in and studied my lashes. "Well, I'll be damned. Good for you. The blush and lip gloss must be jealous, though." She swept her arm around me and planted a kiss on my forehead.

Unlike my mother and sister, Anh was fairly lenient about my image, or lack thereof.

Most Normals agree Grievers should get some slack in the grooming department. I had taken that platitude for granted. I often wondered if Joel peered down from Heaven, wishing I would have some fun again. He was the type of husband who gave me compliments when I looked my worst, bed-head and morning breath included, so it wasn't about what was outside. What bothered me most was that my outside so clearly reflected my inside.

I placed the peanut butter back on its perch. So many Grievers put on the makeup like a mask and I had refused to do it. I would not dress the part of a Normal until I felt it. For the first six months, I couldn't believe he was gone, waiting for him to walk through the door at 5:30 p.m. sharp or step out of the shower or to catch a glimpse of him through the front window, watering the flowers. I searched everywhere for him during those six months, as if imagining him still living would make it so.

What I missed most of all was his presence, his sense of being, and even after two years, I wasn't content in an empty house. But after a year, I no longer had to remind myself to breathe, and though the pain still came in like a tide to shore, the tsunami had lost some of its strength.

When I would tell Anh that my mother dropped hints like little bombs about nice men she'd met, Anh would shrug it off with a laugh and say, "Tell her to send one Grandma's way." Thanks to a one-night-stand in college, her son had produced a daughter, though the union had not produced two willing parents. So Anh ended up with her granddaughter Vi, though she denied she was raising her (which she was). Anh was one of those people who could remove the pricks of pain with a quick jerk and make it all better.

I shuddered. "I've watched those dating reality shows, and I have two words for you: *Hell, no.* I'm happy alone and *that's* why a makeover is a moot point," I said, as if it were justification for my slobwear. The happy part was a lie, and everyone knew it. I hadn't been content in my misery, but it hung around me like thick coat I couldn't shed. I wasn't so naïve as to believe the phony smiles I put on for school or the grocery store were fooling anyone. But what man in his right mind wanted to date a grieving woman with two boys, anyway? I was about as attractive as a bug zapper on a summer's night.

Anh smoothed her jet-black hair and reapplied her red lipstick. I wished I could wear red lipstick, but much like the red suit, you have to have the red inside of you to wear it on the outside, and the one time I tried it in my twenties, I looked like a bad imitation of Anna Nicole Smith.

"What the hell do I know?" she said. "Never listen to a woman who's been divorced thrice, yet still throws herself to the sharks as if she doesn't have a brain in her head."

"I'm *not* listening to you, but thanks for the permission. Besides, I'm going to be much too busy for dating. I've decided to finish my doctorate."

"Look at you! Dusting off the old dissertation. It's about time. You know the world has a shortage of good word doctors."

"You're just jealous because when we go out you won't get to be the only doctor anymore."

"Right. I believe my doctorates in metaphysics and accounting have been a nice repellent to my love life."

"All the more reason I should get mine, stat."

"You'll be Professor Dr. Griffen before we know it. And I can say I knew you when you were just a geek with the *New York Times* crossword."

"Some things will never change."

"Like I've said," Anh continued. "When you're ready, you can get your chakras in alignment again. Especially chakra two." She pointed to my nether region.

I knew enough from listening to her chakra talk over the years that chakra two controlled sexuality. "That chakra's bulb blew out two years ago. How can I possibly have sex with another man and not have it feel like cheating?"

"Have you at least been using Mr. Pleasure 2000?"

"I threw it away," I told her. "Right after my mother nearly had a heart attack when she found it in my nightstand."

Her insistence that connecting mind and body and getting my chakras in order would cure my heartbreak and improve my life was as annoying as my mother's insistence that joining her church would kill two birds with one stone—Jesus would heap blessings on my life *and* land me a nice Christian man, to boot. *When that time comes,* she would add. But the sheer fact she had to add that as a footnote told me that she believed I might shrivel into a lonely cat lady after the boys were grown if I didn't play nice with others.

"It's not about finding a man," Anh said. "It's about living again. That's all we want for you, Ramona. It's the one thing me, your Jesus-freak mothers and your Energizer Bunny sister all have in common." My mother and mother-in-law were both evangamoms at Life Church. Joel used to joke we were book-ended with the Lord. Judith was the first to embrace my mother Barbara when she "found the Lord" at the age of 45. It had been Judith's personal mission to bring all of us into the holy fold thereafter. I was in college, having spent the better part of my childhood bounced from church to church while my mother tried to find one that fit her like a designer suit. She found her fit at Life and a best friend in Judith, which is how Joel and I met.

Joel preferred to tell people we met at a chocolate-wrestling tournament where I was a contestant (and blue-ribbon winner). "One lick and I was hooked," he would tell the shocked listener.

Truthfully, our moms set us up. Joel had just gone through a tremendous break-up, his wedding to the she-devil Monica called off, and besides some quality time with the Lord, Judith thought the best remedy was for him to "get back out there." Sound familiar? As for the remedy for *my* broken heart After, she *only* recommended the Lord. "You'll never find anyone like my Joel," Judith tells me on a weekly basis. And I wholeheartedly agree with her.

The doorbell rang. "Speak of the devil," I said, knowing it would be my mother on her daily visit.

"You mean speak of the Lord," Anh corrected me with a wink as she headed out the garage. "And find da Vinci. American women will be crawling all over him like horny ants at a hunk picnic."

She was gone before I could tell her that finding da Vinci would not be a problem since he was all of ten yards away, and that he was not just a student, but a tenant. If anyone would confirm that I was off my rocker for moving him in, it was Anh. But I couldn't date a student, even if he was an adult, as if the idea weren't preposterous enough if he wasn't.

A little companionship might be nice, though. Dinner had gone well the night before. Da Vinci was a tremendous cook and a quick learner. The boys got a kick out of running around the room pointing at objects and making da Vinci guess what they were in English and giggling when he was wrong. He called a clock a wheel and a fork a spoon and the butter butt. At least he was trying. And if da Vinci could tackle the English language and a foreign world, I could make a go of a new world, too.

I'll admit I liked that they liked him. If they hadn't, I would've handed him his walking papers, gorgeous or not. I'd nearly backed out of letting da Vinci stay in the studio when we entered and I found Joel's things exactly where I'd left them, where *he'd* left them, and I wished for a sign from Joel that I wasn't making a huge mistake, that he was fine with using his space for rent, but the guilt chewed at me like a puppy on a shoe. Unlike some Grievers who claim to "feel" their loved ones with them everywhere they go, I couldn't feel Joel. All I felt was anger, sadness, loneliness. Besides, I didn't believe in signs, did I?

I believed in words. Even if a brisk breeze suddenly whirled through the room knocking his pencil cup off the desk, I'd demand it in writing. A note from the beyond. Still.

Choking back tears, I had moved Joel's coffee cup to the cupboard, left the sketch of the hospital he'd been working on on his drafting table, and asked that da Vinci try to leave everything as is. He seemed to understand, though immigrants often nod their heads when they have no idea what's being said.

"I see you're bright and shining as usual," Barbara said upon entering, in a sing-song voice that was really meant as a put-down of my attire and lack of spit and polish. Pre-Joel's death, I would've gotten a "why-can't-you-be-more-like-your-sister" speech. My dear sister, who, after she found her husband keeping a mistress on the side, lost forty pounds and in two years became the "go-to girl" for fitness in the Lone Star State. After she was nice and rich and famous, she dumped her husband and now dated with incredible ease. I actually preferred her when she was fat.

Now my mom took it relatively easy on me, too busy worrying about me to nag. I had to remind myself that she made her daily invasion into my personal life because she cared. She couldn't imagine a life without my father and she had loved Joel nearly as much I had. As a result, she took my little family on like a full-time job—keeping up on everything from the latest parenting advice to what's cool with boys so she could somehow make up for what my kids were missing without their father. Of course, we knew this wouldn't work, but when Joel died she and my father did turn into Super Grandparents, taking the kids on quarterly vacations and spending more quality time with them than they ever did with my sister and me growing up. With them and Judith and her new banker husband Bob, my kids got plenty of attention, though I still worried every day it wasn't enough because it wasn't from their father.

Barbara handed me a stack of magazines—she hated to be wasteful and throw them away—and I cringed. I don't believe in signs. Anh does. My evangelical mothers do, of course. *God is trying to tell you something*, they would say to me. If this was true, what did it mean that Monica Blevins was on the cover of *Austin Monthly*? I preferred to believe it was just a coincidence; as for the cover, well, she was like Anh, a mover and a shaker. Movers and shakers often get photographed for covers of magazine. It had nothing at all to do with my desire to confront her about Joel.

I placed *Better Homes and Gardens* on top of her picture and sat the stack next to the chair on top of the stack from last week. My mother really should know better. The stack would eventually cause its own avalanche and my boys would step on them, using them as roller skates on the carpet, and eventually my mother would pick them up and throw them in the trash without my ever having read them, which is what she should've done in the first place.

Barbara clicked on my sister's show, *Get Up and Move It, Texas!*, her statewide fitness show that I TiVoed, vowing to work out to it later in the day (unlike her, I wasn't a morning person), but I never got around to it, morning, noon or night. My mother, who watched the show faithfully every morning while sipping her coffee, liked to come over and watch my sister again while she helped me do laundry. (While many single moms take care of these duties on a daily basis without any help and Joel didn't even know how the dryer knobs worked, she insisted.) I'd always hated laundry and wished she would've volunteered for the chore years ago, but after Joel died, I missed doing *his* laundry. Normals believe it is a menial task—wear clothes, dirty clothes, wash clothes—an endless cycle. But a Griever sees laundry as a spoke in the cycle of life. No laundry, no life.

My mother wore slacks and a button-down blouse more appropriate for church or a business office, though she'd never worked a day in her life outside of her home. She considered the church her other full-time job, and belonging to a congregation of 10,000 people meant she was never bored.

Some might say my mother was an enabler, keeping me from cleaning up my own messes, but others might just say she was a mother who loved her daughter and could see that her daughter, for whatever reason, still needed some help. Even with my mother annoying me no end, I weighed the pros and cons and decided that I could put up with whatever she had to dish out—so long as she also did the dishes.

Besides bringing good food and helping hands into the house, she brought commotion with her. It was the stillness of the world without Joel that rattled me the most. I missed the quiet noise of having a partner in my life—the sound of his shuffling down the hall, his heavy breathing in his sleep, his throaty laughter during dinner, his spirited cries during a football game on TV. At first I'd gone to crowded places, believing that any noise could make up for it—the mall, fairs, sporting events. But all I did was prick my ears for the sound in the crowd I longed to hear most, and it never came.

"I met the nicest fellow last night," Mom said as she separated our brights and whites. I started to roll my eyes before reminding myself that I was docking my boys' allowances each time I caught them rolling theirs. It was rude and where there were rolling eyes, there were words not being said. So far I'd be dinged $2 today, but who would hold me accountable?

"Not now, Mom."

Barbara shut the washer door with a thud and shook her head. "Is this what it's come to, Ramona? I can't even have a conversation with you if it involves a person of the opposite sex? I feel like if I even say the word 'man,' you'll snap at me."

I immediately thought of da Vinci pointing to his chest in the doorway of the classroom bellowing the word, *man*. I definitely preferred the way he said it.

My mother flinched (she'd always been sensitive) and I knew that deep down she only wanted the best for me. I apologized and hugged her and went to pour her black coffee, as strong as her religious convictions. "Tell me about the person of the opposite sex if you really think I should know."

We sat on the back patio and drank our coffee. The cool morning required a jacket, and I gazed at the empty flowerbeds thinking how pretty maroon and gold mums would look in them, and orange pansies. They were Joel's favorite, though he made me promise I would never tell anyone a feminine-sounding flower like pansy was his favorite. If I planted flowers, that would mean autumn was here and I wouldn't do anything to speed along its coming.

I hadn't mentioned da Vinci yet, though I could see him stirring through the window of the studio across from us, but as usual, my mother didn't let me get a word in edgewise.

"He's a doctor," she went on. "An anesthesiologist at Mercy. Has a daughter from his first marriage, been divorced for three years and he's on the building committee with your father at church. Noble just thinks the world of him. They're playing golf together this Saturday."

I couldn't take my eyes off of the window, where every few seconds I could see his dark hair pop into view. After awhile I figured out he was doing sit-ups, something I hadn't done since scrunchies were in style. Thinking about his abs, though I'd never seen them, turned me into butter.

"Are you listening to me, Ramona Elise?" Her gaze followed mine, but da Vinci was nowhere in the frame. "Whatever are you looking at?"

"Of course I'm listening. Dad's golfing with a doctor from Mercy this weekend. Just what I need. Someone that puts people to sleep for a living. Is he handsome?"

"Quite handsome, though I only have eyes for your father," she said. My mother pointed out handsome men everywhere we went, yet she always followed it with that statement as if it made her less guilty for noticing. "And what's wrong with an anesthesiologist? He keeps people alive while they're unconscious. It wouldn't hurt to find a new friend. That's all. A friend. Judith and I have discussed it."

"So now you and my mother-in-law are discussing my having male friends? Did the Lord send you a sign?"

Barbara batted her eyelashes. Unlike me, my mother claimed to get signs from the Lord on a near-daily basis. "It just came up. There's a singles mixer we thought you might be interested in. Just for making friends, that's all. Doesn't have to be romantic."

"I have friends," I told her, glancing back up at the garage studio window. In truth, I had Anh and my international friends of my cul-de-sac, mostly former students, and a couple of friends at work. Parenting and Joel had taken up all of my time for the last ten years. More friends would've seemed a luxury I couldn't afford. "Besides, Judith has told me repeatedly how uncomfortable it would make her if I began dating."

"Of course it would. She's not ready for that, but then neither are you, so what does it matter? But a friend wouldn't hurt, darling. Even Judith thinks so."

"Yeah. You said that already."

Barbara sipped her coffee, her bright eyes taking in the outdoors. My mother had a peppy personality (inherited by my sis, not me), but then she wasn't yet a Griever. Even my grandparents were both still living. Judith on the other hand, was a Griever. Her world had been wrapped up into Joel, her only child, and she had transferred that attention to her grandsons, which was both a blessing and a curse. "Why don't we do something fun today, Ramona? What do you say? We could meet your sister for lunch and buy you a new outfit. You haven't let me shop for you in ages."

I recalled the moose sweater she'd given me for Christmas last year and shuddered. I'd cried not because I hated it, but because I couldn't laugh about it later with Joel. I peered at the window again and then down at my slob wear. Well, a new outfit couldn't hurt. Fun had been taken from its dusty box in the basement, brushed off and ready to open.

"Something nice for a singles mixer, maybe?" I said, half-kidding. "Why do I think this won't end well? But what the hell," I said and her right arm shot into the air as if Bob Barker had told her to "come on down, you're the next contestant on *The Price Is Right*."

The one thing my mother loved nearly as much as her church and volunteering was marathon shopping. I had to admit she was devilishly good at it. "Really?" she'd said as if I were pulling her leg. "I'll call Rachel and Judith and we'll make a day of it. You go get washed up and changed then."

While my mother went back into the house to call Rachel, I watched the Panchal taxi cab pull into my side driveway and honk for da Vinci to take him to the center for his job placement interview. A moment later, he emerged wearing corduroy jeans and a T-shirt, his hair still wet from a shower. I imagined how cramped he would've been in the tiny shower stall, and thinking of him naked, stooped under the low shower head, made me feel weak.

Leonardo descended the rickety steps and looked at me, the sun shining on his flawless face, and waved to me. "*Buon giorno.*"

"Good morning," I said back, and meant it.

Like the little devil on my left shoulder, my mother exhaled behind me, "My Lord, Ramona. Who in Heaven is that?"

Chapter 3

RACHEL TALKED ABOUT HER favorite topic while we dined on tuna salad sandwiches (because I was in skinny company) in the food court at lunch: herself. The world according to Rachel contained only three things: her career, her looks, and her love life. While Anh referred to her as the Energizer Bunny, I couldn't help but think she did the opposite of a battery and actually drained my energy instead of boosting it. Her enthusiasm might be contagious to "get off your couch and shake your groove thing, Austin," but it didn't work on me.

She looked fabulous as usual with her tiny, size-2 figure and perky breasts and gleaming blonde hair recently lowlighted. She was two years younger than me, though I'd heard her lie to people and say she was twenty-nine on more than one occasion. She had one daughter, Zoe, who was bowed up and ready for a pageant even on non-pageant days. Her fourth favorite topic, if I were keeping track, would be Zoe and her misadventures in the pageant world. For, unlike her mother, Zoe had no charm, charisma, or personality. She was low-key like me. And she was all of five, for goodness's sake, and her camera-hogging mother couldn't fathom that nature had given her a bookish, inquisitive, athletic girl who questioned everything on the planet instead of a mini-Rachel starlet in the making. I adored her and on a weekly basis thought the best thing for me to do would be to raise her as my own so she'd have a chance.

Zoe joined us for lunch because she only attended a half-day kindergarten, though her afternoons were spent in an endless juggling act of dance, gymnastics, and cheerleading. The only time my otherwise chipper sister had bitten my head off was when I'd suggested, upon seeing a sad dance recital where my niece was two steps behind the other little girls, that perhaps Zoe had inherited my awkward rhythm.

We'd shopped for three hours already and while my mom and sister's bags piled high next to their seats, the only thing I'd gotten is the terrible confirmation that my mid-section needed lipo and some of da Vinci's morning sit-ups. Being a junk food addict did have its side effects, namely thunder thighs and a jiggly badonkadonk.

Having someone like da Vinci as a personal trainer just might make me stick to a workout routine. That doughy area that sits atop the pants' waistline was called a muffin top, my sister informed me after I tried on a pair of pants that would've fit me two years earlier. No wonder I hadn't shopped for myself since Joel died. Jogging suits (not used to jog) were my primary wardrobe.

My stomach growled as soon as I'd finished my sandwich, proof that my appetite was spoiled and indulgent. But no more. Today I was going to start taking back control, starting with what went into my mouth. To prove I was serious, I would pass by the fast-food chains on my way home without even glancing at their evil bright signs, let alone turn into the drive-thru where sadly, all the workers knew me by name. Thanks to the excruciating task of trying to squeeze into sizes I once wore with ease, I realized the huge void in my life could not be filled with powdered donuts and cheeseburgers. If only I'd realized that twenty pounds ago.

"Mom tells me you have a hot Italian living in your studio," Rachel said as she pushed away the cookie I tried to get her to eat.

"What's this?" Judith asked, her red lip pursing in surprise. Judith looked like she'd just had a Mary Kay makeover every time you saw her. Coiffed hair, heavily lined lids, powdered-to-perfection face.

"Oh, he's a student," I said nonchalantly. "He only had $200 for rent so I thought he could stay in the studio for a bit until he starts earning more money."

"That's our bleeding-heart Ramona," my mother said.

Judith crossed her manicured hand over her heart, as if she were having chest pain. "In *Joel's* studio?"

I cleared my throat. "Well, yes. But it hasn't been used."

Judith's brows went up. "I suppose I could come help you pack Joel's things out there."

She had been in the camp that believed you did not have to get rid of the deceased's belongings. In fact, Joel's bedroom in her house was the same as it had been in high school, complete with his trophies and party pics (though Joel had scratched out Monica's face with a black marker after the wedding had been called off) and even the clothes in his closet. Judith was certain, even after we got married, that he might long for a T-shirt or red checked Polo or any number of the clothes she had so lovingly purchased for him over the years.

"Oh, that's not necessary, Mom G," I said, patting her arm. "It's just a few things, and I'm going to keep them."

"Of course you are. But if you decide you don't want them any longer, please give them to me. I couldn't stand his things being thrown out."

I took a sip of diet Coke, while my sister kicked me under the table. She thought Judith's preoccupation with Joel, even in his death, was a bit much. But then she wasn't a Griever, so she would never understand.

"How about giving your sister the hook-up?" Rachel said, turning the conversation back to herself.

I considered my sister's blonde hair, the C-cup breasts "Santa" gave her for Christmas three years earlier and her sparkling white teeth. She wasn't Jessica Simpson, but she was a close clone. He would like her. "He doesn't speak English," I told her.

She flipped her long hair. "Not seeing the problem, Sis. Haven't you heard of the universal language?"

I nearly choked on my diet Coke. "Love? You're not falling in love with da Vinci." Over my dead body.

"Thanks, brainiac. My plans don't include love or verbal communication. Body language of *another sort*." She giggled and my mother shook her head as if to disapprove, but smiled anyway. Judith forced a smile, though I gathered she wasn't one of my sister's biggest fans, something Mom Griffen and I shared besides our love for Joel and the boys. I thought about telling them about my dissertation on the language of love, the one that I'd benched After because it was the last language I wanted to speak and doubted I would ever speak again. If everyone in the world can speak the language of love but me, who am I to write about it?

I grabbed the cookie she wouldn't eat and stuffed it in my mouth. Rachel leaned in and shook her French-manicured finger at me. "Look who's proclaimed herself the bodyguard to the hot immigrants! Well, Mom's setting me up with a handsome doctor, anyway. I hope he lives in a gated community with a pool in his back yard."

Before I could remark on how shallow my sister was I glared at Barbara. "Mother! You're giving her the doctor you were giving me?"

Barbara's face softened. "Just because your sister might go out on a date with Dr. Cortland Andrews doesn't mean you can't also be friends with him."

Judith nodded in agreement. "So your mother told you about our idea for the Life singles group, then?"

My voice shrilled. "I have male friends. Michael, for one." I shot a glare at my sis.

"My ex?" Rachel shrieked. "I wouldn't say that out loud."

"He's not a good influence," Barbara said.

"He broke one of the Ten Commandments," Judith said, then added in case any of us had forgotten, as if Rachel didn't remind us and her public all the time, "Thou shalt not commit adultery."

I kept my tongue to myself to keep from lashing out that perhaps even her own son had broken a commandment, the very same one, and that now I was determined to find out if it was true. Even if I did find out he had cheated with his ex-fiancée, I knew I couldn't burst Judith's bubble about her only son. "Well, Michael's not my only male friend. I have da Vinci now."

My mother giggled. "Oh, Judith. You should see him. He's quite a looker."

"Whatever would you have in common with him?" Judith asked.

I began to formulate a list, but then thought how ludicrous it would be to have to prove to any of them the who and why of my friendships. Da Vinci and I could be friends. And so could this Cortland fellow. Just because I was a widow did not make me unfriendly, though Anh would probably take me to task on that one. She had said the Seven Dwarfs I most resembled were Sleepy, Bashful, and Grumpy. I told *her* to try raising two boys on her own and grieving a soul mate and see if she came up any different.

Rachel flicked her golden hair, giving me the puppy-dog stare she often did her viewers when she looked into the camera and told them she knows how hard it is to get off that couch. "It's okay, sugar. You'll always have us," she said and it dawned on me that this is what my new Normal looked like. If I continued down this path, having my mother visit on a daily basis would turn into a permanent situation. These three musketeers would try to steer my life from here on out.

My new Normal did not seem like a big step up from my Griever life. No way. This couldn't happen to me. If it was time to transition to a Normal, it had to be on my terms, not taking the scraps of others' sympathy to piece together a life without Joel.

I thought about the binder back home in Joel's office—the one where I'd stuffed everyone's articles, magazine ads and letters with ideas on how to deal with my grief. So far the only recommendation

I'd taken was attending a Parents without Partners class, which focused more on parenting needs than personal ones. Because, really, I wasn't worried about *me*. It was my boys, fatherless boys who would grow up into fatherless fathers, who most concerned me. I'd been most concerned about. And luckily they were still young enough that they opened up to me and shared their feelings. It was *I* who hadn't fared so well in the sharing department. It was *I* who hadn't done a single thing to try to recapture *la vita allegra*.

Finding joy would not happen in one lightning strike. Just as my students couldn't swallow big words all at once, I would have to start slow—finding the root and adding prefixes and suffixes until before long I had one word following another, making sense of my life again, creating a new story that may not be the same as my old one, but joyful nonetheless. I had to believe it could happen.

I checked my watch, wishing I could return to spend some time with da Vinci before we had to pick up the boys. Our next class wasn't until the following morning. Muffin top or not, I couldn't give up on at least one slimming outfit first. I would wake up the next day and put on something new, something that I felt confident in, something that a butterfly might wear on her debut into the world.

Who knew one needed courage just to shop for a new look, let alone a new life? I threw down the challenge to my fashion-loving familials and we dove into the shopping sea.

***

"Are we on for Bunko tonight?" Zoya asked as we both pulled groceries out of the trunks of our cars, hers a cherry-red convertible. Zoya was my next-door neighbor in the cul-de-sac, a former student from five years earlier, a pricey mail-order bride from Russia, though Donald had asked her not to tell anyone. (As if we weren't bright enough to know he wouldn't vacation in Russia and during one week, boy meets girl, boy marries girl, and girl leaves for big adventure in the U.S. with a virtual stranger.) With a Russian mother and a German father, she usually spoke German around me since I'm fluent, and Donald didn't seem to mind that he didn't know what his wife was saying half the time. But then couldn't the same be said of English-speaking spouses?

Her family and six brothers and sisters had gotten a sizable sum for her marital commitment (Bunko nights are quite revealing) and the then-nineteen-year-old had been desperate to start a new life in the United States, even if it meant marrying a slightly overweight CPA twice her age.

It might be easy to rush to judgment on a man that would resort to such drastic measures to find a mate, but I understood his desperation. If I hadn't met Joel, I often wondered if I'd still be searching for my soul mate. Donald had tried for twenty years the traditional way with no luck. At least I'd had one true love, more than most people ever get.

I slung my arm through three plastic bags and watched Zoya maneuver the heavy groceries in her platform heels and skin-tight ankle pants. Her dark hair swung down to her hips, the sides pushed up in clips. She was exotic, though not quite beautiful, and Donald kept her happy with all the American luxuries: a red sports car, designer clothes and weekly spa appointments.

"Bunko. I don't think so," I told her. "I have company." Sort of company.

Zoya smacked her gum and shut the trunk with one overly braceleted arm. "You got the man in the backyard. Very handsome man."

I nodded, fighting the temptation to correct her broken English. My vow was once they left my class not to put on my teacher hat again. "He's a student from Italy. Needed a place to stay."

Zoya eyed me suspiciously, then added, "We have you all over for dinner tonight. You, the Italian, and your boys."

"Thanks for the offer, Zoya, but we're working around the kids' schedules so things are crazy. But we'll do it another time. Are things okay between you and Donald?"

She shrugged, her long silver earrings brushing her collarbone. "Husband trying to impregnate me." Zoya, much like Anh, never held back. I don't think it was lost in translation, either.

"Oh. Do you not want a child yet?"

Zoya raised her Prada sunglasses to stare at me as if I should know better. "If I get with child, this body goes kaput. Same goes my mother and three sisters. One day thin and beautiful, after baby like a big Russian housewife."

I suppressed a laugh. I could tell from Zoya's attire that being attractive was very important to her. Unlike me, she did work out to *Get Up and Move It, Texas!* every morning. "Well, I'm sure Donald just wants a child before he gets too old," I said. "And lots of people get their bodies back after they have children." Just not me.

As if a light bulb went off, Zoya pulled out a *National Enquirer* from her bag. "Like article in newspaper. Angelina Jolie gets body back after baby. Zoya too get body back?"

"Yes," I nodded, the grocery bags' handles digging red marks into my forearm. "Zoya gets her body back."

Pleased with this, Zoya waved her long manicured nails through the air and said over her shoulder, "Donald will get baby then. But still want to meet Italian."

As I entered the house I instinctively sang, "I'm home," as I'd done for ten years upon returning from the grocery store. Because the boys asked for everything in the store, they stayed home with Joel, yet in the last two years, it was hard to break the habit. My announcement echoed through the laundry room, my heart sinking when I didn't hear the familiar "It's about time" from my husband. To my surprise, another voice echoed back.

"I'm home," da Vinci said. As if my heart were on an escalator, it rose again from the bottom floor. Besides my class, da Vinci was learning by repeating everything I said and trying to discern its meaning.

He rushed to greet me, wearing soccer shorts and a T-shirt. He'd joined the Panchal soccer league immediately, and I'd told the boys we'd go watch his first game. His muscular thighs and calves drew my eyes down the length of his body, but I quickly rebounded to his large smile. He took the bags from my arms and together we put them away, going item by item for da Vinci to learn their names. A hundred items, the only embarrassing one being tampons. "Tampon for woman," he said, not embarrassed in the least. Well, he did have a family full of females in Italy.

The TV was paused on my own sister in a downward lunge, her boobs front and center. The escalator dropped a few stories again. Bradley had taught da Vinci how to use the TiVo (and TV, as he didn't have it in his village), and obviously da Vinci found programming that he liked. We spoke in Italian.

"Did you work out to my sister?"

"Half of the program."

"Do you like her?"

"I'm sure she's very nice."

"But do you think she's pretty?"

Da Vinci nodded. "She smiles too much. Her voice is irritating."

We laughed. Da Vinci: handsome *and* smart.

Together we set aside the ingredients for the lasagna da Vinci would make us for dinner—his mother's recipe, he had said, starting to tear up at the mention of her name. A handsome Italian cooking me dinner every night? This I could get used to.

When Cecelia had found out da Vinci was living in the studio, she had passed along da Vinci's skills sheet to assess job opportunities at the temp agency also owned by Panchal.

"Have you ever seen anything like it?" Cecelia had asked as we reviewed the sheet. More than a hundred items on the sheet and da Vinci had checked more than half of them.

"He says he's very good with his hands," I had told her.

Cecelia, who looked like a church lady but gossiped like a desperate housewife, had chewed on the end of her glasses and shook her chest. "Oh, I bet he is. Do share with me if you find out, will you?"

Zoe and her father Michael met us at the soccer field because Zoe was staying with him the rest of the week while Rachel flew to San Diego to give a motivational speech to women who had lost their husbands in the Iraq War. If she became as iconic as Richard Simmons, I was going to throw up. At least I had a sympathetic ear in Michael, whose own reputation had been sacrificed for the sake of his ex-wife's career. Rachel's motivational speeches began with the "woe-is-me, my husband cheated, I thought my life was over, I took control, lost forty pounds, and wham-bam, look at me now, I've got my own TV show and get to meet fabulous people like you" spiel.

If I were in the audience (which I swear I won't be), I would raise my hand and ask my sister how she can ever compare a cheating husband to a dead husband, especially a good dead husband, but she would find a way. She always does. The audience would eat her up like an irresistible confection. Pretty, sweet girls have few enemies. At least Michael, da Vinci and I all agreed she smiles too much. It was a start.

Michael, who frequently got dirty looks when he went in public and had bigger hurdles than most guys back in the dating pool, wore his business suit sans jacket, and Zoe, sans mega hair bow, sat between her nephews. She wanted to play soccer, but her mother said she didn't have time with dance/cheer/gymnastics/pageants. So tonight she was skipping one of them because Michael had to exert power in the relationship whenever he could. Besides, Zoe agreed she didn't feel well (she learned quickly) so Rachel wouldn't tear into Michael.

My feeling sorry for Michael (and his mutual sorrow about my loss) had made us much better friends than we ever were when he and Rachel were married. It was probably because he had been Rachel's whipping boy while they'd been married, and I couldn't stand how he never stood up for himself. I was in the small minority who believed Rachel had pushed him into the arms of another woman, but I had only told Joel this and he quickly agreed. He had liked Michael, too, and a friend of Joel's would always be a friend of mine. The other thing about grief is that you divide the universe into two parts: those who knew your dearly departed and those who don't. I'm not sure which is easier, but whenever I meet someone who tells me they knew Joel (a classmate, a client, an associate), I latch on to them and make them tell me anything I may not have known about my husband. You think you know everything about your mate until they die. Some days I feel like I'll never know.

Asking the one person I *really* wanted to talk to, the one person who could tell me the most about my husband, was too painful. If I were honest with myself, I would admit that I could not move on without knowing the truth about Joel and Monica, which is why I couldn't put it off much longer.

I only know what he was willing to give, which was precisely six weeks, two days, and one hour before his death: *We're history. A long, complicated history I don't care to recount if that's okay with you.*

It wasn't okay with me, which is why I had bugged him to death about it, right up *until* his death. In fact, our final argument had been about Monica, the night before he'd died. He was exhausted from a long day at the office; having passed on his work for her law firm to another partner, he was knee-deep in a new hospital project. He'd just gotten back from running and had clutched at his chest, telling me he felt winded, but I hadn't worried. He was athletic and young, always pushing himself to the limit. I wasn't a runner, wasn't even a fast walker, so I knew nothing of a runner's high or why people would push their bodies to the pain limit. I let him catch his breath, but only for a moment, before I'd gingerly asked him if he would tell me honestly and completely if he was over her.

He had looked at me like a stranger might, someone you think you recognize from across the street, only to find out that no, you don't know them at all. I cringed inside that I'd get *that* look—as he continued to pant and left me for a shower without an answer. I took this as a no. *No, I'm not over Monica Blevins.* After I saw her at the funeral, I realized she was the type of woman that no man could ever truly get over. She was someone babies to old men wanted to get to know and once you did, you came back for more. I was no exception.

My obsession with Monica Blevins had not died along with Joel but had been buried underneath the weight of grief. Now that I was digging myself out of it, there she was again, waiting, taunting.

I wished I'd been more trusting, had more faith in our marriage, but Joel's act of passing on the account did not pacify me. A cloud of suspicion hung over our marriage those last weeks and it had not dissipated even in his death. Did I really think he'd pack his bags and go back to her? Truthfully that's what I'd feared ever since our second date when he'd told me that he couldn't get in a relationship because I would just be a rebound and I deserved better than that. My heart's just mush, he'd told me, and though I teased Joel time and again for his comment after we were committed and then long married, I wondered if a piece of it was true. If after eight years of marriage I was still a rebound girl: the one you go to after the one you love has just destroyed you.

"Alrighty then. That's him?" Michael asked as we sat on the bleachers, looking out at da Vinci warming up with his new teammates.

I acted as though I didn't catch the surprise in his voice. "He starts at UT next week. Coming in late because he had some problems with his visa."

Michael, attractive even with a receding hairline, loosened his tie. "At least you're giving him a break. You always were the nice one."

I noted the hint of bitterness, but let it slide when Anh, wearing a business suit and Vi on her hip like an adorable accessory, awkwardly climbed the bleachers in her heels. I grabbed Vi and planted a kiss on her round cheek. Anh sat next to Michael and flipped her hair. She denied that she flirted with him and he with her, but only someone as out of touch with romance as me could identify it in others. Anh firmly believed that opposites only attract out of boredom and she was far from bored. She hated that Michael drove a gas-guzzling SUV and Michael hated that Anh wouldn't eat meat. (Hey, this is Texas! Cattle country!) Don't even get them started on the war and political agendas—he the flag-waving Republican, and she the die-hard Dem. Nonetheless, I thought they would be perfect together. But what did I know?

"I retract my last statement," Anh said as she stared at da Vinci with her mouth agape. "You don't have a chance in hell with a specimen like that. Even if he is a living statue in your backyard."

Michael squinted his eyes. "You like da Vinci?"

"Not in that way."

"Hell, yes, in that way," Anh retorted. "Any woman with a pair of … ovaries would like him in that way."

Michael shook his head and crossed his arms, knowing when to keep his mouth shut.

Anh handed Vi some Cheerios from her oversized black leather purse (she wouldn't dare carry a diaper bag). "So did you call the yogi yet?"

"A yogi," Michael said, shaking his head again. "Don't go getting her involved in your Eastern mumbo-jumbo."

Anh ignored him. "Tell the Repub a little yoga might remove that massive stick up his ass."

"Stop it, you two. You're worse than my boys." Anh claimed that I was like a pipe with massive clogged drains keeping "flow" from happening. It all sounded drippy to me, but I'd promised myself I would try new things and that included the possibility that my body did need some spiritual plumbing.

One thing I knew for certain: the Cheetos/Oreos/sad movies method I had prescribed for myself had done zilch for my grief and even less for my body image. I had always considered myself an open person until my loss sealed the door shut. With the help of—*what?*—I could open it again. I would plow through the ideas in the grief binder like Columbus searching for his New World. Where I would find *me* again, only God, or Buddha, knew.

Then there was da Vinci, whose coming was both timely and oddly welcome. We began our journeys at the same juncture, side by side as we ventured into the unknown; he trying to start a new life in America, me trying to find the meaning of it again. Anh said we were entering our Renaissance period (*Renaissance: a revival of or renewed interest in something*). The original da Vinci had been a key figure in the sixteenth-century Renaissance, and I had no idea if my da Vinci would play a key role in mine.

With one hard kick, da Vinci scored a goal, and raising his arms in the air, searched me out in the bleachers. I cheered for him and felt the deadbolt unlock, the sound echoing through my soul.

Chapter 4

soul \sol\ *n* 1 : the spiritual or immaterial part of a human being regarded as immortal 2 : a person's moral or emotional nature or sense of identity (*Origin*: Old English)

I GAWKED AT DA VINCI'S naked chest a full three minutes before turning the engine off to retrieve him and regretfully see him slide his T-shirt back on his sweaty, dirt-streaked frame. No shock; I wasn't the only spellbound, jaw-slacked female enjoying the view. When I took my eyes off of him for a split second, I saw a woman walking her dog (more like standing still) staring at him, and another just pull over at the side of the road to take a long peek. I thought, *Is this what my life has come to*? Getting my thrills watching a well-built guy planting pansies? Am I so desperate that just watching McDreamy on *Grey's Anatomy* isn't cutting it for me anymore? And wasn't I going to visit my neighbor Gabriella's deacon this afternoon to talk about the very essence of our being: the soul? To prep for it, I should be waxing existential, not staring at eye candy all afternoon.

It wasn't my fault da Vinci got overheated and took off his shirt. It's not like I asked him to. (Would I dare?) I was just an innocent bystander, giving him a ride back home before I hoofed it to the deacon. So if a girl just happens upon a thing of beauty, it would be rude not to appreciate the artistry of a well-sculpted creation. And it somehow calmed my nerves about meeting with a theologian. Because as openminded as I am about life, culture, differences, I haven't firmly grasped any one belief about Heaven, God or that mystery that is the soul. I only knew that I hoped we had one and that I would be reunited with Joel someday and that I would recognize him. Hopefully he wouldn't look thirty-eight and me, eighty-eight, because well, that would just be a cruel joke, now, wouldn't it?

Earlier that morning as Gabriella and I walked through the trails in our neighborhood, she shared with me her view of Heaven, something we hadn't discussed since Joel passed. My friends had trod softly where it came to Joel, and though we talked about him, the conversation consisted of funny stories from his life, not musings about his death.

"It's full of flowers and men like da Vinci walking around with angel wings," she said as her tiny frame kept up with my taller one. Only hours later, as I watched da Vinci among the flowers, I started to believe she could be right. Heaven would be beautiful, right? But no matter how hard I tried, I couldn't picture Joel anywhere other than in my house. Joel was a city boy. If Heaven was more of a countryscape than a cityscape, how could he not feel out of place there? Then again, Heaven surely didn't have mosquitoes, Joel's biggest problem with the outdoors. He also didn't like to get dirt under his nails, so he'd worn gardening gloves. I wondered if they had gardening gloves in Heaven. Would the deacon know the answer to that? Were my questions too basic? I wished I weren't such a spiritual simpleton.

Da Vinci, on the other hand, had the dirtiest nails I'd ever seen and as soon as I saw them, I felt the compulsion to wash them for him, slowly, meticulously, using a file to clean every nail, then finish them off with a vanilla-scented lotion. Instead I said, "Don't touch anything," as he got into the car.

"You like?" da Vinci said, pointing to the exquisite landscaping in front of the office complex.

I said yes without so much as looking at his handiwork. "I like very much," I told him.

As we passed by the Hallmark Stables on the way back to my house, da Vinci's eyes lit up upon seeing the horses grazing in the field. "Da Vinci rides horses," he said longingly.

I glanced at the dozen or so animals in the pasture. I'd passed them nearly every day going home, but I'd never really noticed them before. Like Joel, I'd been raised a city girl in Dallas before moving to Austin to go to college, met Joel and, well, stayed and had babies and did the *New York Times* crossword puzzle every day. Was there more to a happy life than that?

I'd never ridden a horse in my life, save for pony rides at birthday parties. The expansion of Austin from a small city to sprawling suburbia meant occasionally the city and the country collided. "You ride horses? Well, we could arrange that." As a stranger in a strange land, da Vinci was coping well, but I could sense he missed more than just his mama back home. If riding a horse would make him happy, then it was the least I could do.

Da Vinci ran his dirty fingers through his longish hair and instead of cringing at the thought of all that dirt, the idea of washing his hair flitted through my brain. *Here, let me help you with that,* I could say. My favorite part of getting my hair done was the scalp massage, and it was the first time I felt compelled to wash anyone's hair other than my children's. Something could be seriously wrong with me.

We passed by the string of fast food chains I'd sworn off, but da Vinci practically panted like a dog. "What you say, donut holes on way home?"

I hadn't eaten junk food in forty-eight hours. I practically jumped the curb as I screeched into Dunkin Donuts. How I'd missed thee!

Da Vinci and I made a great team. We finished off 36 Munchkins in under ten minutes, dunking them in coffee and rolling our eyes in sugared ecstasy.

"I love American food," da Vinci said, patting his tight abs.

"It's terrible for you," I said, popping the last chocolate-cake donut hole in my mouth, savoring the crunchy outside and doughy center. "It will make you fat."

Da Vinci reached over and gently wiped away a large sugar crumb from my lip. "Then we jog extra mile tomorrow morning to work fat off bodies."

Fireworks went off in my head, proof that da Vinci had an effect on me. I'd sworn the only way anyone was getting me to run was to be chasing me with a machete. But to spend more time with da Vinci and possibly lose a few pounds in the process? I'd be an idiot to turn that down.

I dropped da Vinci off at the house, reminding him about his early classes at UT the next day. I offered to drive him because I needed to visit the library for more research for my dissertation. Honest.

Da Vinci thanked me with his smile, something like a physical tip that was far better than money ever would be. "We ride together," da Vinci said. "Da Vinci teach Mona Lisa to ride." It dawned on me he didn't mean the car, but horses, but I was too caught up by my nickname.

Mona Lisa: the famed art of the pseudo-smiling brunette painted in the 1500s and the nickname given to one blonde widow by her sexy tenant. I had figured out the Mona Lisa within Ramona Elise in college in my first linguistics class. My parents hadn't been that clever on purpose. They had just lumped two family names together as so many expecting parents do: Ramona for my paternal grandmother and Elise for my maternal great-grandmother. It was an accident, yet Anh believed my secret moniker and da Vinci's appearance were no accident at all.

I didn't mind da Vinci giving me a nickname, forming some bond that only we shared. I never considered bonding with da Vinci on purpose. But it was an unwritten rule that no teacher could date students, so my idea of bonding did not go beyond that of one caring teacher helping out a student.

As I stepped into the beautiful marble foyer at the archdiocese where I was to meet with Deacon Friar (a man who had lived up to his moniker, another example of name revealing one's destiny), I stared at the largest reproduction of the da Vinci's *Last Supper* that I'd ever seen. The picture was at least twenty feet wide, so large that I could study the expressions of the disciples and the hands of Jesus, and I shuddered. The work was pure genius.

I thought of Joel and our last supper together, the night before his collapse on the basketball court, an hour after our nonverbal argument; we ate pizza, but not just any pizza: Joel's favorite, the expensive kind we could only afford once a month. It was hand-tossed by an Italian, the short, mustached man who had come to America with only a dream in his back pocket and a recipe for the crispiest yet gooiest pizza I'd ever tasted. I smiled at the memory. I hadn't thought about Joel's last supper before that moment. I'd thought about his last breakfast: Wheaties. And his last snack: peanut butter on crackers before he headed out to the park to play a pickup game with the neighbors. But his last real meal had been his favorite, something that suddenly comforted me greatly.

When Deacon Friar caught me studying the painting, I hadn't realized I had tears in my eyes, but not from the artwork. "It's quite beautiful, isn't it?"

I wiped my eyes and nodded, taking in Deacon Friar's appearance. I expected him to look more like a friar from the seventeenth century, wearing a brown robe beneath a bald head. Yet he appeared very modern, tall and attractive with salt-and-pepper hair and a face full of compassion that fit his profession. Gabriella had told me he was a widower with two grown boys, and that losing his wife had pushed him into the Church in a way that only a loss of such magnitude could. I had said half-jokingly that I should join a convent after losing Joel. Escaping from the world for nothing but 24/7 silence and solitude had seemed like a good fix at the time, but knowing how crazy the quiet around my home made me, I knew it would be even worse if I went somewhere where it was expected. Besides, I was no nun.

I felt a kinship with Deacon Friar before our eyes ever met. When they did, I found his to be kind, chocolate-brown eyes beneath dark brows. He wore glasses with tiny silver frames accentuating what already seemed a very intellectual face. He carried himself with ease, and as his warm handshake met my cold hands, I instantly felt him to be my spiritual superior. If spirituality grew along the lines of biology, mine would be considered a toddler, able only to articulate that I believed, but unable to verbalize a deeper understanding of what it was *exactly* that I believed.

To my surprise, I found it easy to open up to Deacon Friar, how my parents had been lapsed Episcopalians before being moved by the sunshine spirituality offered by the megachurch lifestyle: non-denominational, 100 percent rah-rah Christianity.

We entered a small courtyard with luxurious gardens and a stone path that led to a fountain with two angels. The courtyard itself might resemble Gabriella's idea of Heaven. In the last two years, I had lost all sense of beauty, but sitting amidst the majesty of nature, I could feel the appreciation for it stir within me.

"So Gabriella told me about your loss. Joel, right? My son's name is Joel," he said.

Tears welled in my eyes, but I blinked them back. I didn't get to hear his name said aloud enough. "Yes, Joel. He was thirty-eight. His fortieth birthday would've been in a few weeks, on September 30th, a week before the anniversary of his death."

"What did you do for his last birthday? When he was alive."

His question surprised me. I thought back. "Well, Joel made a big deal of birthdays. He was an only child, so to say his parents didn't spoil him would be an understatement. So we didn't have birth*days*, we had birthday *weeks*. Every day the birthday boy, or girl in my case, would get to pick one fun thing to do each day, ending with a big party on your actual birthdate."

"Sounds like a joyful spirit. You had at least four fun weeks of celebration during the year."

"Oh, that's not all. He was really into decorating for the holidays. Not just the usual ones, either. Christmas, of course, Griswold lights and all. Halloween was one of his favorites—orange lights, lots of spider webs and dressing in costume to trick or treat with the boys. For the Fourth of July, he would buy out the fireworks stand and we would go out into the country and create our own fireworks show. And for Easter, Joel enjoyed hiding the eggs as much as the kids enjoyed finding them."

Deacon Friar dug in his pocket and handed me five shiny pennies. "When I leave, I want you to think long and hard about the five wishes you want most of all to come true. Then when you're ready, you can cast them into the fountain. I like to call them penny prayers. Most people are uncomfortable with the act of praying, and even for devout Christians, praying can be very difficult after you've lost the person you were closest to on earth. So I've found the penny method works."

I stared at the pennies in my hand. I get wishes? Wishes beyond just wanting Joel to come back, for the past to have never happened?

"This is where I'm stuck," I said. "I seem to have lost all of my dreams when Joel died. We had it all figured out, you know? That we were going to go to Hawaii for his fortieth birthday. That we were going to learn to flamenco dance when the kids were older. That we were going to take a road trip on Route 66. Everything centered around *us*. I was always more into the 'we' than the 'me.' And now that it's just me, I'm lost."

The deacon rested his chin on his hand, looking like *The Thinker*. "It's been ten years since I lost my wife. If you're hoping that the grief will go away, that you'll be able to move on from missing your husband, then you'll be disappointed. That will never go away. But if you mean you are ready to start enjoying life again, finding pleasure beyond the pain, then that is possible. But I gathered from Gabriella that you've been worried not just about your moving on, but Joel's."

"We never talked about death. Joel kept things light. When he said he would love me forever, I just want to know what that means. I want to know that we'll be united again."

"Well, if you believe in God and Heaven, then you know that you'll be united again."

I nodded, trying to explain. "As a linguist, I study the origin of words. I'm a researcher. I guess as far as Heaven goes, I just need a little more research. The details, you know? My mom's pastor told me I should be happy for Joel, which kind of turned me off about finding out anything else about it. I mean, I'm sorry, but how can I be happy for Joel when I know he didn't want to die until we grew old together and he got to meet his grandkids and great-grandkids? So even though I should be happy that he is with God, I'm not. There, I said it."

"It's not fair," the deacon said thoughtfully. "Not only unfair that he died, but that everyone tells you he now enjoys perfect union with God in the most majestic place we can imagine while you get to raise two boys alone and deal with the anchors of the life he left behind. I felt the same way."

He had taken the hundred-pound weight on my shoulder and tossed it into the fountain. There it was. It was something the other widows and widowers and divorcees had tiptoed around in Parents without Partners, but we hadn't said those words because it made us sound selfish. Besides the anger and the fear of failure and the enormous sadness, there was jealousy there. I wanted peace and tranquility and to tiptoe through daisies with my husband.

"And his soul?"

"There's a lot of debate about when the soul is reunited with the body, but the Catholics believe it is after purgatory, or the cleansing of the earthly life. And the amazing part is, once our souls are re-united with our bodies, we are freed from its slowness of motion with the quickness to go wherever the soul pleases. The Apostle says, 'It is sown in weakness; it shall rise in power.'"

"So Joel can finally make that jump shot he always dreamed of?"

The deacon nodded. "That's right. And even better the soul takes total dominion over the body. 'It is sown in a natural body, it shall rise a spiritual body.' So the body becomes more like a spirit. Thus the risen Christ was able to pass through material objects."

"Pass through walls. He'd get a kick out of that. Can I ask you something personal?"

"Of course."

"Do you talk to your wife?"

"I do sometimes, but it's normally through prayer. I pray for her soul. It's not like a séance or something silly like that. If we see our-selves at our essence as spiritual beings, then I see no problem with trying to maintain that spiritual connection. We are all made up of en-ergy, in this life and beyond. So sometimes I tell her that I love her and miss her and am praying for her."

"Do you think they know? What's going on down here? Like some sort of big plasma screen in the sky that lets them watch us?" I couldn't help but ask. I hated not knowing if Joel could see Bradley catch the winning pass or how funny William looked with both of his front teeth missing.

"I don't have any evidence on this, of course, so I'm not speaking as a theologian here, but as a widower. I choose to believe they can keep tabs on the lives of loved ones, but it's not like a nightly news ver-sion of what's happening on earth. If TV news is troubling to us on earth, imagine how it might seem from Heaven. Instead, I think it could be more like a highlight reel. They see images of loved ones as if in a reflecting pool. Nothing distressing, only linking of the spirits. I think they can feel us and feel our prayers for them. Don't you feel him, Ramona? He'll always be with you right here." He tapped his own heart with his index finger. I put my hand over mine.

"But I thought it was just me missing him, not feeling him. Just my mind playing tricks on me. And I want it to feel good, not sad."

"I think that's what it really means when we say, 'Love never dies.' The spirit never stops loving. So accept it freely."

I let the tears fall. Each time I thought of Joel, it was followed not by fond remembrance, but by anger that he wasn't there physically or sadness that I could not reach out and touch his wavy brown hair.

Perhaps I was Catholic after all. I had the Catholic guilt part down to a T. I'd felt guilty for any happiness since Joel, as if I were betraying his memory. How could I lose the guilt to make room for healthier emotions?

"I'll work on that," I promised. "And the praying part, too." I thought back to the forty days after Joel's death, how Gabriella and her husband had gone to daily mass to pray for Joel for the repose of his soul. I had gone to church a month after the funeral, and in between I had only bitterly thought of my loss. I hadn't prayed for Joel at all. Had his soul suffered because of it? Did the fact that he'd died with mistrust between us impact his feelings for me now?

"Beyond praying for him, the greatest thing you can do is to honor his memory and live the best life you can. From the little bit you've told me about Joel, I can imagine how sad he might be that his traditions and spirit of your family died along with him. He was the joy conduit."

"He was. I never realized until he died how much I depended on him for happiness. I've been trying for the boys' sake, but it's hard. And it takes four neighbors to put up the lights that Joel could do single-handedly. But I've been doing everything with a heavy heart."

The deacon made a steeple with his fingers and pointed them at me. "So try doing them with a joyful heart."

He made it sound so simple. First I'd have to cut the cables that kept my heart restrained, one by one. I slipped the pennies in the pocket of my jeans, saving them for when I really knew what I wanted. Five wishes almost seemed extravagant; I wouldn't spend them frivolously.

A half hour later, I sat in the car in front of the Socials building around back of the enormous Life Church campus. I'd promised myself I would give it one chance. One singles mixer and if I felt uncomfortable, I would be out of there faster than a rabbit spotting a wolf. I wore my new outfit, a layered ensemble with a black jacket, black tuxedo pants and a red V-neck cami. Red. I couldn't believe I was trying to pull it off before I was ready, but it was a touch, a root, a beginning.

Deacon Friar had lifted my spirits, convincing me it wasn't too late to feel connection with Joel, that I could spend an eternity with him, and this news calmed me. It gave me something to look forward to—not just when I died, but right this minute.

I gathered the courage, feeling the pennies in my pocket, and entered the building where more than a hundred people between the ages of 25 and 45 gathered. The group was attractive, wearing their finest look-at-me attire and chemical elixirs, the perfume and cologne mingling in an overwhelming potpourri scent.

"Welcome to singles," a pretty twenty-something female said to me as she handed me a sign-in sheet and nametag. I surveyed the room, filled with sad people pretending not to be sad. In one way or another, we were all desperate, each wanting to find that something that would make our lives a little better. The never-been-marrieds were searching for fulfillment and family. The divorcées were looking for second chances, and the widowers were just searching, period. I imagined what we all had in common was the desire for connection, only for the living, but I wasn't sure anyone in the room could make me feel that.

I made my way through the crowd to the bar, where, to my chagrin, no alcohol was served. Life Church would not want to be responsible for hook-ups resulting from beer goggles, would they? I accepted an orange spritzer instead, which was just orange juice mixed with Sprite, a sly trick I'd used to get my boys to get their vitamin C.

When I spun around I bumped into a handsome man about my age holding an orange drink, too. "I prefer mine with vodka, but what can you do?" he said.

"I forgot my flask," I said, thinking someone this attractive didn't belong at a singles mixer. He could get any woman he wanted. My blink reaction was that he was either a multiple divorcé or a workaholic womanizer who just came to these things to pick up chicks. (But isn't that what we were all here, for? I had bought into my mother's idea of finding a new friend, but once here I could see friendship was the furthest thing from these people's minds. They were all trying much too hard.) He seemed too happy to be a Griever.

He began to respond when a bosomy redhead grabbed him by the arm and whipped him around in a hug reserved for the overly friendly. She looked his type. Maybe he'd already taken her home before, or maybe she was trying to seal the deal, but I had no desire to wait around just to get his name. In fact, I had no desire to be there at all. Besides, I had a friend at home waiting for me.

I found da Vinci napping on the back patio with a row of golden mums he had planted appearing like the frame on a beautiful picture.

Without thinking, I walked over to his body splayed out in the armchair and ottoman and ran my fingers through his dark hair, causing his lashes to flutter in sleep. He opened his eyes and turned his head, where his lips met the soft skin on the underside of my wrist and kissed it, causing a thousand butterflies to take flight.

His eyes locked with mine and he whispered, half asleep, "*Ché modo buono di svegliarmi.*" He could have said, "Do my laundry," and it would've felt poetic to me at the time, but what he said was far better: "What a nice way to wake up."

Chapter 5

con·nec·tion \ *n* 1 : the linking or joining of two or more parts, things, or people (*Origin:* late Middle English, from Latin)

I COULDN'T STOP THINKING about that kiss the rest of the week. I pretended it hadn't affected me, going about my business as usual, taking da Vinci where he needed to go, his next temp job at a flower shop and classes at UT. I zipped right through the week, soccer and football and chess club and laundry and coffee with my mother and salad with Anh and life should've felt exactly as it had before da Vinci arrived in my classroom, but it felt anything but. The only difference in my life came down to a connection, taking me from the lonely dark cave of my sadness out into the light, led by one strong-armed Italian.

When you lose a spouse, you can suddenly feel as though the strings to your life have been cut forever, as if you're an abandoned kite floating aimlessly in the clouds. Like non-stop static on a television screen, the picture becomes fuzzy, the signal lost. The connection is broken forever, like a baby being separated from its mother after birth or downed power lines in an electric storm. This is the way I felt after Joel died. I had lost my connection and didn't know how to get it back or even if I could.

Most spouses in happy marriages know that the best part is shared experiences: making love, making memories, making a life that becomes richer because you have each other. You understand the other with just one look or sound. It's true what they say about partners starting to look like each other as they age. You eat the same food, breathe the same air, go where the other goes. So the absence of one makes the other feel immobile. You literally feel half the person.

But after meeting with Deacon Friar, I realized I had it all wrong. My connection to Joel had not been lost, and in some ways, we could be closer than ever. Because instead of him being outside of me, he was within me. He was just on the other side of the universal plane, in the spiritual world, and if I believed that our spiritual relationship had been strong in life, it should be just as strong after death. If I believed our spiritual link could never be broken, then "'til death do us part" would only be the physical separation, but could never snip the cord that linked Joel and me for eternity, right? The very meaning of soul mate in action.

Yet doubt had permeated my thoughts since his death, the fear that if we each have only one soul mate, I wasn't his. If he had believed Monica, his first love, was his soul mate, then what was I? The next best thing? I had grown up to believe in the fairy tale of "happily ever after," one person to share your life with. But Joel had loved two women in his life, had felt the awesome power of connection, not once, but twice. I thought of her standing in the back of the crowd at his funeral, dressed impeccably in an expensive black suit, her silky black hair cut in a sharp bob about her refined features. Just like in her pictures, she looked like a model who never left the photo shoot. Even in my anger, I could see that she was in pain. She had loved him as much as I had.

Seeing her in person after only seeing pictures of them together had made my doubt resurface. Was their connection greater than ours? She was the one thing that kept me from believing our love was eternal. The mystery that was Monica pecked at my faith. If I couldn't let go of my jealousy and doubt in his life, how could I possibly after his death? Why had my faith taken such a fall?

What if before I could move on, I would have to go back, to use one copper penny on resolving the issue once and for all? It was as if Deacon Friar had tossed me a special widow key that gave me permission to unlock a forbidden door. I'm not even sure if deacon knew he had given me a key, but those five pennies, five wishes for a better life, became calling cards for something more.

And if I could resolve my issues with Joel and his two great loves, then maybe I could come to terms with the possibility of a connection with somebody *other than* my husband. I would never have believed it until that kiss on my wrist ignited the wick that I could feel go all through my body and straight into my heart—the stirrings of something so familiar, yet so ancient I could barely recognize it. Of course I was fond of da Vinci. I enjoyed his company, and like most women who laid their eyes on him, I was attracted to him. But besides the student/teacher issue, I expected to feel nothing other than a platonic connection. Romance? Never. Just a fantasy? Perhaps. But I didn't believe I would ever act on it.

Yet I did go horseback riding—I, the one who preferred even a smelly human to animals, rode horseback with da Vinci on a sunny fall afternoon when I should've been working on my dissertation. But besides connection, I felt something else: freedom. Freedom to cut loose and do something new and completely unexpected. If I was channeling anything left behind of Joel, it was his passion for adventure, being spontaneous. The next thing I knew, after riding across the field like a painting on a romance novel, da Vinci hopped off of his horse, stopped my horse by grabbing the reins and I nearly leapt into his arms. And on the way down? I kissed him. *On the lips.* I considered it a "thank you for helping me down kiss" though da Vinci seemed to not think anything of it. They probably kissed in Italy the way we shook hands in America. So I didn't make a big deal out of that kiss, either. Yet like the first, I couldn't get it out of my head, either.

I couldn't tell Anh about da Vinci's kiss, because what was there to tell? She might think there was a budding romance, which there certainly wasn't. Not on my end. If you told Anh something, she wouldn't let it go. She would call and ask me about it each day, like a doctor checking charts on rounds.

And with da Vinci just starting college, he was making all kinds of new friends. The fraternities wanted to rush him, the girls were probably pawing all over him, and that's the way it should be. My role as his teacher and landlord and friend was to help him find himself in America and that meant making friends outside of my four walls. I told him not to judge the frat boys so quickly, to give things a chance—something I couldn't believe was coming out of my mouth.

I also had my dissertation to attend to, so when I dropped da Vinci off on campus, where he stood out like a beacon in the throng of students, I made my way through the college crowd to the library, where I would dive back in to my work. It wasn't until I cracked open the notebook that I hadn't touched since the week before Joel died, that the enormity of the work hit. *The Language of Love.* I scanned my notes—more than forty hours of research and thought had already been put into it. Should I scrap the whole thing and ask my professor for a new topic? But what? And my notes were *really good*. I had stopped working on it, in truth, because I had lost connection to the material, too. But now I could begin to appreciate the topic of love again, as someone might appreciate fine art, detached, but drawn to the subject. I would no longer see love through the blurred eyes of grief, but try to be objective. Besides, I wanted to finish what I'd started, a way to prove to myself that love does go on after your husband dies and especially that a dissertation on the *language* of love could survive even death. I did still have dreams, the biggest dream to be a professor with a doctorate.

I grabbed the laptop from my attaché case and clicked it on, the hum causing a few stares from all directions. I slunk into my seat and began typing, the material beginning to pull me in.

The Language of Love
—By Ramona Griffen

Where does love begin, and where does it end? Anthropologists who have studied love claim that for millions of years the ever-changing world has not changed the primal instinct of love, mating, and sexuality. Though technology and evolution have morphed the way in which we live, the language of love is the one constant in the universe, transcending time and cultures. And researchers say it all begins with one look.

The eyes have it.

Across cultures and even species, lovers begin their courtship with a flirting sequence highlighted by the copulatory gaze. As the potential mates stare at each other for two to three seconds, the pupils dilate, indicating a strong interest, and then look away. This powerful gaze is followed by an anxious diversion, fidgeting, or moving away, or it is reciprocated with another universal friendly exchange: the smile.

My cell phone buzzed, causing more angry warning glares, quite the opposite of the copulatory gaze, and I reached into my overstuffed bag to retrieve it. I whispered hello as I beelined for the entrance.

"You've got to help me."

Rachel.

"Don't tell me. You gained a pound in San Francisco and need me to stand by you to make you look slimmer."

"Very funny, though not a bad idea. Zoe is at Cortland's having a play date with his daughter, but my lame-brained assistant double-booked me, and I can't get over there. Can you be a doll and go pick her up for me? Mom's at a church thing and won't leave."

"So you're dating the doctor, huh?"

"He's fabulous. I've been wanting you to meet him, anyway."

"That serious already?"

"Can you do it or not?"

"I'm working on my … okay, fine. What's his address?"

***

I would give my sister the benefit of the doubt and believe she liked Cortland for Cortland and not because of his estate, a 3,500-square-foot, two-story house in a historic neighborhood where all the movers and shakers of Austin lived. Every mover and shaker, that is, except my enviro-friendly Anh who preferred her 1,200-square-foot modern abode near her corporate office.

I stood on the porch wondering if I'd ever seen such a huge front door and felt like a munchkin in the Land of Oz. Even the doorbell's sound was larger than life, echoing through tall ceilings, announcing my arrival as if I were a lady of the court.

When the door opened, our eyes locked. One. Two. Three seconds. Then we both looked away. And back again. I couldn't tell for sure—the afternoon sun could've been playing tricks on me, but I thought maybe his pupils were dilated. Then he raised his arm on the doorframe and puffed out his chest, a classic gesture of dominance and flirtation. It happened so quickly that I hadn't even realized that I had cocked my head slyly and tossed my hair over my shoulder. I was flirting back. Not just with the orange juice spritzer man from the singles mixer who had been nabbed by the redhead, but *with my sister's boyfriend.*

Two thoughts ran through my head: 1) Why was he at a singles mixer if he was dating my sister, and 2) why, oh, why is life not fair? He stuck his hand out for me to shake, yet my eyes never left his. "You must be Rachel's sister," he said.

"Ramona," I said, and my cool hand met his warm embrace and before he let go, he gave my hand a slight squeeze, and I entered the oversized foyer with a beautiful entry table, large sconces with vanilla candles and fresh fall flowers. I thought of da Vinci, spending his days arranging flowers, something that most men would be terrible at, yet da Vinci had the artistic eye for color and contrast and said he loved the work.

"Cortland," he said and put his hand behind his head and scratched his neck, another common flirting tactic. I tried not to smile and wondered if I was reading him wrong. He was handsome for certain, tall and well-built with a natural tan and a full head of blondish-brown hair that shone in the sun. "I was disappointed you disappeared the other night," he said. "Small world, isn't it?"

"Indeed. Are you a singles regular?"

"Hoping to retire," he said, his fingers crossed. "I'm the current president."

"President of the Lonely Hearts Club?"

"Something like that. Your sister didn't tell me you were so funny."

"Surprise, surprise." Who knows what she said about me? Of course the most attractive man at the singles group would be the leader type: the kind who wouldn't stay single for long. My mother had mentioned Rachel and Cortland had seen each other every day since meeting. When my sister saw something she wanted, she put her hooks in and didn't let go. Cortland didn't stand a chance. Not that he'd be squirming to get off the hook, either.

"The girls are upstairs in the playroom," he said.

As I began to follow him up, a German shepherd bolted from around the corner, skidded on the tile and leapt up to kiss my face before sniffing my crotch.

"Down, Leibe," Cortland said.

"*Liebe*. German for love. Great name."

"Thanks. My mother is German, so in a way, I guess I named her after my mom. Sounds better than Phyllis. You have dogs?"

"No, but my boys have been wanting one for years. My husband and I said they could have one as soon as they started keeping their rooms clean and doing all their chores without complaining."

"So, *never,* in other words?"

"Something like that. I've never been a dog person. But I don't know. I'm thinking maybe it's time."

I followed Cortland up the stairs, trying not to stare at his behind, but well, it was right in my face, and I figured he must be a cyclist or runner with such a toned backside. What did I have to lose?

"So I noticed the walking trails in your neighborhood. Do you run or bike?"

"Both," Cortland said.

Of course. A doubly fit behind. "You have a beautiful home."

"Thank you." We reached the playroom, an enormous pink and green room filled with everything a princess, or daughter of a divorced doctor, might desire. "Zoe, your aunt is here to pick you up."

Zoe pouted. "Oh, Auntie. Do I have to go so soon?" Her language of manipulation worked like a charm. "You know how hard it is for me to a be a lonely child."

"You mean an *only* child," I corrected.

Zoe shrugged. "That, too."

Lindsey, Cortland's daughter, put her arm protectively around Zoe. She was a full two heads taller and years older, but the two had clearly bonded. The bond of lonely onlies.

Cortland raised his brow. I could tell he was the type who gave in easily. "We could get a cup of coffee unless you're in a hurry."

I glanced at my watch. Da Vinci would be out of class in an hour and he was going with me to Bradley's football game. I hadn't wanted Bradley to play football—too dangerous, I thought—but he was good at it, a born quarterback, and in the two weeks since da Vinci arrived, he had someone other than the neighbors and me (a terrible passer and receiver) to throw the ball with. Da Vinci was adept at those skills, too.

"One cup," I said, and the girls cheered and Cortland smiled again, this time a wide smile, all teeth showing, eyes turned up on the ends, reserved for the truly happy. I began to think he *wanted* to have a cup of coffee with me for me. A ludicrous thought, really.

While he went into the kitchen to get our coffee, I stepped into his office. You could tell a lot about a person by the books he read, and as a linguist, it was the first thing I studied. Cortland's shelves were full of medical dictionaries—expected, and a few literary works—some Poe and Dickens, and on the bottom shelf, the popular fiction—Nick Hornby and a dozen thrillers. His desk was orderly with only one picture, a silver frame with a close-up of Lindsey when she was younger. Then a neat stack of magazines, *Sports Illustrated, Time,* and on top, *Austin Living,* the local magazine of the affluent. The glossy cover showed a beautiful fall entryway, one as nearly oversized as Cortland's. I picked it up to study it closer, then dropped it as if it had caught fire. *See the home of Austin Young Lawyer of the Year Monica Blevins.*

I'd thrown out the copy my mother had brought me, but as soon as the trash truck had taken it away, I'd regretted throwing it out. I'd made up my mind to confront Monica, but first I had to do my research.

My heart picked up speed, and I plucked it from the desk and turned to page forty-eight where Monica sat in her exquisite living room with her dog at her feet and her daughter Rose lying peacefully in her lap. I stared at Monica's face, thinking if I stared long enough I would feel something, understand something, but the longer I stared, the longer I wanted to rip the magazine to pieces and hated myself for wanting to do it. Because what had Monica done that was so wrong, really? Being born into a wealthy family that could afford private school where she'd met Joel Griffen in elementary school and, later, beginning an eight-year love affair that ended with breaking off their engagement one week before the wedding? Shouldn't I be thankful to her for not going through with it? If she had, I wouldn't have gotten my chance with Joel. And just because she personally hired Joel's architectural firm to build her new law office didn't mean she wanted to have an affair with him or that all those morning, lunch or after-work drinks were anything other than work. Right.

Sure, I could rip the pages out of the magazine but I could not rip Monica out of Joel's history. She would always be there, the woman who had shared nearly one-third of Joel's years on earth. "You know Monica?" Cortland said as he handed me the cup of coffee. The way he said it, so lightly, it was as if everyone knew Monica, and I'm sure everyone who was anyone knew Monica or the ones who read this magazine and who lived in this neighborhood knew Monica, but no one knew Monica the way I knew her.

I cleared my throat. "I know *of* her. I suppose you know her then."

"She's married to a friend of mine."

"A doctor?"

"No. A lawyer."

Two lawyers. No wonder they could afford this neighborhood. I remembered back. Of course. The man she left Joel for, the one she studied with at law school. Not just any guy, but Joel's best friend since they were toddlers. Another part of the story Judith refused to talk with me about. I don't know why I suddenly felt sorry for Joel, but I did. Maybe I believed it should be Joel on the page with Rose and the dog and the designer couch in a house Joel probably would've built, his dream house that we couldn't afford because we'd decided I should stay home and raise our kids, not that Joel would've wanted it any different. My part-time job at the Panchal Center had been more for an intellectual reward than financial. The graduate classes Joel encouraged me to take had meant sacrificing vacations and the extras people like Monica could afford.

"You can take the magazine. I've read it," he said.

And thinking about the copper pennies, I accepted his offer and pushed her from my mind for the moment. There would be time to deal with her later.

I hadn't meant for the article to sour my mood, but thankfully, Cortland was a natural conversationalist. Within no time, I was at ease with him. We drank our coffee on the veranda amidst beautiful gardens not unlike the ones I'd visited at the archdiocese. I scanned my memory for info on Cortland. "I hear you play golf with my dad."

"Yeah. We hit a few balls every now and then. Your dad's a great guy. Mine passed a few years ago."

"I'm sorry to hear that."

"Yeah. It's been interesting. My mom just started dating again. Through church, of course. The Singles Again group. Not an easy thing to see your mother get back out there. I went to two socials with her, and if it's not embarrassing enough to have your mother try to set you up behind your back, it's even worse right in front of you."

"I'm sure your mom's a great matchmaker, but you're kind of an easy sell. The whole handsome doctor thing can't hurt."

Cortland laughed, and I wondered if I'd said too much. My foot-in-mouth disease was aggravated around handsome men. "Well, maybe I should introduce myself as a grocer and see if that makes a difference."

"See if they like you for *you* and not the white coat." I tried to imagine if my sister would be interested in him if he were just a handsome grocer instead of a handsome anesthesiologist. Nope. Afraid not. "I'd stick with the doctor route. Honesty is usually the best policy. So your mom and my mom conspired to get you and Rachel together. You two must've hit it off."

Cortland studied me before answering, clearly thinking before he spoke. "Your sister has more energy than all the doctors at Mercy combined."

So he likes her zest, her zeal for life. Well, who wouldn't? Passion oozed from that sparkly smile, and while I still believed half of it was for show, she did manage to pull it off. "Have you seen her show?"

"No. But I've seen the billboards for more than a year."

The one Anh and I called "the boob billboard." Rachel had the shot done right after her implants, when she was still a little swollen. Her network swears her viewership rose three points after the board went up. "What, no TiVo? I TiVo her. It's the least a sister can do."

He shrugged. "Busy, I guess. But why watch her on TV when you can get the real thing?"

This time I gave him the benefit of the doubt that he didn't mean in bed. I looked beyond the garden at the pool, remembering it was Rachel's first question to my mother about him. "I'm glad Lindsey and Zoe have hit it off, too. Zoe's had a rough couple of years with the divorce and ..." I nearly added *having my sister as a mother.*

"Lindsey's always wanted a sister. Or brothers. Rachel tells me you have two boys. That must be a handful."

Even with a husband. "They're great. They are definitely the bright spot in my day."

"What does your husband do?"

I could feel myself blush. Rachel had told him about the boys, but not that I'm a widow? It had taken me a full year to stop answering yes when someone asked me if I was married. Now I simply said no. If they pressed, I told them I was a widow, but unlike my sister, I didn't seek any sympathy.

He wore what was surely his compassionate doctor's face. The one people saw right before they started counting backwards, imagining little Cortland sheep hurdling over a picket fence. "I'm sorry. Rough subject."

"Oh, it's okay. I just thought Rachel would've told you. My husband died two years ago. Heart attack."

Cortland's smile fell. He seemed embarrassed he hadn't been told as well. "God, I'm sorry. The last couple of years have had to be hell on you."

I caught my breath. "Thank you. Yes. As a matter of fact, it has been exactly like hell. Though Pastor Feelgood never said those words to me."

"Pastor Feelgood. That fits him, doesn't it? I'm afraid I may never be able to call him by his real name again. How come I've never seen you in church?"

"You mean you didn't spot me among the 10,000 other attendees?"

"Fair enough. But I think I could pick you out in a crowd."

He raised his eyebrows. I did the same. I felt the coffee swirl inside of me, and I fidgeted to break whatever connection was forming between us, especially so soon after mentioning my husband's name. My sister wanted this man, or at least his pool. I was just the driver, her personal assistant for the day. I should go.

"Well, thanks for the coffee. I have to pick up da Vinci before Bradley's game."

Cortland stood and stretched again, puffing his chest towards me. "Did you just say you had to pick up *da Vinci*?"

I laughed. "He's an immigrant student of mine that's living in my garage studio. His name really is Leonardo da Vinci. And to answer your question earlier, my husband Joel was an architect. A very good architect. He actually designed your hospital."

"Wow. He did great work. The hospital is a masterpiece."

"Thank you. I'm sure he'd be happy to hear that."

"And I'd love to meet this da Vinci of yours."

"So would my sister. We'll have you over soon." I noticed I had said *we* as if da Vinci and I were together. "I mean, *I'll* have you all over to my house soon. Although it's nothing like this."

Cortland waved it away. "This was my wife's idea. Ex-wife's. She would've wanted the house in the divorce, only the guy she left me for has a house twice this size."

"Ouch."

"Very ouch. But looking back, it's better this way. And I'm actually thinking of downsizing. I prefer a cozy little space."

"Don't tell that to my sister."

He scrunched his brow. "What do you mean?"

I shrugged, regretting opening my big mouth. "Oh, nothing. I just mean I'm sure she really likes your house. And your pool."

"It does have a nice hot tub," he said. "It's nice to get in with a cup of hot chocolate when it's snowy outside. That I'll invite you over for. I mean, Rachel and I will invite you and da Vinci over."

Our eyes locked again, and I wanted to make a snide remark about hell freezing over before I'd get in a hot tub with my hard-bodied sister, but I didn't think that was really the point. The point, if I was really paying attention, was that we had just made two plans to see each other again.

Chapter 6

A FEW THINGS GRIEVERS don't do: We won't tell you to look at the "bright side"; we steer clear of couples' hang-outs; and we absolutely, un-equivocally avoid weddings like vampires shun sunlight. The blushing bride and tearful groom and gaggle of well-wishers and sweet sanctimony don't sit well with my kind. We tend to ignore any nuptial events that come our way. (We have nothing against you lovebirds; it's just best not to throw acid into a seeping wound.)

We normally send a nice Target gift card instead.

But this wedding invite could not be swept under the rug or stashed in a file because the bride was none other than the daughter of Mahatma Panchal, as in *the* Panchal Center for Cultural Diversity, as in my *boss*.

Besides, Griever or not, I had watched his American-born daughter Marcy sprout from a curious ten-year-old to the girl who gave the commencement speech as the valedictorian at her high school and again when she received her engineering degree from UT four years later. And now, how could I not be there to celebrate her next journey just because it involved love? I had attended nearly every type of cultural wedding over the years, and even though Marcy was marrying a white man, she had decided on a traditional Hindu ceremony, one of my favorites.

Before I lost Joel, weddings had become a sort of hobby for us. I rarely turned down a wedding invite and with so many students each semester I got my share of them. I'd seen them all: Jewish and Greek and Christian and Catholic. But a Pakistani wedding was right up there with Vietnamese in my book: colorful and long and full of symbolism, something every great linguist admires.

Joel had made fun of our pastime, and like most guys, generally preferred skipping the wedding ceremony and going straight for the reception, preferably with a stocked bar and lots of food. When we were on a tight budget, sometimes weddings were our very own date nights, and each time, at the close of the reception when we were among the last dancers on the dance floor, Joel would rub his nose against mine and whisper, "I do." And I would answer with a kiss, "I do, too."

This small renewal of our vows had become my favorite part of our wedding nights, and we enjoyed our very own honeymoon each time after, our lovemaking revitalized by the romance of the affair.

Post-Joel, weddings altogether lost their sparkle for me, not just because Joel would not be my date, but because I did not believe I could celebrate in coupledom as a widow. I thought my very presence there would send a signal of half-support, of what "could happen" if the other perishes. I know this half-empty-cup mentality was just my excuse for avoiding any more undue suffering, but this day and this night, I felt like celebrating.

Anh, my date for the evening, remained a strong believer in eloping after three failed marriages, but with the promise of free booze and a buffet, she agreed to come. "I say, 'save your money for the honeymoon, because if you break up later, at least you got a decent vacation out of it.'"

"Please don't repeat that this evening."

"What? As if half the guests wouldn't agree with me. You know I say *half* because that's the divorce rate, right? And what good is having a ceremony and a blessing when you can just change your mind, anyway? No one's going to hold their feet to that sacred fire they're going to walk around tonight, I'll tell you that."

"We're seating you in the bitter section at the far corner of the church," I told her. "Come on. Just suspend your ill will toward Cupid for one evening. Can you do that for me?"

Anh turned to face da Vinci in the back seat, where he sat in perfect view in my mirror. I had stolen glances at him the entire twenty minutes to the church, and it seemed he had never taken his eyes off of the rearview (hence, off of me). "What do you say, da Vinci, are you a hopeless romantic or a skeptic like your namesake?"

Da Vinci smiled broadly. "My namesake loved all beauty, and what can be more beautiful than two people in love?"

Anh stuck her finger in her mouth as if to gag. "I'm seriously going to be sick. This car is full of sappy romantics. So you're telling me that you actually *like* weddings? Because most *American* men despise them."

Da Vinci had shrugged his massive shoulders. "As you say, hopeless romantic. Only Italians maybe ten times more than Americans."

Anh shook her head. "And how you keep this one as far away as the backyard, I'll never understand." She turned back and faced da Vinci again. "Have you met any girls you like at school yet?"

"Many pretty girls, but not mature enough."

Anh raised her hand. "I need to book a one-way ticket to Italy, don't I? See American men *love* immature girls. And Leonardo, if you want mature, I'll give you mature." She raised a brow to me as if to say, *why not?*

When we arrived, da Vinci went through the service entrance where he would work for Panchal's catering company, which was started primarily as a way for Panchal to help employ the new immigrant students. I entered with him to say hello to my former students when Barack, a Nigerian who managed the catering company, spotted me and wrapped me in a hug. "How is my favorite teacher?"

"Excited about the wedding. My purse is full of nothing but Kleenex."

"You always were a sentimental one," Barack said, reminding me of how hard I cried at his graduation. I couldn't help it. To see them come over, sometimes with fewer than a dozen words of English and transform themselves into often brilliant communicators amazed me. "Leonardo is my best employee," Barack said as da Vinci grabbed his first silver platter and headed into the reception hall. "What is it the man cannot do?"

"I haven't figured that out yet," I told him. "Cecelia said he can do everything he's asked to do, but the one complaint we get back is when he thinks he's done with a project, he's done. Just stops working and starts daydreaming. Or writing things in his notebook."

"Well, here there is no time to daydream. Only smile and keep bringing the food." Barack shrugged. "And what about you? You look great. Working out to your sister's show, eh?"

"No. I've actually started running in the mornings after the kids go to school. With da Vinci."

Barack raised his brow. "So he is good personal trainer, too, correct?"

"You could say that," I said, rubbing Barack's arm as a way to end the conversation. Personal trainer. Gardener. Football coach to Bradley. Chess buddy to William. And cook for us all. The only way not to gain weight from having da Vinci in my life was to watch what I ate when he wasn't around and not insult him by not eating when he was. And running three miles every morning, rain or shine, our steps in sync as we drew long stares from the neighbors. The pounds were finally coming off.

I said goodbye to the crew and slipped into the church and next to Anh, who was staring intently at a man three rows up. She elbowed me in the ribs. "You know the only good thing about weddings is that occasionally you can meet a nice man, or at least one who you think is nice at first."

The lights were dimmed so I couldn't make out who she was staring at, but he did have a nice head with thick, blondish-brown hair.

He seemed to be alone, probably why Anh assumed he was available. "Make sure he doesn't slip away," Anh whispered as the music began to play. "I want that one."

We drew our eyes to the back of the church where Marcy and Panchal began to walk down the aisle. Marcy wore a red dress, a sari, symbolizing happiness. Since she was the only one allowed to wear red at the wedding, she could be spotted like a cardinal among sparrows. Her hands and feet were decorated with henna, called *mehandi*, in highly exotic, intricate patterns. It was believed that the deeper the color, the stronger her love for her husband. Her silken black hair was in a bun covered with a crown and veil, and sandalwood had been artistically applied to her face in the same design as her crown.

One look at her made me weep. It wasn't just the red—she embodied happiness and I was at once envious and happy for her. For all the mixers and place settings and toasters she would get, there was no greater gift than that feeling. If only I could've wrapped that up and put it in a time capsule for her to open on a distant day in the future when she may forget what it feels like. Instead, I got her a clock, but not the clock I wanted to give her—the one that allows time to stand still or even go backwards—but had to settle for a regular stainless steel number that ticks on and on infinitely. But still.

Her groom, Thomas, looked equally happy as he awaited her at the altar, wearing a white silk brocade suit, sword and turban— slightly unusual looking on a Caucasian male, but worn with pride. White flowers were tied in suspended strings over his forehead where sandalwood was decorated with gold, red, and white dots.

The Hindu wedding, a sacrament called Sanskara, brings together the spirit (Purush) with matter (Prakritti), emphasizing three core values: happiness, harmony and growth. Though the names of the wedding traditions were different, it shared many of the elements of an American wedding: the father giving away the bride (Kanyadan), and the unity candle (Havan), which is the Lighting of the Sacred Fire. The couple invokes Agni, the god of Fire, to witness their commitment to each other (the part Anh has a problem with). Crushed sandalwood, herbs, sugar, rice and oil are offered by the bride and groom into the fire.

Instead of the exchange of rings, they performed the Tying of the Nuptial Knot (Gath Bandhan), with scarves placed around the bride and groom, symbolizing their eternal bond, and pledged to love each other and remain faithful.

Next, they walked around the fire four times, each circle representing goals in life: Dharma, for religious and moral duties; Artha, for prosperity; Kama, meaning earthly pleasures; and Moksha, spiritual salvation and liberation.

Marcy led the walk first, representing her determination to stand beside her husband in happiness and sorrow. Next they took Seven Steps Together (Saptapardi) to signify the beginning of their lives together, each step signifying a marital vow.

First step: To respect and honor each other

Second step: To share each other's joy and sorrow

Third step: To trust and be loyal to each other

Fourth step: To cultivate appreciation for knowledge, values, sacrifice and service

Fifth step: To reconfirm their vow of purity, love, family duties and spiritual growth

Sixth step: To follow principles of Dharma (righteousness)

Seventh step: To nurture an eternal bond of friendship and love

My heart swelled with pride, as I could honestly say Joel and I had tried to live up to every one of those vows. We had only stumbled on step three, or it felt more like being tripped, when Monica Blevins tried to get Joel back. I wanted to give Joel the benefit of the doubt that he was not the pursuer.

I braced myself for whatever I would learn and then that would be that. No matter what, it would not change the fact that I loved him. It wasn't my love I had doubted. No, that wouldn't falter. I just wish I didn't care so much about his love for *me*.

As I watched Marcy and Thomas receive their blessing, I felt with every fiber of my being that Joel and I had been blessed. Our marriage was not perfect—none are—but we were blessed with joy and two boys who would live on as our legacy.

Thomas applied a small dot of vermilion, a powdered red mineral lead, to the bride's forehead, welcoming her as his partner for life. This was the act that set loose the tears, the simple act of a groom touching his bride. Out of all the things that I missed about Joel, this was highest among them. I often tried to close my eyes and recall his touch—how his body felt pressed up against mine, where my head rested on his collarbone when we hugged, how his fingers felt interlocked with mine. And right there, where Thomas placed the dot in the middle of her forehead, is where Joel kissed me every day after returning home from work. His lips had been soft and warm, and that kiss seemed to release the stress of my day. "You're home," I would say as if now everything in the world would be better because of it.

Anh had dug into my purse and handed me the Kleenex because, as usual, I didn't feel the tears on my face. I was so accustomed to crying, as if it were second nature. But these were happy tears. I could hear Deacon Friar's advice: try them with a joyful heart. I could feel Joel inside of me there and it was good.

When the ceremony ended and we followed the long line to the reception and full seven-course meal, Anh pinched my arm again, tugging and pulling me to reach the man whose back of the head she had fallen for. Just as we entered the reception hall, she purposely bumped into him, and he turned around. As Anh apologized profusely to the handsome man, his eyes met mine. "Don't tell me," I said. "You play golf with Panchal, too."

"Lion's Club," he said.

"When are you not moving and shaking?" I asked, and Anh gasped because I knew this man and she (the mover and shaker among us) did not, or perhaps she had noted the lilt of friendliness in my voice.

"Anh," I said. "This is Dr. Cortland Andrews." And as she tossed her hair and tilted her head flirtatiously, I noticed he did not puff his chest in response. And I hesitated to add, "My sister's boyfriend."

***

As luck would have it, Panchal had seated us at the same table as Cortland. Panchal was not only adept at helping foreigners fit in to America, he helped love misfits fit in, too. Or at least he was skilled at grouping us together.

We were in for a long evening together, and I drank in the glamour of the food and the wine and the conversation like a starved child. I noticed da Vinci had traded with another server to get our table, and he always served me first. I was probably drunk from his attention, too. Halfway into the evening, Cortland leaned behind Anh, who was seated between us, and said, "I think someone is smitten," and I thought he must've meant me until he raised his eyebrow each time da Vinci smiled at me, but only half-smiled (lips closed) to the other guests. The last time Cortland raised his eyebrow, I shrugged an acknowledgement. Perhaps he was right. Perhaps da Vinci was smitten with me, the woman who had taken him in, who had washed his soccer shorts and socks alongside my sons' and made him pancakes on the weekends and run alongside him every morning. For better or for worse, I had become da Vinci's modern patron. I knew we had become friends, but besides that kiss on the wrist and my dismount peck, there had been nothing to indicate our friendship was going anywhere.

"Shall we dance?" Cortland asked, finally. I'd been wanting to dance all evening, but feeling much like a wallflower, had not asked anyone. (Dances are normally considered a Couples activities for Normals, and being a widow wallflower is sadder than being a normal wallflower.)

Joel would've liked this reception, maybe not all the ingredients in the food, but definitely the bar. The American aspect of the reception, Thomas's one request, was the full bar, and the bartender knew how to mix even the latest fad drink.

"Have you decided on a dog yet?" Cortland said as we spun around the dance floor.

"A dog? Oh, a dog. No, I've been pretty busy. Besides, I wouldn't even know where to begin. Big dog, little dog, yappy dog, guard dog, and so on and so on. It's a big commitment."

"Ten to twenty years. My dad was a vet, so I'd be happy to help with your search."

Joel and I thought we had time to get a dog for the boys. Ten or twenty years seems like nothing to a young couple. Now I almost wanted a dog just to prove that I thought I *would* live another twenty, thirty, forty years or more. "I think I'll take you up on that." A date for doggy shopping? I have no idea why the thought of that excited me, but it felt like one thing I wouldn't have to do by myself.

"I found out more about what you do for a living," Cortland added. Rachel says you're kind of like a Mother Theresa. I think her exact words were, "Who else would want to teach English to a bunch of immigrants?'"

"That oozes with pride. She makes me sound like a volunteer who's taken in stray cats. She wouldn't be the first person who doesn't see immigrants as flesh and blood feeling humans. They aren't a charity case."

"I never said they were. Panchal is one of my dear friends. He had nothing but great things to say about you."

"Is there anyone you don't know?"

"My father used to say there are two types of people. Those who know many people a little bit and those who know a few people very well. I guess I fall into the first, but would prefer the second."

"More intimate connections."

He pulled me in closer to him. "Exactly. It's the few people that mean the most that should matter. I get the feeling you're the second type."

"Bingo. Only I *do* know a lot of immigrants."

"And one immigrant very well."

"Da Vinci?"

"Are you two dating?"

"Dating da Vinci? That would be an odd match." Cortland couldn't have been more direct and I couldn't truthfully answer yes or no, because we were somewhere in the middle.

"Really? Well, you know what they say about opposites attracting. And I see the way he looks at you."

I wanted to change the subject. "Did my sister mention I'm getting a PhD in linguistics?"

"Wow. She left that part out. Probably so as not to make me feel dumb. I might start watching every word I say because you might dissect it later."

"Root. Origin. Meaning. Subtext."

"No wonder you knew the meaning of Leibe's name. Then there's the whole body language thing, too. Do you know much about that?"

I could talk on it all evening, but I couldn't share that I had been watching couples everywhere I went for the signals of love through body language. I couldn't tell him that he had shown signs of flirting with me when I first met him and that he exhibited "excuse touching," the next stage in the tactile messages of attraction. He had touched my arm when we talked and had grabbed my hand to lead me on to the dance floor. He might get the wrong idea. Some people were just more touchy-feely than others. It probably came with his profession, and only someone deficient in touch as I had been the last two years would read so much into it. Cortland obviously paid attention to whatever was happening between da Vinci and me.

"Actually my dissertation is on the language of love. Even Rachel doesn't know that."

"I'd love to read it," he said.

"Fascinated with language, are you?"

"You know how we men of science are. We like to prove everything," he said. "Love is the great enigma of the universe. The chemistry, biology, pheromones, hormones and the mystery in falling in love. How can that not be fascinating?"

I began to feel flustered with all the talk of pheromones and chemistry mixed with the smell of his cologne and the vodka coursing through my blood, and nearing that time of night where Joel normally told me he would take me for his wife all over again, and then take me literally.

Fortunately, the song was over and as I headed to get my purse and my inebriated best friend, I noticed da Vinci out of the corner of my eye and when I turned to him, he crossed his arms, his body language clearly angry and jerked the kitchen door open and slipped inside.

Chapter 7

Greek to Me: Ancient Love

The language of love took written form thousands of years ago, with great philosophers like Plato and Aristotle tackling the meaning, seeking truth by Eros.

Eros (*érōs*) is passionate love, with sensual desire and longing. The modern Greek word "eratos" means "romantic love."

Plato believed *eros* helps the soul recall knowledge of beauty and contributes to an understanding of spiritual truth.

"ARE YOU DONE YET?" da Vinci stood over my shoulder, looking down at my laptop. Nothing like a hot Italian to make me forget about my Greek. Of this I was sure: Plato got it right. Love is the Highest Good. Provides the ultimate meaning found in human beings. And I was so sure I'd never experience *eratos* again that the very thought of romance felt Greek to me.

Which made the fact that da Vinci wanted my attention all the more mesmerizing. Being interrupted meant there was someone *to* interrupt me, and it wasn't to find his missing sneaker or fetch him a snack.

"No. I probably won't be done for weeks."

"That won't do," da Vinci said, taking my hand and pulling me out of my seat. "Do you see outside?"

I surveyed the back yard, where the crisp orange leaves had nearly all fallen to the ground. "Time to rake."

Da Vinci shook his head. "No. We do this." He handed me a flyer that he got who knows where. I knew he couldn't read it all, probably the sight words, but his comprehension was aided by the photos of couples drinking wine at a festival. "Eat. Drink."

"Be merry?" The wine festival was at least an hour into the country at a local vineyard that had gotten a lot of press. Joel and I had talked about going to a wine festival for years, but they seemed to always conflict with college football Saturdays, and in fact, so did this one. Bradley was on the couch now, watching the Longhorns play the Sooners in Dallas for their annual Big River rivalry. Bradley was decked out in his burnt-orange football jersey that Joel had given him for his birthday. It was too snug on him now and I'd offered to buy him a new one, but that wasn't the point. He liked it because his father gave it to him, and seeing how much he'd grown was a painful reminder of how quickly things change. The boys were growing every day, while for the longest time, I felt I'd been shrinking. But today seemed like a gorgeous day to grow. Only I couldn't possibly just leave for the day with da Vinci.

William grabbed the flyer from my hands. "Cool. I think you guys should go. I'll rake the leaves, Mom."

I shook my head. "You'll what? Are you feeling okay? You've never offered to do the chores before."

"It's fine. You two go and have a great time and when you get back, we'll make chili for dinner. I found Dad's recipe, and da Vinci has never eaten chili before. Especially good Texas chili."

Da Vinci nodded enthusiastically. Were the two of them in on this together? "But we're supposed to play Scrabble," I told him. "You've been waiting all week."

William pushed his glasses back onto the bridge of his nose and shrugged. "The sunny day won't last forever and Scrabble will. We'll play tomorrow."

"Are you sure?" I could feel the guilt of spending a day with da Vinci in the sun melt away with each reassuring word from my son. "What about you, Bradley?"

"Whatever," Bradley said, which was his way of giving permission.

An hour later, the boys were back home with a neighborhood sitter while we were out in the country, which felt the same as being on another planet. The change in da Vinci was perceptible; he was more at ease in the country, as if we were closer to his homeland. Even though we were in the middle of nowhere, we were surrounded by food vendors and throngs of people who had done just as we had and gotten away from it all.

Da Vinci took my hand as we made our way through the crowd to the wine tables where we could sample a dozen wines, and I was surprised at how comfortable his hand felt in mine. We took our first glass of wine—a white, sweet varietal—and plopped down right in the middle of two dozen blankets around us, filled by couples and even young families. I wondered if we should've brought the boys, but I knew Bradley would've complained about missing the game and I would have to be the mom instead of what, da Vinci's date?

He was progressing further in his English than my other students, something that made me feel guilty because of the individual attention I was giving him. He had begun to make friends at UT, though he felt too old to join a fraternity, where he said they care only about guzzling beer and meeting girls. He surprised me, considering he had asked me the first day if I could hook him up with Jessica Simpson. As far as I could tell, he hadn't dated anyone on campus, though he had gone to a few study groups.

Da Vinci lay back on the blanket, his hands behind his head and stared up at the clouds. "This is my idea of Heaven," he said.

"A wine festival?"

"A beautiful place with a beautiful woman." He reached up and touched his thumb to my cheek. I took his hand and kissed it, forgetting for the moment that we were surrounded by people, but they were safe, *strangers*.

It had been so long since I had just sat and relaxed that it took me two glasses of wine to unwind. Finally I lay on the blanket next to da Vinci, propped on my side. I could've stared at him all afternoon. People pay for cable and you know what? Women would much rather pay to watch a beautiful man breathe, just inches from you, close enough that you can smell his shampoo and aftershave. "Tell me what you think about when you daydream. And what do you write in that notebook of yours?"

Da Vinci removed the notebook from the back pocket of his jeans, but didn't show it to me. "I wondered if you would ask. Inquisitive teacher. I dream about everything. I dream about home, about mother and sisters and nieces and nephews. My grandparents had small vineyard, so my memories of them are going to stomp grapes and even as child, you get to drink wine at dinner table. Make me feel very grown. I think how much they would like you. My sisters always read magazines picturing American women with blonde hair. First woman I saw on uncle's TV was *Three's Company* show, no?"

"Suzanne Somers." Another big-boobed blonde with giant, shiny teeth. Wow. I'm *nothing* like her at all.

"I dream about what can I do in the future for job."

"But you've enjoyed every job you've had so far, right? Being a florist and a landscaper and preparing food."

Da Vinci propped his head on his hand and looked at me eye to eye, just six inches from my face. I was afraid to breathe. "I do them and am good at them, but I get bored and ready for next challenge. Does this make sense? I'd rather do this."

I cleared my throat. By this, I was thinking he meant spend his days at wine festivals and not spend his days with me no matter what we are doing, but I was too embarrassed or shocked to ask him to clarify. "I don't think lounging around in the sun pays much," I teased.

He took my hand and kissed the soft side of my wrist, a place I don't recall ever being kissed by anyone. Then he moved up my arm, kissing it until he reached the velvety paper-thin skin on the inside of my elbow, perhaps the softest skin on the body, where I had never been kissed, either.

Then he leaned in and kissed my lips, slowly, softly, again and again until the noise and the people had all stopped for us, or else I had put them on pause. When I pulled away, da Vinci smiled. "What? Is it okay?"

I smiled back, the noise rushing back into our space. "Very, very okay." Over a loudspeaker, a man made the announcement for the next wine tour so we joined our group. His notebook went back in his pocket, its contents still a mystery. We held hands and listened to the vintner talk about the wine, only I didn't hear a word he said. I was listening for the smaller sounds that felt enormous—the sound of da Vinci's laughter, the sound of our clothes rustling as we walked in unison, the sound of the grass crunching beneath our feet.

And besides listening, I was enraptured by touch—da Vinci pulling me in closer to him, his arm around my waist, hip to hip, lingering behind the group, walking slowly, and when we reached the end of the row and they turned right, we turned left and slipped away, da Vinci pushing me against the vines, grapes like barrettes in my hair as he kissed me deeply, passionately. With each kiss I could feel myself coming back to life, my blood pumping through my veins, my heart beating fast, wild, my skin remembering how good it felt to be touched, to be wanted.

My da Vinci was an explorer. His hands explored my body, he pulled me into him, and then he explored the warm territory of my back, the soft region of my breasts, and just when he headed south, I could see the group coming our way, so I stopped the exploration and we ran, hand in hand down the long row of vines to explore elsewhere. Together.

Chapter 8

Scrabble word: pursuit (22 points)

FOR A LINGUIST, THERE is no better sport than Scrabble. Though doing the crossword had been a couples' sport for Joel and me, Scrabble had always been a family sport. Joel had been very competitive, turning everything we did into a game. The boys loved it. Last one to the ice cream stand doesn't get sprinkles! (Me.) First one to jump in the lake gets to dunk someone! (Me, dunked.) Even the neighborhood weekly basketball game had a prize. Losing team had to buy beer for the winning team on their guys' night out at, yep, a sports bar. The sport didn't matter: football, basketball, hockey, baseball. Joel's last words were about winning. And sex.

He had hooked his arm around my neck and whispered in my ear, "Winner gets the booty prize." Of course I could never tell anyone this. I had attended only one grief group session at Life Church and vowed never to return. We went around the circle sharing what our loved ones last words had been; they had all been rather ordinary, like life: *Honey, can you pick up some milk at the store? We've got dinner reservations at six. Have you seen my black socks?* And my personal favorite: *We're out of hemorrhoid cream.* But just because someone said "hemorrhoid cream" did not mean I would reveal my husband's last words. Besides, some things should be kept private. It was the last thing that could only be shared with Joel and me. I had dissected his words a hundred times over. No matter which way I spliced it, how

I might've wished he would've said "I love you" one last time, he was being Joel. He was a guy's guy who loved having sex with his girl. I should be proud that after nearly ten years of marriage, he still wanted to have sex with me. And better yet, to consider it a "prize."

Still. There were times Joel's competitive nature irked me, but his passionate pursuit for winning was his thing. Being number one was important to him. The kind of person who hangs his plaques and awards and news clippings on the wall where he can remind himself of his achievements and everyone else can see them, too. I felt inferior in this department, not that he did anything to make me feel this way. He preferred the spotlight while I lingered contentedly in the shadows. I was a watcher. He was a doer. In my humble opinion, the doer should never die.

Putting that word, *pursuit*, on the Scrabble board was a small reminder that I could not give up. I had never been a chaser of dreams. But even a bookworm like me could pursue happiness, and if it so happened that *eros* came along with it, then so be it. In fact, I was currently playing footsie with da Vinci under the table. He was seated to my right and I had slipped off my fuzzy slippers and crept my toes inside the leg of his jeans. Da Vinci had responded by putting his hand on my knee and moving his thumb in small circles on my bone. I had no idea even that hard part of my body could have so much feeling.

The boys played with us, William currently in the lead because I wasn't at the top of my game. The footsie and the knee rubbing were distracting my mental capacity for word formation. Da Vinci was holding his own with four- and some five-letter English words. The boys loved to catch him misspelling something, though honestly I would've let him get by with it. I didn't have to be his teacher all the time.

Bradley hated Scrabble, yet he played with us because he was a joiner like his father. He didn't want to be excluded. And he was better at the game than he realized. He thought of words I would never think to assimilate on my tile rack. Defense. Tackle. Touchdown. (That one was on the triple word score.) He collected medals and ribbons and trophies on his bedroom wall on a special shelf put up by his father. (Same for William, only different sorts of prizes.)

I didn't have a single medal, certificate, or plaque in my possession. I'm sure I received them. I got good grades, but my mother had never been one to boast, and while she probably had them tucked somewhere in a chest in the attic to give me before or after she died, we didn't make a big deal out of winning. "It's how you play the game," she had told us a thousand times. We often unconsciously repeat the words our parents put in our mouths from our childhood, and when I said those words to our sons, Joel would shake his head, and add, "But it *is* important to do your best. There's nothing wrong with winning." So he was verbally sort of agreeing with me while physically disagreeing with me. I hated when he did that.

If being an overachiever is a downfall, then I'll take it. It was much better than so many spousal issues. He still made time for fun. If life was a game, then he played it very, very well.

Monica had been just like him. Even in her glossy magazine article, I could tell she was still on the overachiever track. She was a partner in her law firm and had collected all the rewards of her pursuit of riches and fame. Happiness, I wasn't so sure. Why else had she begun to pursue Joel again when she was married? My own journey meant our roads had to converge. I was building up the courage to confront her, but had not yet figured out a way that I wouldn't sound like a total idiot. I began to understand the phrase, "bury the hatchet." (An American English colloquialism meaning "to make peace." Borrowed from the figurative or literal practice of putting away the tomahawk at the cessation of hostilities among or by Native Americans in the Eastern United States. Weapons were to be buried or otherwise cached in time of peace.)

Still, I had to know. I would never achieve inner peace without it.

People like Joel can think of an idea and have a plan formulated in a matter of minutes and then, as the Nike slogan goes, just do it. People like me have to dip their toe into the water first. We do our research. Cover our bases. And then, at a snail's pace, proceed.

Thus far, I have done the research. In my grief binder, I have written both the work and home phone numbers, e-mail addresses and physical addresses for Monica Blevins. I have pulled up her corporate web site and read and re-read her bio. I don't know what I was hoping to find. It was a very bland, lawyer-type bio, packed full of the kind of achievements achievers like to add to such. The fourth time I read it I noticed something: *a clue.* Top 40 Under 40 class, three years ago, same as Joel. There had been a reception and Joel had asked me if I wanted to go, but I usually declined his corporate schmooze-fests and besides, William and Bradley had pizza night at Cub Scouts. I'd take a greasy slice of pepperoni and rowdy kids to a boring business function any day.

I tried to recall that night. I'd seen the plaque. He'd handed it to me when he got in that night.

"It's late," I'd said. 10 p.m. Well, late for married people on a school night. Late I thought for a business reception. "How did it go?"

"Fine," he'd said. "Nothing special."

"Nice plaque. It's even got your name engraved on it."

"I'll live in infamy," he'd joked as he planted the kiss in the middle of my forehead.

"Smells like you had wine."

"You've got a nose like a bloodhound."

"And perfume." Our eyes had locked. "You must stop hugging all the ladies, darling." I'd been joking.

He had laughed. I was never very good at jokes. Joel and Bradley were the good jokesters in the family and William could hold his own where sarcasm was concerned, but Joel had only retreated to the bathroom to brush the wine from his teeth and toss the perfume-scented clothes in the hamper. I hadn't thought it had been anything other than my husband's proclivity to hug his associates—yes, guys, too. It wasn't very PC (you are supposed to do "side hugs" in the office), but still.

It was two weeks after that Joel mentioned he was up for a bid on a new big law firm project. I had been finishing the crossword puzzle. (Joel got it first, answered the ones he knew—typically sports- and business-related items—and then I finished it off, usually two-thirds, not that I'm boasting.) "Oh, yeah. Which one? Don't tell me, it has a bunch of people's last names in it. Like Swarovski, William-Sonoma, Crate & Barrel. Right?"

"Close. Stevens Blevins Polanski."

"Like Roman Polanski." I was always looking for ways to link words, make them familiar to me, place them in the Rolodex of my mind. But the name Blevins had not rung a bell until much later.

A month later, Joel's firm had been awarded the project, and he had been busy in his studio drawing up the designs. "My best work yet," he said, same as he did with every new project.

I recalled breakfast meetings and lunch meetings and even a couple of late-night dinner meetings. This was not altogether uncommon for big projects when the decision makers couldn't carve the time into their day to meet with the architects, so they got creative and involved food. Even so, there were a few more of those meetings than was typical. But when I found out *which* partner he was meeting with, who was *leading* the project and sharing breakfast, lunch, and dinner with my husband, I went ballistic. Monica Blevins. *Beautiful, my-first-love, ex-fiancée Monica Blevins*. Married, but still. Come on.

Then came the fights. *You don't trust me. How can you possibly think I'd cheat on you with her after what she did to me? Did you know how much I loved her? How hard it was for me to love again after what happened? Do you know how humiliating it was to tell our family and friends there would be no wedding after everything they'd invested? How many friendships were ruined because they had to pick sides? Come on, Ramona. Please. Have some faith.*

But I hadn't. I couldn't. My mind raced with the words I thought could ruin us. But it wasn't the hint of adultery that nearly ruined us—it was the crumbling of the faith that could have led to our demise. In fact, I think the more that I obsessed over it, the more he probably considered *having* an affair. I had demanded too much. *What did you talk about? What's her husband like? Are they happily married? Did you talk about me? About the kids? Do you still have feelings for her?* On and on, I'd gone like an idiot missing a shut-off switch. With each question, I had dug us deeper into a hole. For Joel, faith was never an issue. He believed in me, in us. He believed in God and believed he would go to Heaven. He believed you could forgive and be friends with someone who broke your heart. I didn't. I believed *eros* could never fully be erased from one's memory—its magical dust so tiny on the soul, it could never be cleansed. He didn't have to tell me he still loved her. I knew deep in my bones.

He had done what good husbands do and gave the project—his blood, sweat, and tears and drawings—to another partner and said, "Fine. If you can't be mature about this, then I won't see her again." And he died two weeks later.

***

Da Vinci and I hadn't found a moment to be alone together again the entire week after the wine festival. Though we had made out like teenagers in the front seat of my black station wagon in the field parking lot at the festival, I wasn't about to have sex with him in my car. Not even the darkest tinted windows (if I had them) could make me give in to desire. But *almost.* Especially after he whispered, "*Ti desidero.*" *I want you.* And I so badly wanted to be wanted. No, I *needed* to be wanted. But it had to be the right time.

And in the car was not it. If I was going to give up my second virginity, it had to be special.

This, too, became my pursuit, though not a "write it down on paper, put it in a grief binder" kind of pursuit. The pursuit was within, the prick of desire that wouldn't go away, the wheels of our ultimate union were already in motion—the eyes, the flirting, the touching, the kissing—it all led down one road. *If.* If I let it happen. If I gave in to him, though my mind was telling me it might not be a good idea. Because he was my student. Because it was too soon. Because I was afraid what might happen if I did.

Remember, me not being the "just do it" type, also applied to just doing *it.* Everything in time. But soon.

Scheduling time for things like *amore* is difficult enough for married people, but nearly impossible for widows with two busy kids, a nosy mother and a needy sister. Zoe had another something Rachel wanted us to attend. Not sure if it was a recital (modern dance, jazz, ballet, singing), a play (where Rachel fought for the lead role each time) or a beauty pageant, but nonetheless, we were expected to be there for every single one of them. (Not that she returned the attention by going to my boys' events, because though she'd "love to," the mini-celeb, rising star herself was just "too busy.")

Da Vinci asked to come along, and my first instinct was that it was a very bad idea. I didn't want my family thinking there was anything going on with da Vinci, and it might look peculiar to have him tagging along to a family event. But he was lonely. And he loved children, saying often how much he missed his big family back in Italy. I worried that the kids liked him too much now, that da Vinci would move on from us and they would lose another male figure. Protecting my children from future heartbreak was more important than my own.

Yet I acquiesced—it was only an innocent play, I told myself—and we headed out to the production called *Four Seasons,* put on by the creative independent school Zoe attended. Zoe missed way too much school to go to public school, and because Rachel deemed the arts and individual expression the highest standard for an education, Zoe ended up at the Austin Creative Academy where parents hoped for future Mozarts or Dickenses or … well, da Vincis. It also happened to be where the A.D.D. kids who failed in a more regimented environment got stuck, so it was an interesting mix, to say the least.

We arrived late as usual—Bradley couldn't find his lucky socks and William couldn't find his light jacket and da Vinci had to shower in my bathroom because a pipe had busted in the studio. I know what you're thinking. Did I get a sneak peek at da Vinci in the shower to see if reality matched up to my fantasy?

Yes. And no. While I was busy shoveling through my kids' drawers and closets to find their missing items, I remembered that some of Bradley's clean clothes had gotten mixed in with my clothes by mistake. I'd seen them in my closet, which is of course off my bathroom where da Vinci was showering. I opened the door, the steam from the shower rushing out, and slipped into my closet. As I passed by the shower with the clear plexiglass stall, I could see the frame of a naked man and all I could think was that I couldn't believe there was *any* naked man in my shower, let alone a man like da Vinci. I tried to be quiet, but my closet door squeaked and da Vinci hollered out. "Is that you, Mona Lisa?"

And I could feel my whole body tingle from the toes up and answered. "I'm sorry. I'm looking for Bradley's sock."

Da Vinci hollered back. "You've been keeping secret from me, Mona Lisa."

"Oh, yeah? What's that?"

"Your shower is much better than studio shower. Not complaint, though. Only truth. No fix other shower, and I shower with you."

He didn't laugh, but with his broken English, I couldn't always tell when he was kidding. I couldn't see his face. Until I turned, missing sock in hand, and saw da Vinci peek his head out from the shower door. With a big smile on his face. I saw six inches of his naked body from top down, but only the left side. "It's warm in here. Come and join me. I'll wash your hair."

If we didn't have to be at the auditorium in ten minutes and if we were alone in the house, I would've leapt into the shower as if my feet were on fire. If my heart were beating any faster, I was sure it would explode. Still, *eros* would have to wait. "I'll take a raincheck," I said, which da Vinci didn't understand. "That means next time."

He closed the door again and started singing in Italian. I don't know what it was, but I could've listened to it all night long. "Whatever," da Vinci said, which he had picked up from Bradley, only da Vinci didn't infuse the same sarcasm.

Now all I could think about was how badly I needed a shower.

My father hates to be late, and nearly all of my childhood memories involve my dad standing with his elbow in the air, his right eyebrow cocked, staring at his watch as if the house would explode if we didn't get out by the time the minute hand hit whatever magical number he had in mind for us to leave.

In all other regards, my father was an easygoing dad: fair, caring, and noble. Yes, like his name.

Noble: from Latin, *(g)nobilis,* "noted, highborn" from the Indo-European root, *gno.* My father revered education, was a better Scrabble player than I am, and while other dads in my neighborhood hosted poker night, my dad preferred Trivial Pursuit. No one would dare call my dad a nerd. If so, he was a handsome nerd. Or at least I'd give him "distinguished looking." Yes, like his name. He was easy to get along with because he knew enough about any given topic to keep a conversation going and tell you something you didn't know about your favorite topic. I loved that about him. He had also filled my head with many useless facts over the years, which I was surprised to have come back to help me years later. He taught me about anagrams, a word formed by rearranging all the letters of another word, when I was six. It was my favorite car game and before I knew it, everywhere I went I was forming anagrams. It became our "thing."

"Cinema," Dad would say as we were in line for a movie.

"Iceman," I would quickly answer.

"Good girl," he would say and pat my head.

No wonder I was getting a PhD in linguistics. I'd been trained like Pavlov's dog. My love for words grew from there—my pastime looking for root words and keeping a dictionary in my backpack (and later purse) to satiate my thirst whenever I encountered a word I didn't know. Then a notebook much like da Vinci's, though I still didn't know what was in his. Mine was full of words. I had pages of words I loved like:

butter

crème de la crème

avant garde

muse

monkey

poignant

And words that made me cringe:

asparagus

prison

death

And even words that weren't even real words, but ones I thought should exist like "mind-drift" and "love coma." I tried these words (and many others) out over the years, but so far, none of them had caught on. I would have to get them in a Steven Spielberg movie or on MTV to accomplish adding a new popular phrase into the dictionary.

Noble was checking his watch in the dark (yes, it had a light in it, of course) when we arrived. Even in the near dark of the theater, his look spoke volumes. And he sighed as if to say, "Oh, Ramona, still late at thirty-six years of age." Two boys had not improved my proclivity for tardiness. Another word I love: proclivity.

He kissed me on the cheek, my mother hugged the boys and me, and Rachel was nowhere to be found—probably backstage being a stage mom. My father said, "Ramona, this is Dr. Cortland Andrews," and my stomach dropped. I had no idea. What a silly thing for my body to do, just from the mention of someone's name. I squinted and sure enough, Cortland was sitting next to my father, with three empty seats to his left. The boys sat next to my mother, and I introduced da Vinci to my father. My mother was busy mothering da Vinci: how was he liking America, is Ramona feeding you enough, can I come do your laundry. Good. They just thought I was being nice to him. His patron, no more, no less. They wouldn't in a million years believe da Vinci had just propositioned me in the bathroom. I perspired just thinking about it.

"Good to see you," Cortland said as I scooted past him to sit down. Cortland and da Vinci shook hands, though da Vinci told me the night of Panchal's wedding that he didn't like Cortland. Or more specifically, did not like the way he looked at me or danced with me. He'd been jealous. Silly, really. I started to sit two seats over from Cortland to leave room for Rachel, but Cortland said, "She won't come back. She asks me to come to these things, and I never see her until after they're over with." He patted the empty seat with his hand, so I obliged and sat next to him. Da Vinci sat on my left. The last time I was sandwiched by two handsome guys? You guessed it: *never.* "How are you?" I asked Cortland, our shoulders rubbing together as I sat down.

He straightened in his seat. "Hey, I'm glad you came. I have a word for you."

My father used to do this. Try to stump me. I'd gone through dozens of calendars and books on vocabulary, e-mail words of the day, and the thickest dictionaries on the planet trying to keep up. "Hit me."

"Abaction."

"Good one. But we are in Texas, cattle country. It means cattle-stealing."

Cortland frowned. "Okay. Devoir."

"As in, 'It is your devoir to win this spelling bee, Ramona.' Courtesy, my dad before my fourth-grade regional championship."

"And did you do your duty and win?"

"Second place, and don't rub it in."

"I can't believe I'm telling you this, but I was Texas spelling bee champion in 1972. Sixth grade."

"Fine. I'm a little jealous. I lost sixth grade to Morton Fitz."

"With a name like Morton Fitz, how could he lose?"

The lights went off, abruptly ending our conversation. Only our third meeting and I could see why my dad and sister both liked Cortland. Skilled conversationalist, never at a loss for words. Unlike me, who had so many words to choose from I often gave up and remained silent. Cortland knew I liked words, so that's where he started with me. Charming, really. But devoir? Come on. Amateur.

The curtain raised and within a minute, da Vinci held my hand. I could feel my heart quicken as I decided whether or not to let him hold it (which my heart wanted him to do) or to slip it out (which I felt I had to do to save an explanation to my parents). The second option would no doubt hurt da Vinci's feelings, and I really did want the raincheck on the shower and whatever else may come. Why did I care what my parents thought? Hadn't my mother just the week prior said how glad she was I have some company? That I didn't seem quite so lonely anymore? Maybe she didn't think I would have *that kind* of a relationship with da Vinci. But still.

I squeezed da Vinci's hand and then got up, telling him I needed to go to the restroom. I made my way to the back of the theater where I watched my darling niece stumble over her lines, trip across the stage and keep a plastered grin on her face for a solid hour. My knees were weak from standing, but I didn't return to my seat until the final number and then I put my hands in my jacket pocket and shivered as if I were cold in the theater.

When Rachel and the tiny starlet joined us in the aisle, Rachel hugged Cortland and kissed him on the lips, right in front of my parents. I'd always felt funny about public displays of affection, even after Joel and I had been married for years. "Hey, you," she said to him in a flirty voice full of sex appeal. Their language of love was out in full view for the world to see. They were an open book. They were having sex and lots of it. Only later in the bathroom she'd told me I was wrong. No sex yet.

"Believe me, I've practically thrown myself on him, but I can't believe he's the wait-until-marriage type, even if he is a good Christian man," she gushed as she reapplied lip gloss, then tilted her head as if to reconsider. "A few more dates I'm sure he'll give in. How can he resist this?"

"How indeed," I said, my throat catching. Maybe I was feeling a little jealous, and though my sister had enjoyed a spirited sex life since her divorce, this one got to me. I didn't want her to kiss Cortland, let alone have sex with him. He was the only guy she'd ever dated after Michael that I liked. Not *like* liked, just liked in the general humankind sort of way.

"What about you? Knocking boots with Leo yet?"

I brushed through my hair, trying not to compare it to my sister's. It wasn't fair that I'd just spent $125 on a color job that I couldn't afford in the first place and hers still looked shinier and bouncier. "Don't be silly."

"I'm not being silly. I'm being hopeful. For you. If I weren't with Cortland, I'd be in hot pursuit. You're just not interested, huh?"

"Actually, he has kissed me. I mean we've kissed. At a wine festival."

Rachel's wide mouth opened even wider and emitted a squeal of delight. "OhmygodI'msohappyforyou. Is he a great kisser? I always imagined Italians would be the best kissers."

"Very much so. He's young, though. I think kissing improves with age."

"Poo. It's when they're young and hot and full of reckless abandon that it's good. I bet sleeping with him will be …" She rolled her eyes into the back of her head. "OhmygodIcan'tbelieveI'mjealousofyou."

I swelled with pride. Of course I shouldn't have to keep da Vinci a secret. I was a grown woman. I could make my own decisions about my love life. About getting one, that is. I'd just have to deal with the teacher issue and figure out how to break the news to Judith without breaking her heart, and then we were fair game. Not that I'd let my sister's jealousy speed along any decision.

"There you are," Cortland said as I exited the bathroom, and for a split second I thought he'd been waiting for *me* until I saw that my sister was directly behind me. Cortland locked eyes with me, *one, two, three*, then focused on my sister, who put her arm around his waist and led him away from me.

My boys were still at the table, talking football. My boys: William, Bradley, and da Vinci. When I approached, they all three looked up at me with adoration. Not as adorably as when my boys were little and they shouted "Momma!" every time I entered the room, but for growing boys and one young man, I felt very lucky. Especially when da Vinci leaned over and whispered in my ear, "*Usciamo di qui.*"

Let's get out of here.

Chapter 9

Anagrams: Leonardo da Vinci

FOR SOMEONE OF QUESTIONABLE faith, I looked for signs only where I'd felt comfortable: within words. I thought it meant something that Cortland named his dog "love." I thought it meant something that my da Vinci had been named after that da Vinci and that Mona Lisa was a derivative of my full name. Even though I couldn't explain it, I knew that in this time and this space Mona Lisa (me) and da Vinci (him) meant something together though. To figure it out, I searched for meaning within his name, playing the anagram game that had become second nature to me. There were plenty of messages to be found within Leonardo da Vinci:

A candid lore vino. The "lore" of our names.

A candid role vino. The "role vino" had played in our courtship at the wine festival.

A candid rove loin. Having a roving loin could be a bad thing, but as long as it was roving in my direction, I took it as a good sign.

Which led me to:

A candid lover ion. It couldn't be helped. *We* couldn't be helped. It was right there: da Vinci and Mona Lisa's union. Love matter. Right there in his name. All along.

As Anh helped me rake leaves the following day (the thing about leaves is, they keep falling until the last leaf is gone. The trees were now bare, which meant we were only two weeks from Joel's death date), I confessed to Anh my intentions. I'm not sure if I wanted her to give me a high-five or a stern, shake-her-finger-at-me type of warning or do a cartwheel. Instead, she stared at me blankly for a few seconds, which felt more like an hour. Then she threw her rake down and wrapped her skinny arms around me.

"Good for you, Rames." Her hug also felt like it lasted an hour. When she let go, she had tears in her eyes.

"Oh, dear. Why are you crying?"

"Because I'm so happy for you. Because I can tell how much happier you've been lately and if he's the reason for it, then I say, *more amore!*"

"Well, I got him transferred into another class. I'm no longer his teacher, though I am still *a teacher*. Fortunately Panchal met his own wife at the cultural center, so he can't exactly throw stones."

Anh shrugged. "You're both adults and it's not a public university. Besides, sometimes you can't help how you meet who you meet, you know?"

"And besides, it's not like we would be going anywhere relationship-wise. It would just be for companionship."

"And great sex."

I tossed my rake onto the ground. This is why I had to tell Anh. I wasn't looking for consensus or approval. I was looking for a sex pep talk. "I don't think I can go through with it. I'm scared. And don't you dare tell me it's like riding a bike."

Anh put her hands on her hips. "No. It's a helluva lot more fun than getting back on a bike again. And take it from me, someone who's had more sexual partners than should probably be openly admitted and three of them very different husbands in the sack; the fundamentals are the same from guy to guy."

"Uh, yeah. I don't need a diagram. Tab A goes into Slot B, repeat as necessary, thankyouverymuch."

"What I mean is, once things get going, it kind of takes care of itself. The body almost goes into autopilot. Only some autopilots are a lot sexier than others."

"Well, it did feel like if I hadn't stopped things at the wine festival or in the car that I could've gone through with it. If only ..."

" ... you didn't feel guilty about Joel."

"Exactly."

"Well, if Heaven weren't already as great as having sex every minute of the day, then he would be doing it, too. I once read orgasm is the closest thing we experience on earth to the feeling we'll have to the perfect bliss we'll feel in Heaven."

"But you don't believe in Heaven. You believe in reincarnation."

"It doesn't matter what I believe; it matters what *you* believe. And you believe in Heaven, and I do believe in bliss, so go for it."

"A little piece of Heaven might be nice."

"Or a lot of it. A whole lot of bliss."

Bliss: a word missing from my personal vocabulary. What would it be like to have it back in my dictionary? To actually feel it?

"What about you? Gone blissing lately? You haven't shared, which means you either haven't or you're keeping secrets."

Anh shrugged her shoulders. "I swore I wouldn't tell you."

"This can't be good. Maybe I don't wanna know."

"I had a thing the other night ..."

"Great. You're telling me anyway. Fine, you had a mover/shaker thing?"

"Exactly. And who was there, but Michael."

"As in my ex-brother-in-law Michael?"

"Mr. Republican Himself. So we have a few drinks. You know how vodka tonics do me."

"No. Don't even say it." I threw down the rake and covered my ears. "You slept with Michael and now neither of you are going to go to the boys' games with me, and it'll be all awkward and weird, and oh, Jesus, Anh, couldn't you stick to a safe glass of Chardonnay?"

"I'd had a very bad day. My stock dropped."

"And that makes you sleep with people you don't like?"

"No, it makes me drink vodka tonics with extra lime. And sometimes it leads to sleeping with someone I don't like. But it's not that I dislike Michael as a person. He's a good-looking enough man."

"Who fundamentally disagrees with everything you stand for."

"Well, he *has* bought stock in my company, so he can't be all bad, political, social and spiritual views aside."

"What other view is there?"

"The strictly physical view. Nice smile. Nice body. Nice voice. Nice hands."

"I've never noticed his hands."

"That's because they haven't been all over your body."

I cringed. "*Ewww.* Okay. I still think of him as a brother, so you can leave the deets out of your conquest this time."

"He's an amazing lover. Quite aggressive."

"Must be why he and Rachel stayed married so long. So what does this mean? You're not going to start dating him, are you?"

"I can't imagine what we'd possibly do other than what we've already done, which is fine by me. There are four basic human needs. Do you know what they are?"

"I have a feeling you're going to tell me sex is one of them."

"Food, drink, sleep, and sex. And not exactly in that order, either. I'll admit Michael wasn't my first choice, though. I had a drink with Cortland before he had to jaunt off to some play of Zoe's."

"Ohmigod. *You're* the reason Michael was late to Zoe's play?"

"He made it in time for the third act, didn't he? Besides, I think our first two acts were far more interesting."

I shook my head. "No wonder he was in such a good mood when he arrived."

Anh smiled proudly. "Michael was in a good mood? Of course he was in a good mood, what am I saying? And now that I think about it, all Cortland did was ask questions about you before he took off."

I straightened my shoulders. "He did? What sort of questions?"

"About you and da Vinci, for one thing. If you've dated since you lost Joel, how it happened, how you're coping with the boys. He didn't mention your sister once."

"He just wants to get to know her family better is all. I think she might be getting serious about him. They're all coming here for dinner on Sunday. It's Dad's birthday and I get birthday duty."

We bagged up the leaves, and I tried to get Cortland out of my mind. I don't know why I was looking forward to seeing him again. So my sister was dating a nice, sweet, funny guy who asks about me. Big deal.

Anh placed the bags in the trashcan and we went inside. My neighborhood coffee was in thirty minutes, just enough time to shower and put on the coffee and rolls.

"Here's the number you asked for," Anh said, handing me a business card. The chakra specialist. I couldn't believe I was going to see a yogi. "You'll thank me later. I can't wait to see what the new and improved Ramona looks like. Scratch that. What she *feels* like."

After Anh left, I peeled off my clothes and stepped into the shower and began humming a favorite song of Joel and mine: Sonny and Cher's "I Got You, Babe." Sometimes I thought the shower hitting my scalp was like pushing the on button on the stereo in my mind. I only sang Sonny and Cher in the shower, and even then, I sang badly but with fervor.

When I paused to grab the shampoo, the song went on without me. Through the shower glass, I saw a frame, da Vinci's frame, as he peeled off his shirt and hummed the song I didn't even know he knew. "Is okay to shower now, Mona Lisa?" he asked.

I instinctively covered my body parts, which was ridiculous since he obviously meant to get in with me. The very naked me. I sucked in my stomach, stuck out my chest and smoothed my hair back. "Come on in, da Vinci."

When is a shower more than a shower? When you share it with someone else. Especially a someone with a hard, wet body pressed up against yours, thigh to thigh, chest to chest, arms wrapped around each other's slick, soapy bodies. And then? Lips on lips. Lips on collar bone. Lips on breast, stomach, thighs. Anh was right. Enlightenment can come from the simplest things. We hadn't even gotten to actual sex yet, and I was feeling the out of body experience that came with the transition from becoming to being.

I wasn't thinking of anything while we were in the shower, mind you. It was better than getting back on a bike, one thing leading to another and I would have most certainly let nature take its course if it hadn't been for Zoya and Gabriella both calling my name in their thick accents beyond my bedroom door. "Ramona, we're here."

"Shit."

"No stop," da Vinci said as he continued to kiss me.

I began to panic. "Didn't you hear that? My neighbors are here. I can't believe we've been in here thirty minutes already."

"Just five more minutes," da Vinci said, and as much as I would've liked to have gone through with it, I wouldn't be able to enjoy it knowing my neighbors could walk in on us any minute. They had no idea I had company. Why would they?

"Here's the plan. I go out first. You wait five minutes, get dressed. *Fully* dressed, da Vinci. And walk out the front door and around to the studio. Okay?"

Da Vinci scrunched his brow but said okay. "But shower nice, no?"

I kissed him one last time, hard on the lips. "Yes. Shower very nice."

Gabriella, Zoya, and Simone were already eating cinnamon rolls they had heated themselves when I joined them.

Zoya was complaining, her hands flying everywhere as she spoke. "I'm tired of baby-trying," she said. "Used to sex two times a week. Now sex every night. Zoya don't need baby that bad."

Gabriella, who had five children, reassured her. "Just get pregnant, and you'll get sex much less often. He'll be afraid to hurt the baby and after baby comes, you'll get sex hardly ever."

"Really?" Zoya's eyes widened. "Then maybe baby now good thing."

We laughed, but my neighbors stopped laughing, Simone's eyes like saucers, when da Vinci, wearing only a yellow towel that barely closed, walked through the kitchen, his hair still dripping wet. "Da Vinci!" I yelled, wishing I had a dishcloth big enough to cover his whole body. What part of get dressed and go through the front door did he not understand? I swear. Sometimes he says okay when he has no idea what I'm saying.

"*¡Dios Santo!*" Gabriella gasped in Spanish. *Sweet Lord in Heaven.*

"*Pelo amor de Deus!*" Simone whispered in Portugese. *Heaven help us.*

"*Glückliches weibchen,*" Zoya said in German.

"Zoya!" I scolded. She'd called me a lucky bitch.

"Ladies," da Vinci said, walking casually over to me where he planted a kiss on my temple. It didn't take a brain surgeon to figure out we both had wet hair and had come out of the bathroom within minutes of each other. And the kiss said more than any explanation could. "Good morning." He proceeded to pour himself a cup of coffee while we all stared at him. What could I do?

"Good morning, indeed," said Gabriella.

Simone slit her eyes. "You didn't tell us you'd already had breakfast, Ramona."

"The shower in the studio is broken," I told them nonchalantly.

"I'll have Jesús fix it," Gabriella said, then raised a brow. "Or perhaps not so fast?"

We smiled, the chemistry in the room thick with surprise, our eyes all on da Vinci's back where drops of water glistened on his shoulders.

"*Schlechtes Mädchen,*" Zoya said as she wagged her finger at me. *Bad girl.*

Being bad had never felt so good.

Chapter 10

I'D NEARLY CONVINCED MYSELF the shower scene was an anomaly, an erratic blimp in an otherwise normal platonic relationship, yet for the life of me, I couldn't get it—or him—out of my head.

The cursor blinked on the screen, beckoning me to conjure the words, to fill the white space in the quiet hours meant for my dissertation. My outline clearly demanded I write about the history of love letters, but contrarily I'd spent the morning reading the most romantic love letters the world has ever seen and fantasizing about finishing what da Vinci had started.

I, the lover of words, did not wish to write. I only wished to do. Whether I would actually go through with it if and when the time ever came would be a great surprise, like opening a forbidden sex box. I could daydream for hours about the package itself, let alone what I might find inside.

Doing would not be possible for the foreseeable future. Though not nearly as tragic as the love letters written by authors separated by war, da Vinci and I could not pursue our mutual attraction because he was a student first, a worker second, and a lover third. It had been so long since I'd been kissed or whiled away the morning daydreaming about sex that I didn't even care if I came in third place.

Because the real thing wouldn't be home from work until midnight, I spent the rest of the morning researching love in the Renaissance and what secrets I might find in the original da Vinci's past. Anh had dropped off several da Vinci books from her own collection. I had never paid any attention to the origin of da Vinci's works, or wondered about his subjects, until my da Vinci began calling me his Mona Lisa.

The Renaissance, a time of rebirth between the fourteenth and seventeenth centuries, was marked by reflection and resurgence, improvement and perfection. Da Vinci's insatiable curiosity about how the world and everything in it worked gave birth not only to brilliant art, but brilliant ideas. Much like my young Leo, old Leo seemed thrilled to be alive, to make new discoveries in the everyday. Could the scholars be right? Did Leonardo invest in his studies the passion usually reserved for a lover? Out of thousands of pages of notes, not one doodle hinted of a personal affection. Even back then, surely you couldn't resist writing your lover's name just once. Or initials with a heart around it. But maybe that's just me.

Maybe Leonardo was in love with life and that was enough for him. Could it be enough for me?

I stared at the picture of a painting of Ludovico Sforza, the Duke of Milan and da Vinci's patron for several years, who commissioned da Vinci to paint the *Last Supper*. Why did I find the fact that da Vinci orchestrated Ludovico and Beatrice's wedding celebration far more interesting than a great work of art? *Da Vinci: Renaissance Man, Wedding Planner.*

On the next full page, I studied my favorite da Vinci portrait, *The Lady and the Ermine*. Da Vinci was known for using symbolism in his work, and the ermine—the white, short-tailed weasel known for its hatred of dirt—symbolized purity. With mounting disappointment, I read that the "lady" was no lady at all, but Cecelia Gallerani, the favored mistress of the Duke of Milan, and had in fact given birth to the Duke's first son the same year as his and Beatrice's wedding. Was da Vinci a natural jokester, or was it simply so accepted that every husband keep a mistress on the side that no one caught the irony of the ermine in the mistress' lap? At least the ermine was a weasel, and—also fitting—a carnivore.

Poor Beatrice. Four hundred years between us, and I know how you must've felt. As Ludovico lay in your bed, did you not wonder if he was thinking of her? I know. Sharing his heart was far harder than sharing his body, was it not?

I imagined da Vinci painting a portrait of Monica Blevins wearing a shimmery red gown, her dark hair flowing down onto her full bosom, her eyes full of mischief, a fox resting on her lap. A sly, conniving fox, plain and simple. I didn't care for irony. If Monica was in fact a mistress, no use in being cunning about it.

I slammed the book closed, cursing myself that I'd let my pleasant daydreams turn dark at the thought of Monica. I needed some inspiration, both in the form of a second cup of coffee and a visit to my personal collection of love letters. So Joel couldn't compete with the romantic Robert Browning—I was no Elizabeth Barrett Browning, either.

Joel was not a writer. He was not eloquent so much as straightforward, yet his words, in his own handwriting, as opposed to the e-mails our generation is so accustomed to, brought me comfort.

I hurried to my closet, where inside a plastic teddy bear container that once housed animal crackers (yes, Joel loved them with peanut butter), now resided ten years' worth of cards and notes. Unfortunately, ten years only amounted to a jar half full. Or half empty. Whichever way you choose to look at it. This is what remains of our love:

1. William and Bradley
2. Approximately four hundred photographs, a third of them digital, stored on discs.

I'd meant to get them printed for two years, but I wasn't the scrapbooking type. I'd read an article that you need to print off at least one set because of how quickly technology changes. I made a mental note to do this before his Death Day.

3. One VHS tape, ten mini Hi-8 tapes, and two DVDs of home movies (which I have placed in a fireproof safe).

Rachel had offered to have her production team transfer the old tapes to DVD, too, yet I thought watching us from the early days would be painful. I took out the tapes and set them on the dresser to give to Rachel on Sunday.

I unscrewed the bright blue lid, slid down the wall and scooped out the contents like a bear with a jar of honey. One glimpse of his signature was all it took. I hadn't even read the sappy ones (two-third of Joel's cards were humorous, one-third sweet and romantic, probably due to not finding any funny ones he liked on the card aisle that day).

His words: authentically Joel. I read the cards, laughed, cried, and lingered where it mattered most, his own words inked onto the cardstock.

Your bed warmer, J

To many more years of S&S (S&S was code for Sex and Snuggling, two of his favorite things besides peanut butter and basketball)

My lovely

Thanks for putting up with me

And his last cards for Valentine's Day, my birthday, and our anniversary:

Score one for Cupid

You get prettier with age

This card isn't big enough for the love I have for you.

A salty tear fell on the "love" and I caught my breath, afraid the ink would smear, but it merely magnified the word. Of course he loved me. How had I believed that I was the runner-up?

I knew I had to get it over with. The day before, I had called Monica Blevins at work, prepared to set up a quick meet-and-greet over coffee. After all, asking a woman if she'd had a sexual affair with your husband over the phone would never do. It had to be done with grace and aplomb (*n.*, self-confidence or assurance). I was afraid that over the phone I would choke and no words would come at all.

Her number rang the requisite five times before her voice mail picked up. I was at once relieved she did not pick up and say hello, because my own voice had done as I had feared and been constricted by a muscle spasm in my vocal chords. I listened to her voice. Lovely, really. In one of my doctoral classes, we had studied voice. Did you know that most people can accurately determine one's physical properties from one's voice? As beauty is based on one's symmetry, so too can one have a symmetrical voice. Monica Blevins' voice was bold yet beautiful. From her voice alone you could imagine her speaking in front of a jury or making an acceptance speech on stage or whispering sweet nothings into an equally beautiful suitor's ear. I imagined her with Joel. This is why my throat constricted.

Her message said it all: *I can't take your call right now,* and I wondered if she could take my call *ever.* If by confronting whatever it was that happened with my husband would be as painful to her as it would be for me.

I didn't leave a message. I did what most cowards do and hung up and went to Plan B: e-mail. I wondered if my e-mail would go in her spam folder, until I remembered that Joel and I had shared a home e-mail address. She would recognize the last name (had he e-mailed her from our home account?). I had searched the history, mind you, and had not found any, but then my husband was meticulous about keeping his Inbox and Sent box clean. I was the packrat who kept e-mails long after they lost their purpose. If he had e-mailed Monica from our home account, he had efficiently deleted its record.

In my grief book, I ran my finger over her e-mail address, as if I didn't have it etched in my mind like writing on a tombstone. My fingers trembled as I typed in her address in the "To" box.

Subject line: re: you and Joel Griffen. Backspace. *Too specific.*

Re: your past. Delete. *Too mysterious.*

Re: a question. *Too vague.*

I tried again: *Can we meet for coffee?* Yes, this would do. Non-threatening, the message right there in the subject line, meaning I wouldn't have to say much in the text box.

> *Monica,*
>
> > *As you may be aware, the anniversary of Joel's death is approaching and while this time is very hard for me, it is made even more difficult by some unanswered questions I have about his life. I was hoping that you might help me with this. Can we meet for coffee in the next few days?*
> >
> > *Yours,*
> > *Ramona*

Then wondering if she would know who Ramona was, or simply to be possessive, I signed it: Ramona Griffen.

The cursor blinked over the "Send" button. How simple an act just to press my finger down and have it be done with, sent through the cable lines that would cause my message to appear to her within seconds. But I didn't. Instead, I hit "Draft," which would save it for later. I couldn't believe how weak I felt, how powerless, not even mustering the courage to send an e-mail, but the truth was as much I wanted to know the facts, I didn't want to know at all. The same reason that kept me from approaching her at the funeral or reaching her during the last two years remained to this day: knowing would end whatever hope I hung onto that Joel had been faithful to me. That he loved *only* me.

I turned off the computer, realizing I was already late to meet with the yogi. As I let myself feel the heaviness in my heart that I used to believe was sadness, I reconsidered based on Deacon Friar's advice. I changed my mind—it was full of love. If my heart felt like a hundred-pound sack of potatoes in my chest, I would imagine its weight was that of the love that all those eloquent writers spoke of.

It worked, though my mind felt heavy with anxiety over Monica. What if the seven wheels of energy could heal that and everything else that seemed out of sync with my life? It was worth a shot.

Chakra: a Sankrit word meaning wheel, or vortex, referring to each of the seven energy centers of which our consciousness, our energy system, is comprised. If the soul is energy, the mind energy and the universe energy, I had to believe there was some truth in this practice. How else had it survived thousands of years?

Just as the deacon had looked nothing like I'd pictured (because I hadn't spoken to him on the phone), neither did the yogi. The yogi did not look like Gandhi or a Buddhist at all, but rather like a soccer mom from my school. Someone my age had this whole mind/body connection figured out *and* had young kids in school? In fact, she had four kids and one husband who had left her for someone younger, so I had to believe she could've been on par with my life in the stress department.

Her studio looked like any other gym: blue mats rolled up on the left, large mirror in the middle and stereo equipment to the left. This is the room where I would find enlightenment? It seemed like a bubble bath with candles and aromatherapy would make more sense. I nearly turned around and walked out. I didn't know this woman from Adam. Was I supposed to reveal something to her? Share my deepest secrets? Tell her about Joel and Monica and da Vinci? My stomach (which I learned was a part of the solar plexus chakra) was in knots.

If my sister was the Energizer Bunny of the Workout World, then Cynthia Sheffield was the Cool Housecat who owned her domain without a word at all. She was tall and pretty and lean, with cat-shaped green eyes and long black hair. Gray hairs wove through her otherwise Crystal Gayle-looking hair. Wow. She must really have inner peace to allow her hair to show her age. Without the gray, I would've taken her for twenty-five, but I added fifteen years once I saw the silver streaks and the fine lines.

We sat cross-legged on a mat with soft mystical music playing from the stereo. She spoke softly, explaining the seven chakras and their purpose. We discussed the goal of "flow," with no roadblocks within our consciousness. I was a wonderful student, listening intently, asking questions when permissible. I thought I got it—like a biology class, each section matching up like the skeletal system or the organs. I was doing fine right up until she explained the figurative representations of the chakras.

"They aren't physical," she said, "but problems in the chakra can have physical repercussions."

She talked of ego and personality and inner light. It turned out I had multiple roadblocks. If a speedway represented flow, then I wasn't even a quiet country road.

1. My brow chakra was in charge of spirituality and spirit-to-spirit communications. Deacon Friar hadn't put it this way, but my issues with my own spirituality and connectedness to Joel resided here.

2. My throat chakra was responsible for expression and asking for what I really want. No wonder I had choked up when I tried to send the message to Monica. And why had I been avoiding da Vinci ever since our shower? Hadn't I enjoyed the pleasures of our bodies?

3. My heart chakra was involved with sensitivity to touch. I had tried to make up for my heart sensitivity with hugs from my boys—something I'd done right. But I had no idea that the element of air and problems with breathing were associated with love. How often had I woken up and felt that the air in the room had been sucked out, that the air felt different when Joel died and I hadn't been able to breathe the same since?

4. The solar plexus chakra associated with freedom, power, and personality, one's sense of being. No wonder my stomach

ached all the time. My identity had been shredded the day Joel died. My former self was locked up inside that teddy bear jar. Who was I now? Who did I want to be?

5. Even my root chakra was in trouble. Not only because it was associated with my mother, but with Mother Earth and trust and security. It was only because of da Vinci that I had started feeling connected again to Mother Earth—running through the leafy paths of our neighborhood, enjoying a country afternoon riding horses, soaking up the sun and enjoying wine again.

If five of my seven energy centers were on the fritz, how was there any hope for me at all? I had to be the worst case Cynthia had ever seen.

"There is hope for all of us," she said in her soothing tone that I was certain could put me to sleep like a lullaby. She gave me tips on meditation, on how to quiet the chatter in my mind to concentrate on being present, to slowly unwind the knots that hindered my flow. I was still skeptical, but hopeful.

In fact, I was certain that before da Vinci had arrived, all seven of my chakras were out of whack. So as I left that studio, I made the decision that I didn't need less of da Vinci, but more. Much, much more.

Chapter 11

THE STUDIO WAS NOT meant for making love. It was meant for concentration, hunched over a drafting table, the sofa there only to sit a spell until inspiration struck again. Instead, we were bent over the drafting table, and one look at the pencil cup felt like the lead had punctured my heart. I couldn't. This was Joel's sacred place, his refuge. And what was I doing? Seeking refuge in the arms of another man, a passionate man covering me with kisses, warming me in his embrace, whispering, "*Ti desidero, Mona Lisa.*" *I want you.*

And I wanted him, too. God, I wanted him. If I let go, let myself feel the moment, calmed the chatter in my brain that said it wasn't the right time or the right man, then I wanted da Vinci as much as I had wanted any man.

Two glasses of Pinot had helped. My chakras could not be relaxed on their own, mind you. Two glasses and I felt more dream-state than reality. And as a fantasy this, da Vinci's slow, measured concentration on my body, was divine. I knew if I let us, we could create our own masterpiece—like Gustav Klimpt's *The Kiss*, mind, bodies, and souls entwined.

The shower had just been a warm-up. Water had acted as a kind of buffer between us. Now we were nearly naked, nothing between us but silky bra and panties Joel had referred to as "funderwear," strictly reserved for the one or two nights a week we (okay, I) had the energy to make love. To think, before da Vinci had arrived in my classroom, I almost threw my funderwear out. Grievers have no use for funderwear.

If da Vinci represented all Italian men, then may I say Italians make great lovers? He was slow when he needed to be slow and assertive when he wanted to make me gasp; he was soft and firm and dizzying and delicious and always, always sexy.

Within minutes, I forgot all about the pencil holder and the small sofa and the tiny studio and the house in Austin and the great state of Texas and the United States and Italy and the galaxy at large, because I was taken to that place closest to Heaven.

Bliss.

***

Have you ever had a guilty-pleasure hangover? I have. The next morning, after the amazing (God, did I dream it?) lovemaking in the studio, I woke up and felt different. A little more alive. A little peppy, a little less like the Ramona I had gotten used to. A little like the old, fun Ramona of yesteryear.

I breathed in deeply as Cynthia had taught, pushing my breath from my nose all the way down to my toes and back again, filling up every part of me with the breath of life. The air was ripe with sunshine. Florida sunshine on a crisp October morning in Austin. Go figure.

With unusual lightness, I got up and stretched, doing two of the yoga poses that didn't threaten to throw my back out. I couldn't be too exuberant yet, but I felt like I could even do a handstand if I tried. I had used muscles the night before I hadn't used in awhile. I started giggling, a good girlish giggle long overdue. One probably shouldn't giggle while in the downward-facing dog, but my body felt like it wasn't entirely my own. I had shared it with someone else and it felt like a part of me was still with him.

I rolled my shoulders back. The "him" might like bacon and eggs and pancakes. He could join our Sunday brunch that had been a tradition for the boys and me. I wrapped my fuzzy terry robe around me and headed out into my new life. I walked down the hallway, turned the corner and stopped dead in my tracks.

Above my head was a dangling three-foot spider. Webs hung from the chandeliers. A large pumpkin stared up at me with its gap-toothed grin from under the entry hall table. I began to panic—everything was just as it had been that last Halloween Joel had decorated. What was this? A sign from above? Was Joel angry at me for last night? Happy? No way the boys could've done it. They couldn't even reach the heavy box in the top of the closet.

Just as I felt the room spinning around me, I heard their voices and the smell of bacon wafting through the house.

"Mommy!"

"Mother!"

"Mona Lisa!"

When I came to, those three faces stared down at me. How had I not believed in magic, in the power of signs delivered in something other than words? "Is it real?"

"Is what real?" Bradley asked.

"Can you see it? The spider. Is the spider real?"

William's eyes grew large. "No, mom. The spider's not real. I can't believe you thought it was real."

I sat up and did a 360 of the room. Yep. The decorations were all still there. Whoever did this must've taken hours. "So you're telling me that none of you can see what I see? The house is full of Halloween."

"Crazy holiday," da Vinci said. "But boys say lots of candy, so I trick or treat with them."

"Mom, the house *is* full of Halloween," William said.

"It's like the good old days," Bradley said.

"I can't believe your father did this," I said, though I wasn't sure it was out loud until I saw the expressions on my son's faces.

William's lids filled with tears. "Mommy, Daddy didn't do this."

"*We did.* As a surprise," Bradley said.

I looked from one boy to the next, noticing how much they'd changed this year, their faces less babylike, their baby teeth being replaced by the larger ones that seemed much too big for their mouths. Even their voices were losing the cuteness they had when Joel was alive. Could he hear them? Could he hear the change like I could? How ever were they big enough to pull off decorating just as their father had done?

"I helped," da Vinci said. "Da Vinci is tall."

"Well, were you surprised, Mom? Did we do a good job?" Bradley asked.

I couldn't speak—the chakra stopped up again, and I patted and kissed them atop the heads, except for da Vinci, whom I only looked at with dismay, wondering if he knew what he'd done. In one fell swoop, he had replaced Joel in not one, but two ways. I excused myself to go cry in the shower, my flow completely and utterly gone.

When I joined my clan at the table, they were busy eating our traditional breakfast, and I tried to act normal, as if the decorations hadn't bothered me or that da Vinci had not only taken Joel's job, but mine, too. I was the short-order cook around here.

I filled my plate with bacon and eggs, poured coffee and sat down at the table, prepared to eat in silence, thinking how unfair it was that I was so close to becoming a Normal only to have the Griever take over my body again.

I chewed my bacon, vowing not to give da Vinci credit for making it crispier than my own or how much I liked the Tabasco sauce in the scrambled eggs, when Bradley looked at me with a straight face and asked, "Mom, did you and da Vinci have sex last night?"

I could not tell a lie. Which is why even when it came to the Tooth Fairy and leprechauns and the Easter Bunny and Santa Claus, I'd always been rather vague about their existence. "What do *you* think?" I would ask my boys, which would cause them to launch into elaborate fairy tales about the tiny Tooth Fairy kingdom where all the fairies bring the children's teeth to polish and shine and then build themselves pearly mansions, or how Santa probably contracts with NASA, or at the very least, FedEx, to help deliver gifts quickly all over the world.

So when they asked me about sex, and in particular sex with da Vinci, which unlike those fairy tales, had actually happened, I couldn't lie. Instead, I said, "What happens between me and da Vinci is our own personal business. We like each other very much."

I'm not sure if the boys took that as a yes, but it did seemed to satisfy their curiosity for the time being. They stared at each other, stifled a giggle, then earnestly ate their pancakes.

Of course I'd made a huge mistake. As fabulous as the night before had been, how I'd felt the stirring of my soul within me as I allowed passion to be unleashed once again, I knew as a mother I'd made a bad choice. The boys liked da Vinci, had welcomed him into our home, at our table, breaking bread together, laughing and going on as if we were gelling as a family. I couldn't believe I'd allowed it to happen—it was all so soon, wasn't it? How one day you can feel like you're living in a dark cave and the next it's filled with light and you can't believe you've managed to move that boulder all by yourself, yet the world outside of it is so bright and scary. I shuddered. I had to be careful.

"I think it's marvelous," Barbara said six hours later as she viewed my son's Halloween displays, "If it makes them happy." I wondered if she would say the same about me and da Vinci, but I had no intention of telling her anything was going on and I had made the boys' promise not to talk about us, either. Suddenly I was sweating bullets over a simple family meal. I wondered if my nerves had to do with something else, too.

"I think they're in love," Barbara said, referring to Rachel and Cortland, who were a good three minutes late according to my father's watch. "Wouldn't that be lovely to have a spring wedding? Is it too soon? Oh, certainly not. It's not like a second wedding would be an elaborate affair. Now that Rachel's famous, do you think they'll cover their wedding in the society section? I bet *Austin Living* will want a cover story! Do you think the governor will come?"

I let my mom go on and on about her own fantasy while I prepped the tenderloin for the oven. Dad and da Vinci were in the backyard tossing the football with Bradley while William stayed on the patio playing Sudoku. I glanced at them every few minutes to make sure nothing mischievous was going on. (As if I could tell if they were talking about sex.)

When Cortland and Rachel arrived (now fourteen minutes late), my mother went on as if she hadn't seen them in ages. It might make some people feel good to be greeted like those at the airport with the signs and the tears and high-pitched sentiments, but it just made me feel sad. Grievers need more than a cheerleading section to feel good about reunions when you know the one person you truly wish to be reunited with can never happen.

Cortland surprised me, planting a kiss on my cheek and hugging me tightly.

"Oh," I said, patting his broad shoulders. "Yes. Good to see you, too. Wow, this is festive, right?"

"Where's the birthday boy?" Rachel said, practically doing cart-wheels on her way to reach Dad.

Zoe shook her head and shrugged. "He's not a boy, he's a man," she pointed out. "But whatever."

I winked at Zoe and she helped me whip the mashed potatoes in the kitchen. She only got a home-cooked meal when she visited me or her grandma, so helping in the kitchen was her favorite thing. And to think, she didn't have to wear makeup or sequins to get the attention she so craved.

As we were seated around the dining room table set for nine (squishing in a chair for Zoe), I could feel the palpable presence of Joel in the room. I'm not sure if it's because we were surrounded by the Halloween decorations he had so carefully hung each year or because I simply couldn't get him off of my mind.

Both Cortland and da Vinci pulled my chair out for me, one on each side, and da Vinci stiffened as though only he had the right to do so for his lady. As was ritual, Noble began the prayer and we all followed suit. Afterward, forks clanked and my mother began to take a sip of her wine, but holding it in the air, said, "I'm so glad you two are friends."

Da Vinci nodded, lifting his wine glass to propose a toast. "To friends and lovers," he said.

And the rest of us awkwardly joined in while my family members eyeballed me. I would shrug it off as an Italian thing. They wouldn't know the difference.

"To friends and lovers," Cortland said, the one among them who might know the difference.

Zoe piped up, "To friends and lovers."

My boys glanced over and I gave a quick shake, a silent signal for them to stay out of the toast.

My father added, "Hear, hear," and we clinked glasses and began an otherwise normal meal except for the question mark hanging above us like a chandelier: "Who exactly among us are friends, and who are lovers?"

***

"No problem," Rachel said as she stuffed my family videos into her oversized bag after dinner with the promise she would have her editing team transfer the outdated formats onto DVDs, as well as host them on a server.

"I'll give you the photo discs as soon as I print them out," I told her, hesitant to hand over so many pieces of my and Joel's life together at once. After all, Rachel wasn't known for her organizational skills, and she had lost too many of my things over the years to keep track.

"Ooh, I know!" Rachel said, snapping her fingers together. Her bright ideas always arrived with a thunderclap. "Why don't you, me, and Mom have a scrapbooking party?"

I shrugged, internally cringing at the thought of a) spending the day cutting out construction paper with my sister who would be filling her book with more pageant pictures while I laid out my soul with the last pictures of Joel, and b) ever finding the time to do something so crafty and creative.

"You know you can do scrapbooks online now," Cortland said, and Rachel beamed at him as if he were a brilliant anesthesiologist, which I'm sure he was.

"What do you mean?" I asked, intrigued.

"Well, since you already have your digital photos on your computer, you can go to a web site where they have design templates, and you just drag and drop your photos onto the pages and order it and they'll ship it to you."

"Are you serious?" Rachel gasped. "And here I've been spending all that money on glitter and fancy stickers for Zoe's books."

"I'm not very technically inclined," I told him, embarrassed to admit I barely knew how to use e-mail, let alone do something important on the web.

"If you have time, I could show you now."

Rachel shrugged. "Oh, she has oodles of time. I'm going to go out back and talk to the birthday boy. When you two are done, I'll bring out the cake. Think Daddy will mind I had the baker put sixty-nine candles on the cake?"

"Better than the numeral kind," I said, recalling one of my mother's most embarrassing moments; it was when Rachel was in junior high and I was in sixth grade and Rachel asked Mom and Dad at the dinner table what it meant to "69" someone. Besides choking on her chicken, Mother did nothing to satisfy Rachel's curiosity, so Rachel did what most junior high girls would do and went to her girl-friends, who had asked older siblings what it meant.

"God, Mom's such a prude," Rachel said. "And speaking of, I want to hear more about the whole 'friends and lovers' thing when we're not in mixed company."

Cortland raised a brow, but before he could excuse himself, she turned on her heels, leaving us in the kitchen alone, her last state-ment still hanging in the air, but I was unwilling to respond to it.

"It's really none of my business," Cortland said, and I swatted the air where she'd left it.

"Nor hers," I added, and we went into Joel's office, which I couldn't stop referring to as Joel's office, probably because I only used it when trying and failing to e-mail his ex-girlfriend. He hadn't spent much time there, as he preferred his garage studio with the drafting table.

I pulled up the pictures, willing myself not to cry, then let Cortland pull up the web site memorybook.com, where I selected a simple design with photo edges and creamy backgrounds.

"Nice choice," Cortland said. "Now you just have to decide what cover shot you want to use."

I sifted through hundreds of photos, amazed that I didn't mind Cortland sharing the moment, but I couldn't decide which was cover-worthy because every one featuring Joel felt cover-worthy to me, even the ones where he had devil-red eyes or where his head had been lopped off due to a bad camera operator (me).

"Here, we can fix those red eyes," Cortland said, taking over the mouse, blowing up Joel's picture until it filled the frame to life-size. How had I forgotten about that tiny mole on his left cheek or the way his five o'clock shadow grew in faster on his chin than the rest of his face or how the corner of his eyelids rose when he smiled?

And his eyes! Flecked with gold and brown and green, and even the blue of the ocean was in there. When Cortland removed the red eye, Joel looked nearly perfect, lopsided grin and all. I had to look away. I swallowed hard, then realized with surprise that what I felt right then was not grief, but love. For the first time when I viewed Joel's picture, I didn't feel sad at all, but simply happy to see him. Greetings-in-an-airport sort of happy.

"You okay?" Cortland asked, putting his arm lightly around my shoulder, and I nodded.

"I want the picture of the four of us at the beach in Galveston for the cover," I said. "Then I'll just go from there in chronological order. They all have to go in. This might take me weeks."

"Well, in that case," Cortland said, pressing a button that zipped all the photos, the green bar steadily beeping across the screen.

"What did you just do?" I said, starting to panic that he'd messed up my album.

Then the screen blinked: *Done. Your Griffen Family Album is complete and ready for viewing.*

I flipped through the pages, one click at a time, my heart nearly lifting me right out of my seat, and when I was finished, I clicked "Order" for three hardback books, one for each of us. "The boys will love it," I said, beginning to tear up.

Cortland rubbed the back of my neck with his hand, and when I looked up at him, tears in my eyes, I saw that he had tears in his eyes, too. Whatever I was feeling I had passed along to him, but I also saw something else, something that a woman never wants to see in the eyes of her sister's boyfriend, and yet I liked it all the same.

Chapter 12

Two days until Joel's DD (Death Date)

MONICA BLEVINS WAS TALLER than I remembered. Of course, the only times I had seen her in person were among children at the school and standing at the back of the crowd at the funeral, and through my tears, she had looked like the blurriest, yet most beautiful woman I had ever seen.

As I watched her walk to her car, a sleek red Mercedes, I breathed through the pangs of envy I felt in my chest. Before I arrived, I had stopped by the archdiocese to throw two pennies into the fountain. One penny was for resolution. I wished to get rid of that rock of uncertainty and doubt inside my heart, etched with Monica's name. The other penny was for courage.

I didn't have a plan. As I drove up to the pricey new offices that Joel had designed for her law firm, I imagined his hands all over the glass and metal and rock he had picked out personally and thought how happy he would be if, as Deacon Friar thought, he could look down on earth and see the city, and even the state, marked with the buildings of his creation.

No prep. No heads up. No warning. I hadn't called or e-mailed her, deciding just two days from Joel's death date that I wanted it over and done with, and the best way to achieve it would just be to go find her. She wasn't hard to find, and even now, as she fumbled for the keys to unlock her car, I wondered why it had taken me so long to get to this moment. I could've called her when Joel was alive, but I was too afraid my suspicions were true and I'd have to make a decision to forgive Joel and stay with him or … what? Leave him? Go to counseling? It had all seemed too nightmarish to deal with in his life, and it was only when my motive was pure, when I had dropped that penny in the fountain, that I knew what I really wanted.

No matter what she told me, it would be over with. Done. *Finito.* I would be okay with it either way. Joel loved me, and if this temptress—for she very much looked like a high-class version of one—had caused him to stray, then I would forgive him and still honor his memory. I loved him no matter. My love—no, *our love*—was strong enough to withstand whatever came of it. Still. I had to know.

I got out of my car, feeling sloppy in my blue track suit compared to her fitted Armani number and stiletto heels, but I held my head high and walked fervently across the hundred feet between us, getting halfway there when she opened her door, plucked her cell phone from her briefcase and began talking as she slid into the leather seat and closed the door, shutting me out.

What would I do? Pound on her window? *Excuse me, Monica. I'm Joel's widow. Remember me?*

Instead, I turned thirty degrees, stepped up on the sidewalk and watched her back out and speed away. I did not take this as a sign, only that I was too slow and had once again let fear keep me from acting fast enough. I retrieved my cell phone out of my jacket pocket and dialed her number, which I had memorized. I know this isn't a nice thing to say, but her number really did spell out SHE-SLUT, although a kinder person might instead use SHE-PJ88.

I didn't feel like being kind.

***

Monica hadn't answered, probably still on the call she'd taken when she sped away, and *again!* I choked when I heard her voice in her mailbox. But I cleared my throat (not becoming) and spoke through my fear, "Monica. You may not remember me, but I'm Ramona Griffen, Joel's wife. I was wondering if we could meet for coffee and talk for a while." I left my number and reminded myself I still used the term "wife"; I didn't like to refer to myself as his widow, even if it were true.

I hung up, feeling both scared and proud of myself for doing it. Of course, there was the distinct possibility that she wouldn't call me back, which is why I thought surprising her in person would be more productive. If Joel had loved her, she had to be a decent person, but who in their right mind wouldn't return the call of a widow?

What I did next truly surprised me. It was a warm October day, one away until fall break, when the boys would be spending the weekend with my parents. Although they certainly remember the time of year that their father died, we did not talk about his death date. I know some of my friends, such as Catholic Gabriella, regularly visited their friends' and families' graves on their death dates as well as their birthdays, but I had only visited Joel's grave three times in two years, and none of them were significant days. I did not want to spend his birthday or our anniversary, or even his death date, at the cemetery.

Two days prior seemed like a good day to visit. It wasn't as if I had to keep up with maintenance—I would never allow even one weed to grow on my husband's grave, but I did every so often wonder how often the cemetery cleaned off bird poop off the tombstones. Joel never had this kind of bad luck when he was alive, but I have been shat on from above four times in my life! Four! And it wasn't even after I'd done anything that deserved it.

I had selected his gravesite with as much care as a Griever can muster—one that was near a tree to get partial shade during the summer and a beautiful view of autumn leaves and icicles when the weather permitted. This was, of course, just the kind of thing a Griever does: think about the deceased as if they were still living—

as if the deceased in the coffin could actually "see" the tree to enjoy it, as if he were napping and needed a good place to lay his head and catch a cool breeze. Still, I knew he would like it, even though he wasn't much of an outdoorsman.

The clouds rolled by and I watched the puffy train become a tiger become a lollipop. If the deceased could see anything from their spot in the earth, then watching the clouds, not to mention the occasional thunderstorm, would have to be a highlight.

I lay on my back beside Joel, six feet above the pearlescent burnt-orange coffin I'd spent too much money on, again falsely believing that Joel would care that he would rest in eternity in a box the color of his favorite college team, the Texas Longhorns. Hey, it seemed like a good idea at the time. The dead grass tickled my hand, which I had laid, fingers spread, above Joel's resting place, as if in some karmic way we were holding hands, or perhaps my hand was above his heart, the one that gave up on him at least forty years too soon. The autopsy indicated a heart defect that he was most likely born with, one that was exacerbated by too much physical activity. I couldn't imagine Joel's life without sports. If they had found the defect when he was younger, he wouldn't have played youth soccer or junior high basketball or high school football or intramural sports. Or those weekly pick-up games with the guys in the cul-de-sac. His life would have been completely different. Not the same person at all.

Of course, I had immediately had my sons' hearts checked out. People told me I was crazy, but by now, you've figured out that Grievers do crazy things, and high among them is to check the health of those left behind. I didn't just stop at heart checks, either. I had every organ, every bone, even our blood tested for the rarest of rare diseases. After several tests, I was found to be completely normal, barring a few extra pounds that could come off with, you guessed it, physical activity. *Stick to your daily vitamin.* That was it. That was the magic cure to keep me alive to raise my boys? Of course not. Still. I took that daily vitamin as if I were drinking from the Holy Grail. I had to live, even if some days I hadn't wanted to live at all.

And the boys, well, you couldn't find two healthier boys than Bradley and William. "As normal as boys could be," the doctor had said.

I had argued with the doctor. "I don't feel normal at all," I had told him. I wanted to tell him I was dying, I was certain of it. But aren't we all dying a bit every day? It's morbid to admit, but I knew my pain wasn't my body giving up on me, but my bruised soul wilting within me.

The wind picked up, and I rolled over on my stomach, on top of Joel's grave. I wondered if I was turned the right way, if our faces were in alignment, or however unfortunate, my head were at his feet. I couldn't remember. But I pretended we were lying chest to chest, my cheek on his cheek, and I breathed deeply, slowly, fully trying to feel our spirits connect until I watered his grave with my tears. I imagined they traveled through the earth and landed right on Joel's cheek as they had done when we found out we were pregnant with Bradley.

A recent best-selling book asked what you would do if you had one more day with a loved one that had died. I thought of this often—something the author obviously knew Grievers do. But as many times as I played out that One More Day, the more it looked like Any Day and it was a good day—not a great day, but a typical day in our marriage: being parents, running errands, and successfully completing the crossword puzzle. There was nothing I would ask him or say to him that I hadn't already said in his life. Even the question about Monica.

Maybe our spirits were intertwined or the autumn sunshine had soaked some sense into me, because suddenly Knowing did not matter anymore. I let it all go. I could have closure without Her. He was Mine and would be for eternity.

Without meaning to, I'd fallen asleep. When I awoke, my muscles ached, and the sun was beginning to set. I had dreamed of Joel, something I'd only done once since his death and even then, it hadn't been the powerful dream I'd been looking for. Grievers hope to dream of their loved ones telling them they are fine, they'll be fine, they still love you, and they'll watch over you. My dream had fallen far from my aspirations; it was simply Joel asking me if I'd bought more peanut butter.

But on this day, my dream startled me. It started out well enough, Joel and I and the boys at an amusement park, eating cotton candy and going on all the rides I hated, the fast ones that made my insides switch places. We all got on the Tilt-A-Whirl and began spinning, Joel making it go even faster by turning the wheel in the middle until my body was crushed against his and I rested my head on his shoulders until our ride came to a stop, and when he lifted the safety bar and reached out his hand for me to take, it wasn't Joel at all.

"You okay?" he asked, and I nodded my head and took his hand—one that did not belong to my Joel or my da Vinci, but to my sister's beau.

***

I'd almost forgotten that you get as much time on break from college as you actually spend in college, so when my father came to pick up the boys that morning for the long weekend, it meant that da Vinci and I would be alone. Entirely alone. For four whole days.

I tried to act nonchalant. After all, da Vinci *did* spend most of his time in the studio but came and went as he pleased through the back door for dinner or snacks or for stealing kisses when the boys were asleep. It was bad enough having sex with da Vinci in the studio—I vowed I would never be with da Vinci in Joel and my marital bed, Lumpy. I had begun to wonder if da Vinci and I were more "friends" than "lovers," as we hadn't been together since that night in the studio, but with the boys safely out of the house, the idea to have some fun of my own sounded better every minute.

When I had returned from the gravesite the day before, da Vinci had tenderly wiped the dirt from my cheek where the grass has made an imprint, but he hadn't asked where I'd been. He seemed to notice when I didn't want to talk, but then again, we rarely needed to talk. Words were for whom? Journalists? Novelists? Linguists? Sure. But not always for friends and truly not necessary for lovers. Rachel had been right about that.

When the boys pulled away, waving from their backseats of my father's SUV, I instinctively pulled da Vinci closer to me, and when the car rounded the corner out of sight, da Vinci pulled me into him in a long, urgent kiss that sent us tumbling back into the house for privacy.

I hadn't eaten breakfast yet, but it wasn't food I was hungry for. Da Vinci lifted my flannel nightshirt over my head, kissed my shoulder blade and steered us to the bedroom. I put the brakes on, my feet firmly planted on the hardwood floor, my arm reaching out to grab the wall, but da Vinci was much stronger than I. Before I could protest, we were already on the king-sized bed, much softer than the drafting table in the studio, and I got lost in the heat of our bodies pressing together, forgetting that this bed ever had any other purpose than a soft place to make love in that moment.

"I should've known you'd be blissing," Anh said, arms crossed in the doorway. I shrieked, awkwardly grabbing for the sheet to cover us, but we were still nearly fully clothed. We hadn't even gotten to third base yet.

Da Vinci's groan turned from pleasure to annoyance. Something was always getting in the way of our togetherness, and it wasn't because of him. My boys. My family. My best friend who really, *really* should've known better. Nothing should break the spell of a Fantasy Sex Day. It wasn't fair. And I only got one, maybe two, my whole lifetime.

Da Vinci's arm was wrapped around my waist, his hot breaths at my shoulder blade, warming me from the outside in. I couldn't believe I wouldn't get to do what we were about to do. "What are you doing here?"

Anh gave an apologetic shrug, but obviously she wasn't sorry enough to turn around and leave when she saw us. "You said you'd watch Vi for me, remember?"

Vi appeared from behind Anh's legs and stared up at me with her big brown eyes, a sucker stick hanging from her mouth, sugary goo dripping onto my carpet. "I did? Why would I do a crazy thing like that?"

"Because I have the conference in Galveston this weekend, remember?"

I pounded my head against the pillow. So much for a free weekend. "I'm sorry. I can't believe I forgot."

Anh knelt down, a worried look on her face. "I hate to ask this, but do I look as bad as I feel? I've felt like crap all morning."

I pressed my cool hand against her head and quickly removed it. "You definitely have a fever."

Just then Vi removed her sucker and threw up all over the floor beside my bed. She was so shocked at her own vomit that she ran out of the room and straight for the couch, where she promptly spewed again.

Good thing Joel and I had a plan not to get new furniture until our kids were older. Little tykes believe couches are their personal wipe rag. Because our boys had finally reached the age where they knew potato chip grease was meant for napkins instead of seat cushions (well, half the time anyway), we'd been looking for a new couch the week before Joel died, but couldn't agree on one we both liked. Vi began to wail. "Oh-up. Oh-up."

"Dammit!" Anh said. "My son was sick earlier this week. He must've given us his bug."

I began tending to my friends. Another clue da Vinci was not a typical American male: he cleaned up the throw-up without even being asked. Actually, I wouldn't have asked him to do it at all, but by the time I'd retrieved the thermometer and trashcan from the bathroom, he had already grabbed a towel and began cleaning the mess. "Carpet cleaner?" he asked, and I directed him to the Oxy10. I'd almost forgotten his last temp job had been cleaning office buildings.

"Oh, God," Anh said, laying on the clean part of the couch. "He's sexy *and* he cleans. I'm the world's biggest bitch for breaking up your sexfest."

"Yes, you are," I said, shoving the thermometer in her mouth. "But as usual, I'll forgive you. Besides, we have three more days to be together. *If* he'll forgive me."

"This can't be happening," Anh said, closing her eyes.

"Yeah. Tell me about it. Don't talk. We want an accurate read."

Anh lay moaning on the couch while I scooped up Vi and bathed her and brushed her teeth with my finger. I wrapped her in a towel, and when I returned, I took the thermometer from Anh's hand.

"Yikes. 103," I said. "On the bright side, you won't have to go to a boring conference."

"It *better* not be boring. I'm the one who planned it."

"You work too hard. A little R&R won't kill you."

"That's what the conference was *supposed* to be. Do you know how much my hotel room is? And how much I was looking forward to getting away? And for all intents and purposes, I'm a single mom, you know. Her biological mother hasn't taken her the last four weekends, and her father, well, let's just say he takes after his own father. He's dating some hot college student and hasn't told her about Vi yet, the putz."

"Well, let's just worry about getting you better now."

Anh's cell phone rang.

"Don't answer that," I said just before she answered.

Anh's voice turned from corporate cool to fun and flirty. Nothing in my dissertation research said anything about being able to flirt with a fever. "You don't need to do that," she cooed.

I mouthed, "Who is it?" but she shooed me away. A moment later, she hung up.

"Nobody," she said.

"This no-named nobody sure seemed to turn your frown upside down."

Anh shook her head. "Fine. It's Michael. He said he'd come over and take care of Vi and me this weekend."

"Seriously? As in my Michael that you couldn't see doing anything other than blissing with?"

Anh put her hand over her head. "Weird, isn't it? Well, I'm sure even Republicans can make chicken noodle soup." She groaned. "The conference! My room! I even splurged for a suite. It's too late to cancel now."

"On the bright side, at least it's tax deductible."

She shook her fevered head. "You know where you can stick that 'bright side' Miss Sex-a-lot?" She removed her washcloth. "Wait a minute. I've got a great idea. You and da Vinci should go stay in my room. That way, it's not $350 down the drain. Come on, my treat."

"Me and da Vinci vacationing on Galveston Island? On the beach? That's crazy talk."

"You said you needed to take a vacation anyway, right? Wasn't that on The List? So do it! And I do mean, 'just do it.'"

Da Vinci's hands were folded in prayer. He clearly understood the words "island" and "beach" … and probably even "sex-a-lot."

"*Fallo e basta,*" he said urgently. *Just do it.*

Chapter 13

SIX HOURS LATER, WE were naked on the king-sized bed in an expensive suite I would've never been able to afford, living out the Fantasy Sex Day I couldn't believe was a reality. If a best friend could get any *bester*, then Anh had done so. Getting away unleashed any inhibitions I'd had about being with da Vinci. I felt young again, beautiful again and sexy again. Me, the thirty-six-year-old widowed wordsmith. Da Vinci became sweeter and more real by the minute. He cradled me, caressed me, and made love to me like I was the only thing he desired on the planet.

Getting away from Austin was like shedding a protective skin. As da Vinci and I walked along the shoreline after dinner, I realized I wasn't the same person at all. I still didn't know who I was, but getting outside of my comfort zone, my wall of imprisoned grief, I let myself smile again and really, really meant it. I let him hold my hand in public and didn't mind being seen by others. I could see the way other women looked at him, how they all wondered what I'd done to get a man as striking as him. They probably assumed I had money, though I didn't look it, or I was incredibly famous to land a boy toy such as this, though I saw him as so much more than a handsome man on my arm.

If I had been feeling poetic, I could have thought of him as my savior, my rescue pilot, my wake-up call. Mostly, though I just thought of him as da Vinci, the man I taught English to who taught me about so much more.

I sat next to him, our arms touching as we ate ice cream on the dock while we watched boats coming into the harbor. The night smelled salty and sweet, and I breathed in the air as if I'd never get enough of it. "What do you think?"

He raised his brows. Most of the time I was still too vague with him, even for a teacher. "Think of life? Love? Galveston?"

"Yes. All of it. Every last bit of it. Tell me everything."

Da Vinci's eyes crinkled in the moonlight, and I couldn't believe how romantic he looked under the stars. I wanted to capture the moment and put it on postcard and mail it to every woman I knew to tell them I was doing okay. Ramona Griffen would survive. *Look what I did.* Otherwise, would they ever believe me? I couldn't believe it myself.

"All of it, yes? Okay, then. I like this place very much. This beach is breathtaking. I like your place very much. Your shower nice. Your bed is lumpy. Your pancakes not hold candle to my pancakes. I like school, so-so, but am learning. What I like most about America so far, though," he said, leaning toward me, "is my Mona Lisa."

He kissed me softly, and I threw my ice cream into the lake, and he did the same. Then I heard two teenagers yell, "Get a room."

"What a marvelous idea! Our room," I said, relishing the sound of it, and we went back to the suite and drank champagne until I got tipsy, which didn't take but one glass because I never drink it. Champagne is for celebrations, and I hadn't felt like celebrating in so long. I'd forgotten how much I like the taste of it, the bubbly sweetness that feels like little fireworks in my mouth. The room began to spin when da Vinci lay on top of me, making love to me again. I was overwhelmed with his scent, the feel of his soft skin and hard muscles and the beat of his heart against mine that told me he was very much alive and very much mine for the moment.

Between kisses, he gazed into my eyes and clearly whispered, "*Ti amo*," and though my translation is sluggish when I'm inebriated, I am fairly certain that da Vinci had told me that he loved me.

***

My cell phone blared "Bootylicious," awaking me the next morning. The song was a cruel practical joke Bradley pulled on me after I'd told him and his brother to stop singing it in the car one day. He'd taken my cell phone, and for the past six months, his tech-idiot mother couldn't figure out how to reprogram it. Like so many other things about widowhood, I didn't ask someone to do it for me.

The bedside alarm clock blinked its red digits—7:30 a.m. Not *my* bedside alarm clock—the one Joel bought me for our fifth anniversary from Pottery Barn—but a boring, old brown one better suited for a cheap hotel than a pricey suite. No one ever calls me in the morning, so I assumed the worst. Something had happened to my boys, or Anh and Vi had actually caught the bird flu and were in ICU, or my boss was calling me to fire me because he'd found out da Vinci and I had gone on a sexcapade.

"Hello?" I mumbled as the morning sun cut through the hotel blinds, my head pounding from the champagne. I remembered where I was, which caught me by surprise, and yet there lay the proof: da Vinci in gorgeous sleep. He didn't even snore. My life couldn't get any better.

I began to recall that da Vinci had said he loved me when the voice on the other end spoke. "Ramona? Hi. I hope it's not too early to call, but I'm actually in the airport and thought I'd return your call before I'm on my long flight."

"I'm sorry," I said, still dreary from sleep. "Who is this?"

"Oh, I apologize. Silly me. It's Monica Blevins. Returning your call."

My pounding head pounded harder, my mouth so dry I couldn't speak. I had to get water before I could respond.

"Are you there? Ramona?"

While downing a glass of water in the bathroom, I stared at my naked frame, vowing to double my sit-up regimen from zero to at least ten per day, then covered up with a towel and sat on the toilet lid. I couldn't talk to Monica while naked, if I could speak to her at all. Composure seemed impossible. "No. I mean, yes, I'm here. I'm just surprised is all. I mean, it's early. Yes. I'm out of town."

"Is it a bad time, then? I can call you back at a later date."

A later date? Would *any* time be better? Maybe after a cup of joe, some bacon and eggs, and a good hour-long meditation to prepare for her call? "No, it's fine." I told myself to calm down. To think clearly. I wanted to sound composed and smart and not embarrass Joel. After all, he'd married me and not her. She'd probably downed two cups of Starbucks and looked smashing in another designer suit. But it didn't matter. It was only the phone. What was I so afraid of?

Monica continued. "Okay, then. So you said you wanted to speak with me. It was good to hear from you, actually. I've been wondering how you and the boys have been."

I blinked back tears, trying hard not to dissect her every word. She'd really been thinking about us or is that something that you just say to widows? To the family your fiancé creates after you've dumped him? "I did want to talk to you, but it's really not important now. I thought it was, but I guess it's not. It's fine. I'm sorry to have bothered you, really."

"No. I'm glad you did," she said. "I've been meaning to call you, too, and I didn't have the nerve to do it. I want to set some things straight about Joel, and I have a few questions that only you can answer."

In my hangover haze, I wasn't sure if she'd said the words I had intended to say. SHE-SLUT had questions for *me*? Questions only *I* could answer? What was going on here? "You do?"

"It would mean a lot to me. Oh, shoot. They just called us to board. Can we get together for coffee when I get back from Tokyo?"

I slumped over the toilet and held up my head with my hand. I didn't even sound like myself when I said, "Absolutely. Let's have coffee when you get back from Japan."

***

I'm not going to lie. Monica Blevins *ruined* my Fantasy Sex Weekend. My sexcapade was officially over the very moment bootylicious Beyoncé sang. Even my young hot Italian couldn't improve my mood. Which is too bad, really. Because I had moved on. Until. *She* wanted to "set some things straight." She had Questions and not just The Answer?

I had exactly 149 questions formulated in my mind that *she* might ask me. They went from bad to worse:

- Did Joel tell you we went to Cabo that long weekend he said he was at a conference in D.C.?
- Did you find the receipt for the hotel rooms we rented Friday afternoons?
- Did Joel tell you he was leaving you to come back to me?
- Did he tell you he never loved you as much as he loved me?

The last one really got me. I could barely eat lunch over that one. *No*, I would tell her. *He said he loved me and only me.* He was lying.

Da Vinci did his best to take my mind off the call. Not just making love to me again, but his insistence on making the most of every moment: going sailing, feeding the birds, buying me a balloon with a big yellow happy face on it. Okay. I finally smiled. I laughed even. But *She* was never far from my mind.

I wanted to be happy for me because da Vinci had told me he loved me, or I was fairly sure he'd said it, but I didn't have the nerve to ask him to repeat it, and I knew, call or no call, that I wasn't ready to say it back.

***

The Chemistry of Love

With nearly 7,000 languages in the world, there are nearly as many ways to say, "I love you."

Albanian: "*Te dua.*"

Chinese: "*Wo ie ni.*"

Dutch: "*Ik hou van jou.*"

Greek: "*S' agapo.*"

Italian: "*Ti amo.*"

Zuni: "*Tom ho' ichema.*"

The words may be different, but scientists say the chemistry behind the words is the same. Love is, in effect, a chemical reaction. The cuddling chemical is known as oxytocin, linked to milk production in women, making both men and women calmer and more sensitive to others. Oxytocin levels are highest for women just after childbirth, which can explain how moms are able to cope with screaming newborns and care for them.

The hormone also plays a huge role in romantic love during sexual arousal, prompting couples to pair up and cuddle before, during, and after lovemaking. Production of this love hormone can come from both emotional and physical cues, including the loved one's voice and look or even just thinking about the lover.

So, what? The Duke of Milan's *hormones* made him drop his royal drawers for every blushing countess he had chemistry with? *Sorry, lovey, the oxytocin made me do it!* Right.

Addicted to Love

Oxytocin then passes the love baton to a new group of hormones, morphine-like opiates that calm and reassure lovers with intimacy, dependability, warmth, and experiences.

These steady hormones are more addictive, explaining why the longer two people have been married, the more likely they will stay married. Staying together becomes addictive, with lovers relying on the endorphins and marital serenity they bring one another. Absent lovers yearn for each other when they are apart because, like a drug, they yearn for the steady high endorphins bring. Similarly, the absence of endorphins plays a part in grief over the death of a spouse.

I lifted my hands from the keyboard and noticed they were shaking. So I wasn't crazy after all. It was those pesky absent endorphins making me miss him so. Making all those absent lovers write such eloquent love letters across the miles. *How long?* I wondered. How long does it take to come down off of a lover's high? After I had been bonded, addicted to Joel for so many years? If a part of my grief was chemical, then could falling in love cure me of my grief once and for all?

I stared at the date on the calendar, Joel's death date, and yearned for my boys to return home from my parents so I could hug them. I couldn't even go hug da Vinci because he was gone again at another temp job and then to a study group with kids his own age. There I go again, calling him a kid. If our age difference wasn't a big deal to him, why did I think of it at all?

I took a sip of hot tea and picked up the album Cortland helped me create on Joel's computer. It arrived while I was gone with da Vinci in Galveston. I tried not to be sad that I wasn't here when the postman delivered it. I didn't want him to think I didn't care about the delivery, that the album meant nothing, because in fact, it meant everything. Of course the "him" I was referring to wasn't the postman at all, but Joel.

I had carefully laid copies of the book on the pillows of the boys' beds to surprise them when they returned. I took my own copy and lay with it on Lumpy, a bed I knew I had to replace sooner rather than later, and carefully looked through its glossy four-color pages at the happy family we had been. By the tenth time I viewed it, I saw the pictures through clear eyes, the tears dried, and my heart was full once again.

When I returned to the computer, I could finish the section, now three-quarters complete. Besides, I had to know about the Monogamy drug, and even more so, if my husband had it in his system when he'd died.

Monogamous Mating

Only three percent of mammals are monogamous, and scientists say humans are not among them. *Monogamous: mating and bonding with one partner for life.* Scientists claim a drug called vasopressin would help. It is called the monogamy chemical.

Lifelong mating is linked to the action of vasopressin, which kicks in within 24 hours after mating, at least for the male vole (a mouse-like rodent) that falls into that small three percent of monogamous mammals.

Once vasopressin kicks in, he is indifferent to all other lady voles, no matter how comely or come-hither. In addition, he becomes aggressive toward other males, a classic exhibition of the jealous husband syndrome.

What keeps a lover from straying, then, may not be one isolated chemical, but the love potion created by all of them: a dose of oxytocin, a scoop of endorphins, and a dash of vasopressin for long-lasting kick.

If humans were ruled by one drug, vasopressin, then might their ability for long-lasting love die along with their spouse? Would they never love again, forced to live out the rest of their lives alone and loveless?

If I had wanted a monogamous mate, I should've married a rat. Literally. I turned off the computer, thinking again about Monica and trying the breathing exercises Cynthia had recommended for when I felt anxious. After twenty-one counts, I had stopped thinking about Her and decided to get out of the house.

Sometimes Grievers do irrational things such as sit on the porch, willing their loved ones to return home, even when those loved ones have passed on. For months after his death, I imagined Joel would walk through the door. "Where have you been?" I would ask him, half-angry, half-relieved he had returned. He would wrap me into his embrace and say, "I love it when you worry about me," and kiss me, and we'd go on with our lives.

I waited on the bench in the yard on Joel's DD, not awaiting his return, but that of my boys. I craved time away from them until I got it, and it didn't take long before separation anxiety kicked in. It had, in fact, kicked in back in Galveston, but I tried to be a Normal and just enjoy time alone with da Vinci. Still. Sometimes I felt as though I needed my boys to verify my existence. I couldn't survive another two days without them, and I needed the strength of their smiles to get me through that day.

Gabriella spotted me and waved, and I silently wished she wouldn't come over, but she did anyway, dressed in a warm brown and blue floral dress that fell to her calves. From across the street, she looked like a bunch of violets drifting towards me. Sometimes I thought Gabriella paid no mind to seasons. She dressed as if it were spring year-round. She carried something in her hand—food, I presumed. With her steady stream of casseroles and baked goods, Gabriella had kept the boys and me alive after Joel had died. The boys must've thought the food train would never end, because the first day she didn't bring us food, Bradley said, "Great. I guess it's back to eating Mom's type of cooking," which is to say not very good, and I'd relied too much on fast food to nourish us.

Today it was a meatloaf; I could smell it before she even told me what lay beneath the aluminum foil. "We just got back from Joel's grave," she said with a bright smile, inhaling as she sat next to me on the bench. "Such a beautiful day." Yes, I thought, as beautiful as it had been two years before, same blue sky and spotted puffy clouds and warm October afternoon. A beautiful day to die.

"I was there a few days ago," I whispered.

"The orange pansy was a nice touch. They were his favorite, weren't they?"

"Orange pansy?"

"The one on his grave."

There was no pansy. If there had been, I would've smashed it when I had lain on his grave. "Only one pansy?"

Gabriella nodded. "As if it had been planted there on purpose. No other pansies as far as I could see, either direction."

I wondered how I could miss an orange pansy and who might've planted one there. But *one*? Who would plant one pansy? I squelched the thought that Monica had done it; that my call had brought up old feelings for Joel that sent her to his grave with his favorite flower.

Down the block, two men from the neighborhood walked side by side in their basketball gear, ready for the 2 p.m. pick-up game. Dave the banker and Tom the car dealer, both average players at best, not half as good as Joel. Dave bounced the basketball and with each hit on the pavement, my heart caved in a little more.

"Shall we go inside?" Gabriella asked, noticing them, too. I had spent Joel's first DD in bed all day, telling the boys I was sick while my father took them out for bowling and ice cream. I had lain there all day, waiting for the moment the clock ticked 2:37 p.m., half-expecting something to happen when it did, whether it was an external sign or an internal combustion, but the minute was just like the one before it: heavy with sadness. I had even closed my eyes and imagined him lying beside me on Lumpy, his leg crossed over mine, as he did so often, and curling my hands into his chest where I could feel his heart beat. I felt that Joel deserved something from me in that moment, some eulogy or prayer, but all I could muster was one simple sentence, "I love you, Bear," and in my mind, I could hear him say back, "Love you big, Ramey."

Forty-five minutes until the exact moment Joel collapsed on the basketball court. "I'd rather sit here," I said. "I'm waiting for the boys."

Donald emerged from his front door, wearing red warm-up pants and a white T-shirt. In an effort to stay fit for Zoya, he played with the guys, though I couldn't recall him ever making a basket, something that inevitably wound up in our conversation after each game. "Missed it by a mile," he would say. Or, "So close it had to hurt."

"Howdy there," Donald said, followed by Zoya, who was dressed unusually normal, meaning no low-cut tops or tight jeans or massive amounts of jewelry and make-up. She wore her thick hair in a ponytail. While Donald met up with the guys and they greeted and then waved to me, probably feeling badly that they were playing today, Zoya joined us on the bench, now full. She held her arms around her stomach, and I could see she'd been crying.

"You okay?" I asked. I liked that someone other than me could be having a crappy day.

Zoya nodded. "Donald impregnated me."

Gabriella gasped and hugged Zoya, and I did the same. "Congratulations."

Zoya began crying. "He gave me bad baby that makes me sick and ugly. I can't do workout or eat food or drink my coffee or fit into my sexy pants."

"A baby is worth all those things," Gabriella said, shaking her finger for emphasis. "We'll go shopping for sexy maternity clothes if that's *really* important to you."

Zoya wiped the raccoon eyes from her face with her sleeve. "They make such things?"

I nodded. "Very stylish, indeed."

Zoya's mood lifted. "I love America. Then Zoya happy about baby. Thanks for friends like you." Zoya took our hands and held them in her lap. "I am sorry for telling you on day of mourning, Ramona. I lit candle for Joel this morning."

"Do Russians do that?"

"Gabriella taught me. When I am thinking of someone I miss, I light a candle and say a prayer for them. It made me think of Halloween party three years ago when Joel drug chains in attic to scare us."

Gabriella laughed. "Joel would stop at nothing to try to get the last laugh. God rest his soul."

I remembered that night, how Joel had begged me to be Franken-stein's bride and, as usual, I agreed. I tried to get the picture of us in my mind, but only bits and pieces of our costume flashed in my mind. How could I forget such an odd image, the two of us in green paint and that black beehive wig with a white lightning stripe? Dur-ing the middle of the party, Joel had grunted something about mak-ing a Frankenbaby with me later, and we had sex in our costumes, which turned out to be sexier than I imagined.

I silently vowed to get every printed photo from our ten years' worth of Halloween costume parties, and put them out as decora-tions for Halloween. The crispy orange leaves fell toward us, one perfectly shaped oak leaf sailing onto my lap. I grabbed it by its stem and twirled it. "Let's put those little ghost things Joel liked so much on the branches."

"Oh, the kids will love that," Gabriella said.

"Joel will love it, too," Zoya said, catching herself after she'd said it, wondering, I assumed, if I believed Joel still had the capacity to feel such an emotion.

I patted her knee. "You're right. Joel will absolutely love it."

A hundred little white ghosts swung in the wind when the boys and I walked down to the park. It was 2:48 p.m. I imagined my father, the timekeeper, had known exactly when to pull up, to cause some sort of distraction so I wouldn't be sad. My father's grief had to include how sad he felt for the boys and me. Gabriella had insisted we stop and pray when the time came, so we stood underneath our white ghosts and she prayed us through the minute of his death. I don't even recall what she said, but it sounded like a song: smooth and rhythmic and full of emotion.

William hugged me tightly and let me kiss him on the head and—probably instructed by his grandfather—Bradley allowed me to hug him, too. "We want to go to the park and make a basket for Daddy," William said, pushing up the frames on his button nose. "I've been practicing at Grandpa's house."

I felt the tug of a cry, but kept the tears at bay. William was terrible at basketball, perhaps worse than Donald. When William was younger, Joel had tried to get him to make the shot on the regulation court, but the then-five-year-old was much too short for it.

Bradley raised his brows and nodded. "I think he can do it, Mom," he said. "He wants to make Daddy proud."

My father turned away to wipe a tear from his face, and Zoya and Gabriella had tears streaming down theirs. I couldn't possibly go to the court while the other men were playing, but I couldn't let my boys down, either.

"We'll all go," Gabriella said, and my father nodded and retrieved a basketball from the backseat. It was a blue and red Globetrotters basketball, one I had gotten Joel for our first anniversary after we had seen the team perform at an exhibition game.

My father walked beside me and grabbed my hand and squeezed it. "How you holdin' up, pumpkin?"

"On the bright side, it's a pretty day." Growing up, my father had told my sister and me to always look at the bright side. I often heard him say the same thing to my sons. It had annoyed me growing up, but now I appreciated his optimism. Somebody had to do it.

"That it is, darlin'. Never a bluer sky."

When we arrived at the park, the players were gathered in a circle, their shirts covered in sweat, their heads bowed in prayer. We stopped until the moment passed and they dispersed. I wondered if Deacon Friar had been right and the deceased could feel our prayers in Heaven. Gabriella had told me once that her mother believed it was like a game show in Heaven, and the person with the most prayers said for them had the highest score, allowing them to move closer to God, like cosmic board spaces, but I hated to think of getting to Heaven like a contest. How many lonely people died that no one prayed for, save the nuns? If Gabriella's mom was right, Joel probably skipped ahead a few spaces that day.

After we said our hellos and goodbyes to the men, we had the park to ourselves and sat on the cool cement bench that the neighborhood had bought in remembrance of Joel, with a silver plaque in the middle that read, "In Loving Memory of Joel Bradford Griffen." The boys began to warm up and peered over their tiny shoulders at their small audience.

"Ready?" Bradley asked, and before we could answer, he lobbed the ball from the free throw line, sinking it. "Nothin' but net!"

William retrieved the ball, and I said a tiny prayer that he would make it because it meant the world to him. He bounced it once, twice, and the third time, it landed on his foot, causing the ball to veer left, but he caught it before it escaped, and he started over again. With his tongue stuck onto the top of his lip, his brow furrowed in concentration, William heaved the ball to the sky, causing it to soar toward the goal … and hit just underneath the rim before catapulting back to earth.

His shoulders fell in defeat.

"It's okay, bro," Bradley said, and I couldn't believe how uncharacteristically nice he was being to his little brother. "Go again." He bounced the ball to William.

A second time, knees bent, William hurled the ball upward, this time landing on top of the rim, but circling it and falling to the right and down.

"This is the money shot," Bradley said, and William turned back to us. "This is the money shot!" he yelled.

He positioned his right palm underneath the ball, his elbows bent, feet planted firmly on the free-shot line, and in one sweeping motion, he jumped up high into the air, the ball sailing toward the rim and falling straight through the net. "That's what I'm talkin' 'bout!" William said, and Bradley high-fived him before we gathered him in a hug. *Thank God.* I meant it. I would've sat there until sundown to make sure William got the shot he wanted. Surely the boys' guardian angels had given that ball a little lift on its journey to the net.

I knelt down beside my seven-year-old, eyes moist with tears, and beamed. "Daddy would be very proud," I said. "And so is Mommy."

An hour later, I knelt down again, this time at Joel's grave. I had never asked the boys to visit their father's grave, believing it was too macabre for young children, though Gabriella's children had visited his grave numerous times.

Bradley and William folded their hands and stared at their father's gravestone. Bradley knelt down and traced his fingers in his father's name, while I stared at the orange pansy, which had not been planted at all. No earth had been moved, the grass perfectly grown in around the flower's stem, and upon closer inspection, I saw that the flower had grown up precisely where my tears had fallen two days prior.

Chapter 14

I AM NOT CERTAIN of the exact moment da Vinci became my boyfriend. It snuck up on me, not as a private revelation, but as a public display of affection.

I had no idea he was my boyfriend, in fact, until da Vinci referred to *me* as his girlfriend. To make matters worse, I discovered it at the same moment that a group of his friends from college did: outside of the movie theater the Friday night before Halloween. I don't care what older people say: Friday nights at the local cinema is reserved for young couples, and I should've remembered this, but it had been so long since I'd been on a date that I had forgotten.

While the cool twenty-something wore sporty decaled sweatshirts and ripped jeans, I wore a smart cardigan and khakis and boots. Not cool cowboy boots like this young girl Katie wore, mind you, but boring brown boots that I'd had for eons. I wondered why I hadn't taken my sister's advice on updating my wardrobe, but it hadn't seemed out of date to me until I was around other college students. I'd just been thankful I fit into my pants with buttons again. The moment you find out you are a girlfriend is one you'll never forget. Here's how it went down for me:

Da Vinci and I were in line to see a romantic comedy, my mood light and relaxed until we saw his friends coming toward us. I could feel my cheeks begin to burn, and scolded myself for thinking that it mattered. Of course it was time I met some of da Vinci's friends. After all, we'd been sleeping together for three weeks—not long by any means, but long enough to figure that sleeping together might continue or, by some standards, this would mean we had a "relationship." I don't know what I thought, except for that I was very much enjoying sleeping with someone again and with da Vinci in particular.

Every last one of them gave me the up–down, the look that I had read about in my flirting research, which is the moment I realized I must look more like da Vinci's mother than his girlfriend. Okay, big sister. But still.

I showed my age further by sticking out my hand when da Vinci introduced them. College students don't shake hands. They nod and utter, "Hey, wassup?" or "How's it goin'?" Hand-shaking is saved for the truly adult moments such as interviewing for a job or meeting someone's parents. If shaking their hands wasn't shocking enough, what came out of da Vinci's beautiful mouth next did the trick: "Everybody, this is Ramona," he said proudly. "My girlfriend."

Katie's jaw dropped. Just a little. Maybe she didn't mean to, but I saw it, I swear. One guy—Paul, was it?—muttered, "Cool," but I'm sure he was thinking it was anything other than cool.

After an embarrassing, awkward moment where da Vinci told them that I had been his English teacher (how cool is that?), we walked into the dark theater. "You didn't have to tell them I was your teacher," I said. "Or your girlfriend."

"Why not?" da Vinci said, stuffing his mouth with way too much popcorn. "You *were* my teacher. I have you to thank for good English speaking. And you *are* my girlfriend, correct?"

Instead of answering him, I took a long slurp of Dr. Pepper while da Vinci pulled me into him and kissed me atop the head with his buttery mouth, and it occurred to me that I had to ask myself if I really *wanted* to be da Vinci's girlfriend. I hadn't considered what we were doing was *dating*. If I had known *that's* what we were doing, I would've said no to the Italian dinner we had the weekend before at an actual restaurant, and the day after that when we walked hand in hand at the arts festival, and the week after that at the movies. I did think we were hanging out, having fun and some amazing sex, but surely not "dating."

And girlfriend/boyfriend? Such a juvenile expression for someone who had been married for ten years and wears khakis and boots while her boyfriend wears ripped jeans and athletic shoes.

"Face it," Anh said later that evening while the boys were watching a rerun of *America's Funniest Home Videos,* and we ate greasy potato chips with onion dip when I should've been eating carrot sticks with fat-free ranch. "You're dating."

I moaned. "I knew you were going to take his side."

"This coming from a walking, talking dictionary. Seriously, Ramona. When two people go out on a social engagement with just each other, then it's a date. Especially when the date ends with kissing and sex."

I stuffed another chip in my mouth. "Fine. We're dating. But that doesn't mean we have to be exclusive."

Anh eyed me suspiciously. "You've got other hot young guys beating down your door you haven't told me about?"

"Not me, *him.* I mean da Vinci should definitely be dating other people."

Anh made a sour face. "Not in this day and age. All those diseases. Besides, who cares? What difference does it make if you're exclusive?"

I wiped my greasy fingers on my jeans—not mom jeans, but cool ones I'd picked up at Abercrombie the day before, proof I obviously *did* care. "Well, because I don't want him to become too emotionally attached."

"Him or you?"

"So what if I don't want to fall for him and get my heart broken when he dumps me for a younger coed? That makes me a normal woman. And I'm not ready for a serious relationship, anyway. I can't have my boys believing da Vinci is my boyfriend. What would they think? That he'll be their next daddy? It's ludicrous. Preposterous. Ridiculously absurd. Besides, I think about Monica Blevins more than I think about da Vinci. How screwed up is that?"

"Has she called you back yet?"

"No, but her flight came in yesterday, according to her assistant, so I'm expecting her to call any day now."

Anh grabbed the chip bag and rolled it up. "I knew something was eating at you. You inhale Lays and onion dip when you're nervous. But you keep this up, you're going to gain back those pounds you've lost."

I admired my slimmer frame. My new jeans were a size smaller than anything I had in my closet. A little tight after half a bag of Lays, but they still fit. I'd lost twelve pounds without even trying, or rather, I lost pounds without obsessing over losing them. Much like da Vinci becoming my boyfriend, the weight loss had surprised me. I didn't lose the weight to *Get Up and Move It, Texas!* like my mother and Rachel assumed. I didn't lose the weight by eating any less, either, or at least I don't think I ate any less with chocolate and ice cream and non-stop carbs from da Vinci's pasta.

Anh claimed it was falling in love that did it, but I don't think it was falling in love with da Vinci, but falling in love with life again. I was more active than I had been in years. As my sister said on a daily basis, "When you move it, you lose it."

"Speaking of dating, you and Michael still a thing?"

"Not dating," Anh said, reapplying her lipstick. "Unlike some people I know, we are not going out on social engagements. Just my house and his. Taking care of me and Vi when we were sick did score him a few brownie points, though."

"I don't know. I think you're closet dating. How many affairs go on that never make it out into the public? Are they not dating?"

"No. That's why it's called 'having an affair.' Two different things. See, if you'd have asked if Michael and I are having a sexual affair, I would've said yes."

"Thanks for setting the record straight. We'll see how long it takes before you slip up and wind up in public like da Vinci and I did."

"Not gonna happen. Besides, I'm still holding out for Cortland. He dumped your sister yet?"

"So not gonna happen. If anything, she'll dump him. She brags about how often she gets hit on every day. I just want to shake her and scream, 'I get it! You're hot! But you're still not good enough for Cortland!'

"I may not be the only one with a little crush on Cortland."

"You mean *me?* Don't be ridiculous. But he did call me earlier to see if I needed any help dog shopping. I'm going to surprise the boys."

"Maybe he's a little hot for sister."

I waved my hand as if to swat away the absurdity of her idea, though I secretly thought she could be on to something. "More like feeling sorry for his girlfriend's widowed sister. But I may take him up on it. I'm terrified of picking out the wrong dog. And he's done all the research on the best dog for kids. He knows a breeder who has pups for sale."

"I don't know," Anh said, slinging her purse over her shoulder. "Sounds like a date to me."

***

"I don't see you as the yappy dog type," Cortland said the following day as we sipped coffee at Starbucks. He thought it would be easier to meet up and drive out into the country together, as it was twenty minutes into the middle of nowhere.

"What? You can't see me dressing a little Chihuahua in a cute striped sweater and carrying it around in my purse?"

Cortland's face broke into a smile and I wondered if it was the caffeine that made my heart begin to race or that smile. Now here was a man who knew how to dress sexy for his age. He wore a black mock turtleneck with pressed dark denim jeans and black boots.

"You need a dog like my Leibe. Good dog for growing boys. And a great jogging companion, too. Of course, *you* already have a jogging companion."

"I do? Oh, you mean da Vinci? I guess so."

"You two serious?"

I shook my head. I vaguely remembered how this happens. You start dating someone, people ask you if you're serious, will you get married, do you want more kids? I couldn't believe people assumed that romantic evolution for da Vinci and me. Either I was delusional or I didn't like da Vinci as much as he liked me. "I can't see getting into a serious relationship right now," I said. "Maybe it's the timing. Or maybe it's just him. I don't know."

Cortland's smile turned down, though the twinkle in his eye showed the opposite. "Well, that's too bad. You deserve to be happy, Ramona."

I wrapped my fingers around the hot ceramic mug. "I am happy. Okay, *happier*, anyway. But I'm not sure I need a man to feel that. The way I see it, it either happens or it doesn't. I've done some research on those pesky love hormones. I'd like your professional opinion, actually."

"A professional opinion about love? Didn't know there was such a thing, but I'll give it my best shot."

"Vasopressin."

"The monogamy drug."

"So you've heard of it?"

"I happen to believe humans can very much be monogamous."

"By choice or biology?"

"Everything in life is a choice, whether inspired by biology or not."

"But you agree love is a chemical attraction? That the endorphins cause us to fall in love and stay in love?"

He crossed his arms in front of him and I found myself staring at his large hands, and longed to reach out and touch them. Anh had to be wrong. I couldn't have feelings for him. It would not only be crazy, but wrong.

"I think chemistry is a huge part of it," he said, leaning in to the table. "But in the end, our brains have to tell us if it's the right thing or not. Otherwise, who knows who we might end up with?"

He may not have meant it as a put down, but that's how I took it. That he thought my loving da Vinci was a colossally bad idea. "You're right," I said, holding my head high. "We might end up with someone like a fame-obsessed TV star with fake boobs. *For instance.*"

I could feel my cheeks flame and Cortland stared at me for a long moment before he spoke. "Or an immigrant preying on a lonely widow."

If he hadn't meant it as a put-down *before* … "Oh, is *that* what you think?"

"If it's not love, it's at least convenient. A backyard beefcake at your beck and call."

He hadn't sounded snappish—it's the women who come off that way—and I couldn't control the shrill of my tone. "Who do you think you are?" I grabbed my jacket to get up and leave, but he grabbed my hand.

"I'm sorry. I don't know why I said that. It was rude and completely out of line."

I stood and fought back the tears, releasing his hand. "I started it. I'm sorry. I shouldn't speak that way about my own sister. I don't know what got into me."

"No, *I'm* sorry. Now that I've acted like a complete dog, perhaps it's time we go look for one. If you'll still get in a car with me?"

His apology sounded sincere, and I really did want to surprise the boys with a dog. They'd been getting along so much better lately, and while their rooms still weren't immaculate, I didn't exactly set the best example in the good housekeeping department. We drove in silence most of the way to the breeder's house, my head pressed against the cool window as I watched the sunflower fields sway in the wind. The temperature had dropped considerably, and by the time we played with the litter of German Shepherd puppies in the breeder's backyard, it began to drizzle.

"Which one?" the breeder asked, tugging at his rain slicker, clearly ready to take cover.

A wooly gray furball pounced over and playfully bit my hand. Love at first bite. "I think he picked me," I said, looking up at Cortland.

"You three will be very happy together," the breeder said dryly, as he led us into the house to do the paperwork. Obviously, he thought Cortland and I were a couple, but I didn't correct him. Neither did Cortland.

"They can be tough to house-train," the breeder said, handing the puppy over to me.

"I've done it before," Cortland said assuredly, and I grinned at the prospect of his help. Presumptuous, but kind. I was probably his future sister-in-law and my sons, his future nephews. He was helping out family, was all.

"Could be fun," he said as he peered over the backseat at the little pup whimpering in the crate, and then looked back to me again.

I don't know who needed more help at the moment—me or the dog—but I looked forward to it all the same.

Chapter 15

I LAY IN THE early light and swept my arms over Joel's side of the bed, sunken in where his body had lain. Joel used to joke he was climbing into his cocoon every night. I wondered if it would be weird just to move it to the garage to keep for old time's sake? Weird for a Normal, but perfectly normal for a Griever.

I'd progressed in leaps and bounds by adding a dog into our lives, but I couldn't get rid of Lumpy, even when I woke up with a backache because the mattress had given up support long ago. I'd had emotional attachments to objects before—my first designer bag in college, my grandmother's diamond earrings—but an ugly, worn-out, king-sized bed? I decided a marriage is a triangle made up of a man, a woman, and their bed. It was one of the last physical remnants of our union, and yet my back knew it was time to say goodbye; finally, so did I. If only I could gather the courage.

Da Vinci would've preferred Lumpy to the pull-out couch that became our regular venue for late-night romps. On Halloween night, after the boys had finally come down from their sugar high and gone to bed, I had slipped out to the studio, where more than two dozen candy wrappers littered his floor.

A few things began to bother me about da Vinci, high among them his trail of clutter wherever he went—this coming from the Clutter Queen. How could I tolerate it in myself, but despise it in others? Talk about a hypocrite. Used paper towels and wadded-up homework and wrappers of every size, shape, and color. Didn't they have wastebaskets in the Italian countryside, too? He was worse than my boys, and I already had to pick up after them. I forgot when you get a boyfriend, you get more than a late-night body warmer. It wasn't just his mess, either.

His work ethic was questionable. While he was good at a lot of things, he didn't like to finish anything he started. After a few days on a temp job, he was ready to move on. If they kept him on too long, he just didn't show up, which caused reprimands all the way up the ladder, and ended up being reported to Panchal, who had high expectations of his immigrants: *on time, best effort, no excuses.*

I dismissed it as his age, not knowing what he wanted to do with his life yet, or not yet feeling like he fit in, but the more time that passed, the more I thought it could just be da Vinci's personality. I wondered if he would wake up one day and see that I wasn't so interesting after all—just a regular woman with two boys and a mortgage she could barely pay.

And what was with that notebook? He carried it with him everywhere, but when I tried to find it, it was nowhere to be found. What could be inside? Sketches of me and the boys? Love poems? A journal of his new life in America? Da Vinci was still a mystery to me. On any given day, he went from incredibly simple to preposterously complex. He was both or neither or I was just overthinking him. Well, I had a right to, hadn't I? Wasn't he my boyfriend now?

Halloween night, after a quickie on top of the sheets, we lay naked on our bellies and ate more bite-sized candies. He threw his wrappers on the floor and I tossed mine on the side table.

"There are three trashcans in here," I said, motioning to the one just a foot from where he was tossing the trash.

Da Vinci stuck a Tootsie Roll in his mouth. "You sound like my mother."

Ouch. "I was just pointing out an obvious fact. Fine. Whatever. You're a grown man. If stepping on candy wrappers and getting chocolate goo on your bare feet doesn't bother you, then why should I care?"

"You shouldn't."

"Fine."

"Fine."

I tried to lighten the mood. "I guess you enjoyed trick or treating? From the looks of it, you really cleaned up."

"Stop with clean house. Got lots of candy."

"Sorry. That's an expression: 'Cleaned up' can mean you really did well. As it, got lots of candy."

"Yes, lots of candy. Candy bars very big in America."

"Chocolate releases endorphins in the brain," I said. "Mimics the feelings of love."

"I don't need chocolate," he said, playfully hitting my foot with his. "You are one big chocolate factory."

I kissed him, one chocolatey kiss that had the power to pull me on top of him. "So I saw you writing in your notebook when you and the boys got back. What do you put in there?"

"I already told you. Things."

"So it's like a diary, then? Anh thinks you write down observations about life, like your namesake did. Is that what it is? Borrowing an old trick from the old man da Vinci?"

In fact, Anh believed he could *be* da Vinci reincarnated, finally getting to visit America. I would not share this with him, or anyone else, for that matter. I liked to keep my friend's loopy ideas under cover. Besides, it wasn't reincarnation that gave him so many similarities with the genius da Vinci, but his name. Perhaps his parents, even in their small Italian village, fostered creativity and curiosity in their little da Vinci, hoping he might grow up one day to master any of the many things in which the genius da Vinci was gifted. Many people didn't know the old da Vinci had done everything from party planning to war strategy and everything in between: scientist, horseman, astrologer, artist. I had never seen my da Vinci draw or paint anything, though I'd tempted him a few times when the boys were doing crafts, but he never did. Perhaps that's what I was hoping I would find in his notebooks: proof that he was or wasn't da Vinci reincarnate. Besides my da Vinci's skill at landscaping, horseback riding, and taking care of his body, the most obvious shared trait was his proclivity to leave projects half-finished. Hardly a way for him to make his own name for himself, let alone the old guy's.

Da Vinci shook his head and ran a finger down from my neck down to my belly button. "My notebook is personal. Now let's get it on so I can do my sit-ups before bed."

He was nearly as fitness obsessed as my sister. The only difference was he ate whatever he wanted, but he made up for it with marathon workout sessions: jogging, biking, lifting weights, Pilates. Rachel had asked him to come on her show for the next taping, so he'd been even more obsessive than usual. His hundred sit-ups turned into a thousand. Not that I let his one-armed push-ups make me feel bad about my still soft body. Well, maybe a little.

"I thought you said America cared too much about TV? That we should get out and enjoy nature more?"

"This true," da Vinci said. "But TV makes you star, no? And maybe I could be star."

I picked up a pillow and threw it at him, hitting him in the head. "I already have one star too many in my family, thank you very much."

The puppy whimpered from inside the house, his bark becoming more persistent, needy. Bellezza. Da Vinci had named him for beauty, but I was beginning to think we should've named him Cane Terribile for "holy terror."

I grabbed my sweatshirt and sweatpants, thinking I must be an old, uninteresting girlfriend to not even wear sexy lingerie for da Vinci after only four weeks together. I made a mental note to pick up some when I went to the department store to look for a bed. Oh, God. I was going shopping for a bed? I'd have to pop a Xanax just to get through it. For some reason, it felt like more of a betrayal than being with da Vinci.

"Don't go," da Vinci said, tugging at my arm. "Puppy can wait."

Another annoying trait: da Vinci could be selfish. Maybe a younger, more interesting girlfriend would've stayed with him, but I was a regular woman with two boys and a puppy, which was a lot like having a newborn. "Da Vinci, I've got to take care of Bellezza. I'll see you tomorrow."

He sat up in bed, pulling the sheets over him. "Is that man coming tomorrow?"

I slipped on my house shoes. "Cortland? I have no idea. Why do you ask?"

"He's been over too lot."

I rolled my eyes. "He's been over *a* lot. He's just helping with the puppy. He's being *nice*. I haven't had a dog since I was a kid."

"I had six sheepdogs back home."

"Well, Bellezza isn't a sheepdog, is she? She's a German shepherd, and if Cortland wants to help, I appreciate it."

"Something not right about him. How you say, fishy? He's not welcome in house."

"I can't believe this," I said, grabbing the door, the sound of Bellezza's barks growing louder. "You're jealous of my sister's boyfriend? Do you know how crazy that sounds? And since when is it *your* house?"

He clicked off his lamp and turned away from me in a huff. *What a baby*, I thought, unsure of whether I should be flattered or turned off by his behavior. I decided to blame it on too much sugar and retreated to take care of my other baby.

***

She caught me off guard. Again.

I was walking Bellezza around the park when I got The Call. It felt out of the blue, though my heart had skipped a beat every time my cell phone rang the last week and a half. This time, I was too preoccupied with waiting for my puppy to pee to think that it could be Her.

"Ramona? Hey, sorry it's taken me so long to get back to you."

Her voice was unmistakable, like an angel's, though not a sweet cherub, but a powerful angel like Raphael or Gabriel.

"God, I did it again. Sorry. It's Monica. Blevins. I was going to call you when I returned from Japan?"

"Yes, of course. How are you?" I looked down to find Bellezza urinating on my sneaker. A half-acre to roam, and he picks my Nike. "Dammit."

"Excuse me?"

"No. Not you. My puppy just peed on my shoe."

Monica laughed. "I don't hear that every day. Shall I call you back?"

"No, no. Don't hang up. It'll dry, right?"

"Well, if you need to, call me back when you have your calendar in front of you."

I imagined Monica was the type of person who couldn't live without her planner directing her every move, but my schedule was in my brain: Monday, Wednesday, Friday at the Panchal Center, Tuesdays and Thursdays volunteering at the school, and every day from 3:30 to 8 p.m. was booked with boys' activities, and then dinner, homework and bed. "Not at all. What works for you?"

Monica made exasperated noises on the other end: moans, sighs, ticks, as she moved through her frenzied days. She must be important to be so booked up. "Okay. Got it! I was nervous for a minute there, but I have thirty minutes two weeks from Monday."

"Two weeks?" I'd already been a nervous wreck waiting for her to return and call me back. Now I had to wait two *more* weeks for her confession? For those huge Unanswered Questions she was going to hit me with?

"You're right. That's too long, isn't it? Let's see what I can move around."

"Oh, you don't have to do that for me."

"It's no big deal. Besides, Joel was special to me. It's the least I can do."

I nearly dropped the phone. I wanted to say, "Forget it. Let's just get this over with on the phone. What do you mean by *special*? What *precisely* is your definition?"

"What about tomorrow then? Coffee at 8 a.m.? That Starbucks on 89th?"

The one where Cortland and I had our spat. "I might be a few minutes late. I drop the boys off at 8."

"That's fine. I'll see you then." And she was gone. I was left standing in the park, staring at Joel's bench, with warm dog piss on my shoe.

***

The next morning, I woke up with a racing heart as though I had anxiety even in sleep. It was 6:30 a.m., just enough time to look half as good as Monica. It would have to do. I would exfoliate my entire body in the shower and use the expensive lotion my sister got me last Christmas. I would even wear eye shadow and attempt to curl my hair.

Forty-five minutes later, when it was time to wake the boys, William wasn't in bed. My adrenaline still pumping, my voice rose an octave. "Bradley?" I shouted, shaking him awake. "Where's your brother?"

Then I heard it. Gagging noises from the bathroom. I followed the trail of spaghetti vomit down the hall and to the bathroom, where William sat hunched over the toilet, puking.

He looked up at me with those big, sad eyes, drool hanging from his mouth. "Mommy, I don't feel so good."

I leaned against the doorframe. "You don't say, buddy." I caught my reflection in the mirror and hardly recognized the woman staring back at me. Dare I say she was pretty?

After I washed his face, cleaned up the mess, and put him back in bed, William, hot with fever, held my hand in his. "Why are you so dressed up? Is it a special day?"

I thought of Monica and our fated meeting that wasn't meant to be. "Nope. Just a day to get you better. Now I'll call Grandma to give your brother a ride to school, and you and I can stay home and be bums."

Monica didn't answer when I called her, which was for the best. As a mother herself, I was sure she'd understand. I'd waited for two years for the truth. What was two more weeks?

When da Vinci came into the kitchen later wearing only a pair of khaki shorts and flip-flops—much too cool for early November—he shrugged me off when I hugged him from behind. He was not a morning person and on this day, perhaps he had a sugar hangover.

He sipped his coffee and scrutinized my face. "Too much makeup," he said. "I like you plain."

So *that's* what it was. Someone like da Vinci is attracted to Plain Janes with soft tushes. Go figure. "Well, you can't please everybody."

"I won't be home tonight. Study hall at the fraternity."

"You joined a fraternity? But you said they were juvenile." I felt hurt he hadn't asked me first.

"They are juvenile, but they promised free tutoring. And they have nice gym in basement."

There was no way in hell I would let da Vinci drag me to frat parties. Why didn't he just break up with me now and get it over with? "Well, if that's what you want."

He sat at the breakfast bar and I tossed dry toast to him. In the last few days, I'd felt more like his short-order cook than his girlfriend. Hadn't I thought just the opposite weeks ago? When he'd first moved in, he had cooked more for me than I had for him. Da Vinci took a bite of the toast and eyed me evenly. "We are learning American history slaves," he said. "Did you know the masters used to keep their black lovers in small house in back of property?"

I could feel my cheeks burn and wondered if I should let it slide. Had Cortland been planting something in da Vinci's ear? Da Vinci, love slave? How could he possibly think that? "I've heard that," I said coolly. "Perhaps you should move into the fraternity house, then. You can work out all the time that way."

"Smells like urine and beer," he said, shaking his head. "Besides, I want to move into *your* bed. I'm beginning to think I not good enough for you."

I exhaled. Here I thought I was the jealous one. Da Vinci wasn't just jealous of Cortland, but of my dead husband, and rightly so. Though Joel was gone, his territory was still clearly marked. "Oh, honey. It's not that. It's doesn't feel right. I'm going to buy a new bed, then I promise you are welcome in it." I couldn't take it back after I'd said it, and it had clearly pleased him.

Da Vinci softened. "Really? For true?" He got out of his seat and wrapped his arms around me. "This makes me happy. Let's go for run. Work off Tootsie candies."

"Sorry, can't. William's sick in bed. Better stay inside in case he needs me."

Da Vinci groaned and took his mug with him. "*Ciao.*"

"Don't party too hard at the frat house."

"No party. Only study," he said.

Right. As if I were born yesterday.

***

He didn't come home that night. I knew because I'd snuck into his studio at 2 a.m. and then again at 7 a.m., and his futon was still in couch mode. I took the opportunity to pick up his candy wrappers because *I* minded getting chocolate goo on my slippers and grabbed the six coffee mugs that were beginning to grow mold. Da Vinci was looking more like Homer Simpson and less like Romeo with each passing day.

With the boys both healthy and back in school, I decided to venture to the department stores for lingerie and a bed, not my typical shopping excursion. I'd never been good at shopping for frilly undergarments, so I'd just grabbed a black teddy (widows wear black, right?) and a few silk panties, and got the hell out of Dodge. I always feared I would run into a parent from the school, but I hadn't considered that they might be worried about what I thought, too. Parents were supposed to pretend we didn't have a sex life, especially a saucy one that included sexy, lacy things.

As for the bed, I couldn't afford anything nice, I was sure, but I could at least get a firm mattress and something with a headboard and footboard. Nothing fancy. Joel was practical and frugal, and so was I. So *am* I. That wouldn't change.

An hour later, I lay on a king-sized bed that seemed to swallow me, wondering if I should just get a nice double bed for when I would be all alone again. Da Vinci had probably hooked up with a loose college hottie, and I would spend all this money on a big bed, only to find myself drowning in its space.

The salesperson, a fidgety fellow named Carl, grew tired of my indecision. I was tired of it, too. I had sat, lain and even booty-bounced on all twelve beds they offered, but I recalled that this is why I had never bought new furniture with Joel. I was certain whatever I picked in the store would look terrible once I got it home.

"This is an excellent choice," Carl said, as he rolled a pen between his fingers.

"Yes, but you said that about the last three," I reminded him. This headboard was mission-style. Too casual? But the Victorian one was too formal and none of them felt just right.

"What's the matter, Goldilocks? Can't get comfortable?" a voice said, emerging from behind a Ralph Lauren rack.

"Cortland," I said, my voice singing with surprise.

Carl rolled his eyes. "Thank goodness. Your husband to the rescue, I presume?"

"No."

"A friend to the rescue," Cortland corrected.

"My sister's boyfriend," I told Carl, who began tapping his pen on a clipboard. I noticed his fingernails had been chewed back. Customers like me probably drove the man crazy.

"I'm happy to help," Cortland said.

"Shouldn't you be putting someone to sleep right now?"

"Oh, boy," Carl said.

"Goldilocks not get her porridge today? Need some beauty sleep?"

"Very funny. I just can't pick a bed." I tried to maintain my composure, but felt myself whither inside. I should just call it a day and stick with Lumpy.

"How about this? I'll help you find your bed if you help me find a new comforter for my daughter. I'm drowning in purple and pink flowers, and I'm certain I'll pick something she'll hate."

I slapped my hands on the bed. "Oh, fine. Whatever. And you're right about the porridge. I haven't eaten all day. Da Vinci joined a fraternity and didn't come home last night, and he complains I haven't let him sleep in my bed, and oh, my God, why am I telling you this?"

Cortland sat beside me on the bed, causing me to lean his way. "Because I'm your friend."

"You're not my friend. You're my sister's boyfriend. Big difference."

"Are you not Michael's friend?"

"That's different. We became friends *after* the divorce. We are united in our shared history with Rachel. It forms a special bond, believe me."

"So maybe we'll form a special bond."

I bounced off the bed. "Let's just find a bed, shall we? And your daughter is growing out of the cutesy phase, so let's go with something a little more grown up. Like leopard print."

Cortland scrunched up his face. "Isn't that a bit 'teen diva' for my little girl?"

"Right. Well, if you want her to hate what you get her, then you just stick with your flowers."

"Fine. I'm gonna trust you on this."

Carl excused himself to let us look and bicker in peace. Cortland pivoted on his heels, checking out the selection. "That one," he said, pointing to a king-sized sleigh bed.

"Seriously? It doesn't remind you of Santa Claus?"

"It's you," Cortland said, walking over to it and laying down on what would have been Joel's side of the bed.

I climbed over and lay down next to him, albeit with a good foot between us. "How so?"

"Well, it's whimsical, but not silly. Slightly intellectual, but not stuffy. And your blonde hair looks good against the mahogany."

I felt my insides swirl and had to catch my breath. I turned to face him, not quite believing what I heard. I don't think that's something even a good friend would say. Getting horizontal made my lingerie slip out from the Victoria's Secret bag, and I stuffed it back in quickly, hoping Cortland hadn't noticed.

"Black's not your color," he said matter-of-factly. "I'd have gone with pink if I were you." Cortland turned to face me and we held our gaze, longer than the flirting research indicated was the norm, and I wanted to say something, but wasn't sure what.

"You'll thank me later," he said, tapping the bed with his hand. He motioned to Carl, who was all too happy to schedule the delivery to my house for the following day.

"It's too expensive," I said, already feeling buyer's remorse. "I don't deserve a bed like this."

"You do, and that's that. Now let's go get Goldilocks some porridge. Great little Italian place in the mall."

"I get quite enough Italian," I said.

"I bet you do. A burger, then?"

"I've been dying for a cheeseburger for weeks."

I told myself it wasn't a date. It wasn't as if we'd planned to meet at the mall and grab lunch. It just worked out that way, which Anh told me was fate throwing us together. "Your energies are in sync," she said and I had no idea what that meant, but I still insisted he was just being nice to me because I was his girlfriend's widowed sister.

Chapter 16

THE LIBRARIAN AT UT handed me the *Glamourpuss* article as if she were passing me porn, tucked in a brown paper bag. "I saved this for you," Betty said with a wink. "For your dissertation. I presume you'll have a section in there on sex, right?"

I nodded, taking the magazine from her. A women's magazine? Was she kidding? What could possibly be kinky about this?

"And one more thing," Betty said, pushing her wire frames up on her nose. "Can I read your paper when you're through? I've always been fascinated with love. I never married, but I've been in love at least two dozen times. You might say I'm more in love with love than with any of the blokes I dated. Fortunately, I realized it at exactly the moment each of them asked me to marry them."

After thanking the octogenarian love-adrenaline junkie, I retreated to my favorite corner of the library, where the morning sun warmed the carpet and the brown leather chair. I curled into it like a cat and read the article Betty thought was so risqué: Hindu love voodoo and Indonesian spousal swapping? What did she think this was, a dissertation for Playboy University? Instead, I gathered my notes on the linguistic origin of the most common sex words and plugged in my laptop so I could get my thoughts down before they dissipated.

"Sex is emotion in motion." —Mae West

"Is sex dirty? Only if it's done right." —Woody Allen

One cannot write about the language of love without at least acknowledging the language of sex. Contrary to popular belief, the term "French kiss" did not originate in France, but entered the English language in 1923 as a slur on the French, who to this day are deemed highly sexualized. The French don't call it a French kiss at all, but a "tongue kiss," or "soul kissing."

The slang expression "petting" is an American word, originally meant "to stroke or caress." The word was used worldwide during the twentieth century, but has now become old fashioned. In the UK, it is more common to use, "touching someone up," "frigging someone," "rubbing someone up," "bringing someone off." Petting is now often referred to as "foreplay."

Once the sex act commences, lovers hope for climax, called "orgasm," from Greek *orgasmos*, "to swell up, be excited," tracing back to 1684.

My cell phone blared "Bootylicious," but it took me a moment to get my head out of my research before I could answer. It wasn't often homework could turn me on. "What are you doing?" Cortland asked.

I closed my laptop. I hadn't heard from him in three days. Not that I was keeping track. With my own hormones activated from all those sex definitions, he couldn't have picked a worse time to call. I didn't want to think of him in that way. "Writing about sex. You?"

"Not writing about sex I'm afraid," he said smoothly.

"And people think linguists are boring intellectuals." I tried to calm the flirt in my tone. My voice was lilted, thick with lust.

"Depends on if they only write about it."

"*Touché.*"

"French origin, I presume?"

"That pesky accent gives it away every time. Literally it means 'you touched me, you got me.' Originally it came from fencing and sword fighting. A fencer says it when his opponent scores a point by making contact to alert his opponent he's got him. It's used as an insult or to devalue what the other person is saying."

"So you're insulting me, then? Funny, I don't feel insulted. Turned on, perhaps."

"Maybe I just don't want to talk about my sex life with you, not that it doesn't warrant it," I said playfully.

"Well, you're the one that brought it up."

"Not so. I brought up my dissertation," I corrected.

"Most dissertations aren't this exciting to discuss. Tell me more."

"Funny, I thought doctors knew everything."

"*Touché.*"

"Fine, then. Speaking of the French, what do you know about the origin of the term 'French kiss'?"

"I know I'm strongly in favor of it. What about it?"

"Not French at all. American term. Seems the French/American wars have their linguistic side, too."

"Interesting. So what do the French call it?"

"Soul kissing, for one."

"Goldilocks, you're always full of information."

"I'm always good for useless sex trivia," I said, packing up my bag. I spotted one of da Vinci's friends at the checkout counter—the one who'd said "cool" when da Vinci had introduced me as his girlfriend. He wore Greek letters on his sweatshirt, from the same frat that da Vinci had joined. I slunk in my seat, hoping he wouldn't recognize me. I turned my attention back to Cortland, trying not to show that I cared he'd called. "So to what do I owe the pleasure, anyway?"

"Wanted to see how you liked your bed. Good enough for Goldilocks?"

"Quite," I said, thinking how nice it was to not wake up without a backache and to have da Vinci's strong frame beside me all night long. I'd hated to admit to myself how much I'd missed a sleeping companion. The bed seemed just the thing to keep my frat boy at home, at least in the wee hours of the night, but there were some things I wouldn't share with Cortland, friend or not.

"Glad to hear it," he said. "I also called to thank you for the recommendation on the comforter. My daughter loved it. Said it was her favorite birthday gift. And anytime I can one-up my ex-wife is a good day."

"Glad to see you're not above tacky one-upping," I said, turning back around to find da Vinci's friend standing in front of me, apparently waiting for me to get off of my call.

"I'm gonna have to let you go," I said, really not wanting to. It wasn't fair that the one male I felt I could really talk to was my sister's beau.

"Before you do, what do you say we take Bellezza on her first jaunt at the dog park?"

Not a date, I told myself. Safe enough to tell my sister. A boring old dog park is all. In fact, my sister should come along. "Do you think she's ready? I mean, that's sort of like taking your daughter to the first day at kindergarten. What if the other doggies are mean to her?"

"That's why I thought we should go together. She'll have Liebe there to protect her."

After we'd made plans to meet after da Vinci's taping at Rachel's studio, I instantly regretted it. Taping, dog park, double dating. It would be worse than water torture. I'd have to listen to my sister brag about herself all night and deal with da Vinci's jealousy of Cortland.

First things first, like getting rid of da Vinci's young, grungy playmate. "Todd, right?" I asked, nearly sticking my hand out before remembering what had happened the last time I'd made that mistake, my hand just hanging there in mid-air while his friends had looked at me like a weird old person.

"Wassup?" Todd asked. "I forgot Leo said you're a student here. English or something?"

"Linguistics."

"Yeah. Same thing," he said, but—not wanting to look like a superior, which I so clearly was—I didn't argue with him.

"So, you coming to the party with Leo tonight?"

I shook my head, pretending I knew what the hell he was talking about. It didn't matter. I had told da Vinci—*Leo* as the young 'uns called him—that I would not be partying with kids half my age, or even two-thirds my age. I really needed to get out with people my own age. Like the double date with Cortland and my sister. "I've got a thing," I said, wanting to add, "a grownup thing, like two boys and a real life."

"Too bad. Gonna be rockin'. The Grey Pincers are gonna play."

"Really?" I said, feigning being impressed, whoever they were. "Well, take good care of Leo for me."

I stood and felt Todd give me the up down. "Oh, he doesn't flirt with the girls, if that's what you mean. Not that he couldn't jump on that if he wanted. He's the talk on campus. That's why we wanted to pledge him so bad. With Leo around, the rest of us can be his wingman and get all the girls, you know? Of course, if I were him, I would probably stay in if I had you to keep me warm. You know what they say about older women lovers—experience and all that? No wonder Leo's hot for teacher." He flashed a lopsided grin and turned on his heels, not bothering to say goodbye.

I resisted the urge to kick him in those saggy, overpriced jeans and pull him by the ear into the ladies' room, where I would wash his mouth out with dispenser soap.

On second thought, if da Vinci's friends believed he was with me because I was an incredible lover, I could live with that.

***

The next morning, da Vinci woke up with a hangover the size of Texas. I know because after we'd made love (which had begun feeling more like a booty call after his late-night partying at the frat house), he had thrown up, brushed his teeth, and passed out in the bed.

I'd lain there until 4 a.m. wondering how I'd arrived at this point. For all intents and purposes, da Vinci had moved in. Just as getting rid of my marital bed had marked another step forward in my journey to Normalhood, the new bed had lured da Vinci to my side like bait: comfortable, supportive, high-thread-count bed bait. Anything was better than his old pullout couch and Lumpy. We were both the winners, really. I got a warm bedmate who happened to still be a great lover (and strangely better at certain sex acts when inebriated) and we both got a good night's sleep.

Until he wet the bed. My new, amazing, waited-fifteen-years-for-this miracle bed. Peed on like a cardboard box in a downtown alley.

I wouldn't have even minded if it had been Bellezza that did the bedwetting, but my twenty-five-year-old boyfriend?

"You have *got* to be kidding me," I said, as I stared at the huge wet spot in disgust.

"Those fucking Jäger shots," he said.

"Excuse me? Since when do you say the F-word? You join a fraternity and suddenly you've got a potty mouth and you start using my bed as one?"

"Get off the back," he said, holding his head. "Going to take shower now."

"And don't think I don't know you pee in there, too," I said, standing on the bed. "From now on, if you think you can hold it until you hit the shower, my awesome bed and I would sure appreciate it."

Da Vinci turned back to me and winced in the sunlight. "You going to complain all day or come in and make love to me in shower?"

"And another thing," I said, wagging my finger at him. "I don't want you telling your frat buddies about our sex life."

Stepping out of his boxers, he revealed an erection I could've hung a dozen suit jackets on. I tried not to look at it, but it was a beacon in the morning sun. A thing of beauty, work of art. "You take shower with me or what? I'm horny. And I only tell them you are very good at blow job. Most girls terrible at this."

I dropped to my knees. I'd never been complimented on sex before. Joel had told me I was a good lover, but when he'd said it I felt like I was good as in *average,* not good as in good enough to brag about to all your buddies. "I am? Wait a minute, *you did*? How am I ever going to get a teaching job at the university if you're talking about our sex life? I'll be the laughingstock on campus. Professor Blow Job! I'll be forced to work at a community college the rest of my life."

"Don't get panties in a twist," he said, which was another terrible catchphrase he'd learned from college. He'd be Americanized in no time and ruined beyond repair. "Speaking of, I like your new panties very much. Black very sexy." Da Vinci rubbed his belly and scratched his balls. I should've been terribly turned off by this, especially after what he'd done, but I was strangely turned on. There was something terribly wrong with me. He was no good for me, but all I could think about was having sex with him in the shower. Which I did. Twice. And we still made it to Rachel's studio in time for the taping.

After two Tylenol and two pieces of dry toast, da Vinci began feeling better and turned on the charm for the camera. I loved watching him work out, and he followed direction from my sister very well. He made the other four people on stage with him look like amateurs. You couldn't help but stare at him the whole time, and I heard the producer tell camera 2 to stay on him. I could see it now: *Get Up and Move It with da Vinci, Texas!* in big, neon lights. I silently wished he would kick my sister out of her time slot. See what *that* did to her precious ego.

Yet as I watched, I wondered if this was when the countdown to his leaving began. I couldn't imagine after 25,000 households saw the show that he would stay with me much longer, expert fellatio or no. I needed to have a grown-up conversation with him before things got out of hand, before the boys got too attached, and then there was my own attachment to consider.

Rachel beamed with pride as if she had discovered him. "Come on. Squeeze that tush or no one else will," she said, which I'd only heard at least a hundred times on her show. She called it a "Rachelism." *Ugh.*

When they wrapped, I picked up the boys at my mom and dad's and met Cortland at the dog park, where I'd hoped he would show up looking disheveled and unattractive, but there he was, dressed sharply in a brown wool sweater and tan corduroy jeans, looking handsome and approachable. So approachable, in fact, three women were talking to him.

When I walked up, they must've thought I was the wife or girl-friend, because they quickly dispersed with disappointment in their eyes. No wedding ring, but obviously taken. I'm surprised Rachel didn't force him to wear a neon necklace that read, "Back off. I'm dating Fitness Star Rachel Taylor."

"Hey, you," he said coolly. Bellezza took off, leading the boys around the park, eager to run and play with the other dogs. It was William who seemed to be on the leash and not the puppy. I had been a worried parent for no reason.

"Bet you've picked up a lot of women at the dog park," I said, noting the women who had left and eyed me with envy.

He shrugged. "I don't date women I meet at the dog park any-more. It's where I met my ex-wife."

"Fair enough. Where's Rach and Princess?" Princess was Rachel's Chihuahua, an obnoxious little lapdog she had bought the day after Cortland and I had picked up Bellezza. She hated to be left out.

Cortland and I had gotten a good laugh out of the fact that she *was* the type to want a toy dog, but I knew it was more than that.

My whole life Rachel had wanted whatever I had. The week after I'd announced that Joel and I were getting married and planning a summer wedding, she and Michael announced their engagement and *spring* wedding. When I told her Joel and I were trying to get pregnant, she said she and Michael were also trying. It took her three years to get pregnant with Zoe, and knowing what she puts Zoe through, I was thankful she never reproduced again. I wondered if she and Cortland were going anywhere. Were they a fling? Getting serious? Would they have babies together? God, they'd be obnoxiously cute.

Like a punch to the gut, I realized this was the first time *I* wanted something my sister had. "The taping went so well that they decided to do another. I left so I wouldn't be late."

"I appreciate that. Your sister always makes me wait. I can't stand that."

"No wonder my dad likes you. He's a stickler for time, too."

"Don't I know it? A surgery ran over a couple weeks ago and I was five minutes late for our tee time and he let me know about it. I felt like a kid in the principal's office."

"It's best to know how crazy we are before you join our family."

Cortland raised his left brow. "Why? You think I should marry your sister?"

I began feeling flustered and couldn't think straight. "Of course not. Or of course. I mean, what do I know? Or care? Of course, you should do what you want to do."

"You still don't like your sister very much."

"I love her. I'm just glad I don't have to live with her. It's you that has to make that decision."

"Well, I did give her my house key," he said, sticking his hands into his pocket.

"Oh," I said, feeling my throat close up. "Well, looks like you're moving in that direction then."

"Not necessarily. I don't know why I did it, truthfully. I guess I was feeling some pressure that she wanted our relationship to be going somewhere, so instead of saying anything, I handed her a key. Dopey caveman sort of move, I know. At least she can come and go as she pleases."

"Right," I said. "Like a maid."

Cortland began to laugh and it was contagious, an icebreaker, demolishing something—sexual tension or jealousy or I don't know what, but it felt good. A house key meant they'd be having sex soon. Again, *not that I cared.*

Out of the corner of my eye, I saw movement among the upper-class women wearing their cashmere jackets and designer jeans and boots that I half-hoped would get covered in dog poo. Were they talking about me? One woman stepped apart from the pack and I recognized her, even thirty feet away. *Monica.*

I couldn't run. Couldn't hide. She was coming toward me and I would have to think of something to say. My day that began with da Vinci peeing in my bed followed by great sex followed by meeting Cruella Fiancée. Life was one wicked roller coaster ride.

"You know Monica, right?" Cortland said as he wrapped Monica's lithe, tight body in a side hug.

"Not officially," I said, nearly forgetting to stick my hand out for her to shake, but of course she would know what to do with it and she did. Very lawyery, firm handshake.

"Nice to meet you, Ramona," she said, her white teeth shining even in the overcast afternoon.

"You, too," I said stammering and wishing Cortland would go away.

"Sorry I haven't called you back yet," Monica said. "It's been a crazy week."

"Oh, same here," I said. "We can get together another time."

Monica pulled her Blackberry out of her jacket pocket and clicked a few times before looking back up at me. "What about Tuesday morning then? Same place?"

I—of the no-PDA, no-calendar, no-big life—stammered some more. "Perfect, fine, sure. That works. See you then."

Monica turned her attention to Cortland. "You and Rachel still on for dinner at my place Sunday night?"

I could feel my jaw dropping. My sister dining with my pseudo-archenemy? No way.

"Rachel moved some stuff around so she can make it," Cortland said. "We'll see you then."

"We'll eat light," Monica said. "Maybe Rachel can show me some exercises for my little baby gut here." She patted her flatter than flat tummy. Her "baby" was two, and if a person's stomach could get any flatter, it would be concave.

"Oh, she loves personal lessons," I said dryly.

Monica shook her head, puzzled.

"I'm sorry. I thought you knew," Cortland said. "Rachel is Ramona's sister."

"I didn't connect the dots," Monica said.

But why would she? We didn't look a thing alike. If it weren't for inheriting the weird earlobe shape from my father, I would've sworn I belonged to the mailman. Mom always said she was a bored housewife before she found the Lord. I wouldn't have put an affair past her, back in what she called her "sinning days."

As Monica left, her firm buttocks rocking to and fro in her jeans, we both watched her, and then I watched Cortland watching her, obviously liking what he saw, and I hated that I had to be jealous of *him* liking her, too.

"She's something else," Cortland said, diverting his eyes from her finally. "I mean her success. And she's a nice person, too."

"Yeah, I know what you mean," I said, willing my voice not to give out on me. Nice I wasn't so sure about, but she was *something else*, something irresistible. Clearly every man admired her.

By the time Cortland and I had left in separate cars, we'd both gotten calls from our respective other halves, telling us that they were on such a roll, they wanted to record just one more show and to go ahead and start without them at the restaurant. No arguments here.

"Story of my life," Cortland said, as we ordered our second bottle of wine. "Women always keep me waiting."

"Look," I said, feeling drunk-happy. "You told me I deserved a worthy bed, and I'm telling you that you deserve a worthy mate. Not one that keeps you waiting every time you turn around."

"Is that so?" He refilled my glass of wine, though I certainly didn't need it. "You think I should dump your sister, then?"

"If I wouldn't miss you coming around, I'd say 'Hell, yes' to that," I said, clinking my glass with his.

"You think I call and come around because you're Rachel's sister?"

I snorted, an unattractive result of having drunk too much. "Um, duh? Why else would you call and come over all the time? Look, it's fine. Widow sympathy is a natural human phenomenon."

Cortland reached his hand across the table and placed it over mine. "And here I thought you were the smart one in the family."

Our eyes locked and I pulled away, excusing myself to go to the restroom and vowing to myself not to return until I knew da Vinci and Rachel had arrived. In the bathroom, I splashed water in my face, drank water out of my hand from the sink to try to sober up and stared at my raccoon eyes in the mirror. "What are you doing, Ramona Griffen?"

I freshened up my makeup and eventually felt clear-headed enough to return. I was an adult. I could tell Cortland that while I appreciated that he wanted to be friends, perhaps our flirtation had gone a little far, and it wasn't fair to either of our mates to ever be alone with each other again. *Ever.* After all, hadn't da Vinci said something about Cortland seeming fishy?

When I swung open the swanky bathroom door into the darkly lit hallway, arms reached around my waist, pulling me into the even darker corner. Cortland's face was inches from mine, his hot breath on my cheek. "Do you think I wanted this to happen? Because, believe me, the last few times we've been together have been sheer torture for me. I've felt something since the first time I saw you. I wanted to kiss you in my office and on the patio next to the pool and at the Starbucks and on that country road with the puppy asleep in the back and outside in the rain. How do you think it made me feel to lie on that bed with you in the department store with that lingerie you would wear for another guy? Or how just talking to you on the phone makes me feel weak inside, especially when you're talking about French kissing when I've wanted to know what it's like to kiss you for so long? I'm sorry, Goldilocks, but I just can't wait another minute."

He pressed his lips against mine, and I let my body take over, my mouth on autopilot. The kiss became a French kiss. A soul kiss. A kiss that muddied my normally logical brain, and when he finally stopped, I pulled him into me, our bodies touching in the darkness, and I wanted to tell him that I had felt something, too, especially in the rain, when I could smell his aftershave in the car and on the bed when I secretly wished he could see me in that lingerie, and all the times I had pretended the tone in his voice wasn't tinged with wanting something more.

"Oh, my God," I said when we broke apart. I wasn't sure if I wanted to run away or run away with him.

Cortland held my gaze. "I won't apologize."

"Me neither," I said, straightening my blouse.

"But I don't know where we go from here."

Da Vinci. Rachel. Of course. I had selfishly forgotten them. "We do nothing," I said. "Look, we got that kiss out of our system, right?

We'll just play it cool. I'll just tell da Vinci I'm not feeling well, and you can have a nice dinner with Rachel."

"You're feeling fine," he said, his finger brushing against my cheek. "In fact, I want to feel more of you."

I held his hand and pressed it against my chest, between my breasts. "You're wrong. I'm not feeling well at all. I need some time to think about this."

He nodded, his eyes full of yearning. "I have to see you again. Soon. Tonight. Even that's not soon enough. Let's leave right now."

If I looked at him too long, I'd be lost and we'd do something I'd truly regret. I could feel tears well in my eyes. "I'll call you in a few days."

The yearning turned to disappointment. "I'll wait."

Just minutes after I'd told him he deserved a woman that didn't make him wait, I was doing it to him, too, but what choice did I have? He was my sister's boyfriend, for God's sake. And da Vinci, Leonardo da Vinci, was mine.

Chapter 17

"I don't want to live—I want to love first, and live incidentally."
—Zelda Fitzgerald, letter to F. Scott Fitzgerald, 1919

PANCHAL WANTED TO SEE me. Panchal *never* wants to see me, which could mean only one thing: da Vinci and I had been found out. If he had been bragging about me to his frat buddies, what kept him from saying anything to his classmates? The English class bonded like family. And foreigners were whip-smart, reading the physical cues of others long before they even knew the English words to describe them. But, like da Vinci, they all clearly knew the word "sex" by now, and "affair" and "wrong."

Panchal was a small man, 5'5" in his black dress shoes, tiny frames around his large brown eyes, silvery black hair around his outturned ears. He sat in an oversized, elevated office chair with a wooden box on which to rest his feet. We made small talk about his daughter and how well his son-in-law fit into his family when Panchal cut to the chase. "We hab a bery big brobleb," which, after ten years of working for him, I could clearly understand as, "We have a very big problem."

I began sweating and removed my jacket. "I don't know what to say," I said full of shame. Panchal had been a mentor to me, urging me to get my PhD and supporting me through my loss. Disappointing Panchal was worse than disappointing my parents.

Panchal shrugged. "Well, it's not your fault, is it?"

"I suppose not. Not exactly. Still."

"Don't be ridiculous. You can't help that Leonardo is Leonardo any more than I can."

"Right. And?"

"We must correct the bad behavior." Panchal came around the front of the desk and sat on the corner.

I began to think of all the bad things I'd done with da Vinci in the last month. Panchal knowing about even one of them would be devastating. Correcting the bad behavior would mean giving up da Vinci, breaking things off with him.

Panchal waved his hands in the air. "Tardiness. Absenteeism. Total disrespect for the Panchal Way of Immersion."

That bad behavior? Not the sleeping-with-the-teacher kind of bad behavior? The Way of Immersion was Panchal's method for smooth integration. While every immigrant is expected to struggle, Panchal's "way" should work if only they followed the rules. Panchal continued: "I expected him to be different. It is his birthright, see? I expected him to make his own path, but something has happened to him in the last month. Something big. Would you know what this is?"

I nearly blurted the first thing that came to mind: da Vinci was my lover. But that was the biggest thing that had happened *to me* in the last thirty days, not da Vinci. No, he likely had bigger worries, like making his grades and learning English and finding his way in a new country. But Panchal knew all of this. All immigrants dealt with these dilemmas. It was something else. "He joined a fraternity," I said, wiping the sweat on my brow with the back of my hand.

Panchal crossed his arms. "American fraternities can be hard for Americans, let alone someone like da Vinci. Frat houses are not a part of Panchal immersion."

"Yes, sir. But they offered him free tutoring and a nice gym."

"And beer and girls," he added in disgust. "I can see the lure, Ramona. But I thought da Vinci was smarter than that. Perhaps he is just big, dumb jock after all?"

I vacillated between wanting to defend da Vinci and agreeing with Panchal. Da Vinci had started spending more and more time at the frat house and on campus, partying four or five nights out of the week and crashing at the frat house half the time instead of our new bed. I missed him, but what choice did I have? I knew I would lose him if I pushed him too hard.

"You have a special relationship," Panchal said. "You can talk some sense into him. He must be on time and finish every job he is assigned. He must not miss English class. Is this understood?"

"I'll see what I can do."

Panchal put his hand gently on my shoulder. "And Ramona? Be careful. Your heart is still tender."

Long exhale. He knew. Of course he knew, and he cared too much about me to stand in the way of my happiness. I could see it there—the light at the end of the tunnel—when I would feel *la vita allegra*, but I had never expected I would stumble so much on my journey. Joel, da Vinci, Monica, Cortland.

Panchal was right. My heart was still bruised, and there was only one way to avoid further heartbreak: institute the arm's length policy. "Arm's length!" I would yell at the boys when they picked on each other. If I kept everyone at arm's length, not only would they not be able to reach my lips, but they'd be at a safe distance from my heart, too.

***

"What are you doing here?" I said as I entered the Starbucks Tuesday morning, my vocal cords tightening. I froze in place. Cortland sat in the corner booth where we had sat together two weeks prior. He was unshaven and wild eyed. He didn't look or act himself.

Cortland stood and grabbed my arms. "You haven't called me."

I shook loose of him, remembering my arm's length policy. He was already breaking it, and his touch felt like lightning on my skin. "I said it would be a few days."

Sadness and longing flickered in his eyes. "My God. You look beautiful."

I hadn't dolled up for him, but her. I had gotten up early to look good for Monica, and fortunately, neither of my boys threw up that morning to foil our meeting, but instead I found something even worse. I had thought about calling Cortland a hundred times since Saturday night, but I had stopped short of it, because what good would it do? Avoiding the issue seemed a far smarter way to go. If only there weren't another human being on the other end of it.

"Please don't," I said, looking behind him to see if Monica had arrived. I could see he was hurting, and it made pretending it didn't happen all the harder. "I'm meeting Monica here. I guess you remembered that."

He shoved hands in his jacket pocket. "I'm sorry. Maybe I shouldn't have come, but I haven't been able to stop thinking about you. I haven't felt this way in … in a long time. Maybe ever."

I cocked my head, trying to brush off the weight of his words. *Arm's length, Ramona!* "You're forgetting one key fact: you're with my sister. You were with her all weekend, were you not? Didn't you have a dinner date at Monica's last night?"

"I couldn't cancel. But things aren't serious with Rachel. We haven't even been together yet."

I leaned in. "In case you've forgotten, you keyed her. What are you going to do, put a lock on your bedroom door to keep her out?"

Cortland stiffened. "So you're telling me things are that serious between you and da Vinci? Just say the word and I'll back off. But I have to know. It's driving me crazy."

Through the window, I could see Monica emerge from her red Mercedes, wearing a crisp red suit, different than the first one I'd seen her in that day at school. A power suit. The color of love. A suit that said, *Stop! Pay attention to me! I'm important.* "I'm sorry, Cortland. I can't do this."

He bit his lip and nodded slowly. "Thanks for clearing that up." He turned to leave, and I could feel my bruised heart beating within me, aching, yearning, begging me to go after him and plan a grown-up kind of talk in a private place. This was crazy. It was all crazy, the whole lot of it. I had to be careful, just as Panchal had said. I wasn't thinking rationally. My heart had made me do some stupid things in the last month. In my effort to find joy and adventure, I had inadvertently opened the dam. But I had Monica to deal with. I had to resolve my past before I could think about my future.

Monica shook hands with Cortland on her way in, and I surveyed my outfit, black dress pants and a fitted black sweater, wishing I had the confidence to wear a color—*any* color—other than black. I was still dressed in mourning gear.

"Your sister is amazing," Monica said as we wrapped our hands around our steaming cups minutes later. I had figured Monica as the no-fat latte kind of girl, but she surprised me. Like me, her favorite was the café mocha.

"Chocolate fiend," she said, flashing a white smile at me. Where were the coffee stains?

"Me, too," I confessed.

"Joel used to say we were like a Reese's cup—him with the peanut butter and me with the chocolate."

My heart burned at the mention of his name. Of course, Joel's peanut butter addiction did not belong to me. And thankfully he had never called us Reese's. I would've been offended if he'd used the same term of endearment. I wished I could've been the bigger person and let my jealousy wash away, but it was there. I was jealous of all the years she had Joel before me and all the space she had occupied in his mind and heart after she had left him.

"Yes, the peanut butter," I said. "I couldn't bear to throw away the last jar of it. I know a food can't define a person, but he wouldn't have been Joel without the peanut butter."

Monica laughed. "Or the way he made a pizza sandwich by putting one piece on top of the other."

"My kids still do that," I said, then lowered my voice. "Thanks for meeting me."

"No, thank you. Like I said before, I've thought about you often. How you and your family are doing, and I guess I have some unresolved issues where Joel is concerned."

I could feel my throat strain and I forced down some of my coffee. I had to stay strong. "Well, he had an unresolved life. Isn't that the worst part of dying young?"

Monica's voice softened. "The worst part is that you're left behind. God, I can't even imagine. Even though things have never been great with my husband, I can't believe how dependent on him I am. I can't imagine."

"I get by. We get by. I mean, it's not easy, but you have to keep going. For the sake of the kids."

"I don't know how to say this without just coming right out and saying it, Ramona. I feel selfish for even bringing it up. I have such respect for your marriage. I do."

"I appreciate your saying that, but I can't take away the history that you two had together. I know he loved you. I'd be a fool to think that went away when you left him."

Monica cringed. "Is that what he told you? That I left him?"

"That you broke off the engagement."

"It's complicated."

"Look, you don't have to tell me. It's none of my business."

"But it is," she said earnestly, her voice rising. "I've lived with such guilt over the years. Some days I worry I'll die without talking to you. And I can't let this go unfinished."

My hands began to shake. "I don't know if I'm strong enough to hear what you have to tell me. Maybe that's why I never called you before now."

Monica's eyes glistened with tears. "What did he tell you about me?"

"At first, it was just that you broke off the engagement because you were in love with another man. I often thought I should thank you for doing that. If you'd married him, I wouldn't have ever met him."

Monica shook her head. "I cheated on him with his best friend."

"I'd heard it was something like that. Judith refuses to talk about it."

"She hates me and rightly so I guess. He was humiliated. The whole family was."

"You have to admit, it's a soap opera moment."

"We were all best friends, since junior high. The guys since they were babies. They were inseparable. I guess by dating one, in some ways I thought I was dating both of them. Joel was the nice one, the funny guy. The boy-next-door type, you know? I had dated Jonathon first, in junior high. We were king and queen of our eighth-grade dance. But then Jonathon got seriously girl-crazy and he broke my heart. So to get back at him, I started dating his best friend."

"Joel."

"Exactly. And the thing is, Joel was my best friend, too, so it was easy to love him. I pined for Jonathon off and on, and when Joel and I would break up, Jonathon was there to console me, and one thing would lead to another. I was on and off with Joel in the public and Jonathon in private."

I'd never known. How could Joel not tell me? "But you were kids then."

"I don't buy that. Teenagers and college students may not have the logic yet, but they have the passion. I was passionately in love with both Jonathon and Joel, but it was different. I was more attracted to Jonathon, but knew that Joel was the one I should marry. I knew this even when I was fifteen. And that never changed."

"So what happened?"

"Something I never expected: Jonathon finally grew up. He quit his womanizing ways. He'd slept with half the sorority girls on campus already. He was a player, but as my wedding with Joel approached, Jonathan came to me and said he was done with other girls—that I was the one that he wanted to spend the rest of his life with."

"So you broke things off with Joel?"

Monica grabbed a napkin and dabbed the corners of her eyes. "No. Even though I wanted to believe Jonathon, I couldn't believe he'd changed. We were twenty-five. I was in law school, Joel was at his first architecture firm and we were planning on getting married two months later. Joel had wanted to elope in college, but I wasn't ready. I convinced him we should wait until after I graduated from law school, but Joel insisted we not wait another year. I guess I was putting it off because I wasn't sure I should marry Joel. Not without him knowing the truth."

"But all the while you were sleeping with Jonathon?"

Monica shook her head. "Not after we got engaged. But Joel and I had been going to premarital counseling and they talked about the importance of being truthful and not keeping secrets, and I couldn't marry Joel with the guilt of what I'd done with his best friend over the years. So I confessed that I'd been in love with Jonathon, that I'd been with him off and on since I was thirteen, but that it was all behind us now."

"Your confession broke off your engagement."

"I lost him for good. I destroyed our love, and I ruined their friendship. I think that's what hurt Joel the most. He lost his fiancée *and* his best friend."

My heart ached, but for once it wasn't for me. I hurt for Joel. "It must've been too painful for Joel to talk about."

"My crime was that I was in love with two men. Two men who I often confused as one. I was immature and selfish. And when I tried to do the right thing, it cost me Joel."

"But you married Jonathon."

"Yes, but not until *you* married Joel. I begged for him to come back to me, but he told me he was dating someone. Someone completely the opposite of me. Someone who would never hurt him."

"Someone safe," I whispered.

"I don't know. I guess so. But my marriage has been strained since the beginning. Joel is still very much alive in my marriage. I'm not sure if it will keep us together or tear us apart. I don't know how to fix it, except to try to do the right thing again."

I could feel my temples pound. The boy next door had married the girl next door, not out of passion, but for security. I would never cheat on him; he knew that. I wasn't the type. He had picked me carefully, someone so different than Monica that I would never remind him of his old flame. Monica's Blackberry buzzed. I began to panic. "You can't leave. We're not done here."

Monica gathered her things. "I wish I didn't have to. Judges are sticklers for promptness. Let's get together again soon, though. Wow. I already feel better talking to you like this."

And I felt strangely worse. "I can't wait another two weeks. Can you come over tonight?"

"My daughter has a basketball game and then I have to take the red eye to New York. As soon as I get back, though. I promise."

"How long?"

"Three days. Four tops."

I watched her leave as elegantly as she had arrived, though she was now a different person in my eyes. I knew her secrets. Some of them, but not all. Not the one I needed to know the most. I knew she was a cheater. Jonathon was a cheater. But what about Joel? What about my husband? And was I the rebound girl that became the rebound wife?

Was Joel just seeking revenge when he took me as a wife?

***

Alfred Lord Tennyson once wrote, "It is better to have loved and lost, than never to have loved at all." With all due respect to Lord T, he didn't know what the hell he was talking about. It is *far* better to have never loved at all, for never knowing love means you will never know what you are missing. But then this is a Griever talking. I have a distinct feeling Alfred was a Normal when he wrote that. I doubted he would've said it just after he had lost the love of his life. In fact, he probably wrote it while in the throes of a passionate love affair and said it off-handedly to a Griever. It's just the type of smart-ass remark a Normal says to a Griever, believing he is making them feel better.

I knew I needed escape. I took Bellezza for a jog around the neighborhood when I *really* wanted to jog to the local 7-Eleven for a box of Ding Dongs. I had helped the boys with their homework and began putting away the mountain of clothes in my closet. I found pieces of apparel I had forgotten I even had. Brightly colored clothing. Blues, greens, reds, purples. I told my mother I didn't need help this week. I told Anh I was cutting off the organizational umbilical cord. I had to do it myself, for myself. If she and my mother kept cleaning up my messes, I would never learn. I knew I could not become Normal when my world was still so cluttered.

As I vacuumed the dust bunnies (how quickly they procreate) underneath the couch at 1 a.m., waiting for da Vinci to come home, it hit me: *I deserved more than this.* I had become a doormat with him—a highly sexual doormat, but a doormat all the same.

I had become da Vinci's security blanket, making America a little easier for him, just like he had made life a little easier for me.

And I owed it to da Vinci, Panchal, and especially myself, to straighten things out.

So I implored Zoya, who was usually up eating a bowl of cereal with her pregnant appetite, to stay at the house with the boys so I could go fetch some Italian.

I had expected to find the frat house pumping with party music, but it was strangely quiet, the side door propped open with a large rock, making it all too easy to sneak in. I had no idea where I would find him, but I began climbing the stairs when a young freckled-faced frat descended the stairs with a beer in his hand. He immediately put the brew behind his back. I must look like someone's mother and he assumed he was in trouble. "Are you here to apply for the house mom job?"

My ego deflated, but fortunately, it wasn't that big to begin with. "House mom? Definitely not. I'm looking for Leonardo da Vinci."

"Einstein? Oh, he crashed in Pickler's room."

Einstein? Pretty rude, wasn't it? Just because a person doesn't know English very well doesn't make him dumb. "Could you show me the way?"

"Sure thing. Right this way. I really think you should consider the house mom thing, though. You get free room and board, and I'm sure the guys would like you. Our last one was a real old bat."

I couldn't even get my own boys to clean their rooms, let alone a hundred hormone-crazed frat boys. I wasn't sure if I should feel complimented or insulted.

The frat boy—who told me his name was T-Bone, which seemed like an awfully big name for such a small man—led me through the stained-carpeted hallways, passing by the TV room with three guys asleep on the couches. The pungent odor was worse than da Vinci had described, a combination of alcohol, urine and gym socks.

T-Bone rapped lightly on the door, then peeked inside and turned to me with a grin. "He's busy," he said taking a swig of his beer. "Sure you want me to disturb him?"

I shook my head, feeling hot tears rush to the surface. I should've left it alone. A few more weeks and da Vinci would've weaned himself from me. Why rush it? I heard moaning from inside the room and considered rushing in to surprise him and just end it right there.

"She's sick," T-Bone said as he walked away. Intrigued, I stuck my head in and saw that a girl was throwing up in the trashcan next to the bed. Da Vinci lay on the bed, in the position I was so familiar with: one arm on his belly, the other above his head, in a deep sleep.

I entered the room to help the girl. I held her hair as she threw up and helped her to the bathroom to wash her face. "Jell-O shots," she said, clutching her stomach.

I'd forgotten all about those lethal jiggly things. Jell-O was strictly a kids' thing in my world. "Guys use them to wear down your resistance," I told her, thinking it didn't seem like da Vinci to get a girl drunk to take advantage of her. A girl didn't need to be inebriated to want da Vinci.

The girl studied my face, the color returning to hers. "I'm Cheyenne."

"I'm Ramona."

Cheyenne's eyes widened. "*You're* Mona Lisa?"

I could hear da Vinci begin to snore. "That's right. How did you know?"

Cheyenne rolled her small shoulders back. "Leo talks about you all the time."

"He does? But I thought ... well, you were in here with him."

Cheyenne shook her head. "Oh, that. Sorry. Passed out. I'm with Pickler, but he's still out partying at the Phi Delt house. Leo and I are just friends. He's crazy about you."

"He is?" I looked back and watched da Vinci's chest rise and fall, and longed to touch him. He'd been so distant lately, so not the guy that had strolled into my classroom two months before.

Cheyenne nodded. "Yeah. And you're even prettier than he said you were. Younger, too. Not that I really know any thirty year olds."

"He said I was thirty?"

"Think so."

Bless him. He gave me six years. Then again, he didn't even know my real age. The only time he'd spoken of our age difference was to say that it didn't matter. "So he's never been with a girl here? Even when he's drunk and not knowing what he's doing?"

"What? Oh, no. The girls try, but he says he's with Mona Lisa. He's kind of become the big brother of the house. All the guys look up to him."

"Really? Because he's been skipping his English class and not showing up to work."

Cheyenne shrugged. "Dunno, but he helped one guy move last week, and then he fixed the plumbing in the sorority house next door when they had a huge water leak in the middle of the night and then he's always studying. Frats call him Einstein, which is kind of funny, since I think the real da Vinci was a bigger genius than Einstein, but that's just my opinion."

"So they mean it as a compliment? But what about his drinking? Doesn't he party all the time?" God, I wasn't sure if I sounded like his jealous girlfriend or his nosy mother.

Cheyenne closed the toilet lid and sat down. "No way. Said he learned his lesson after he peed in your new bed. He doesn't hold much back. But he worries about his frat brothers. Makes sure they're all safe before he goes home."

"*My* da Vinci does that?" My heart swelled with pride.

Da Vinci rustled and opened his eyes and leaned up on his arms. "Mona Lisa? Is that you?"

Cheyenne kept the washcloth on her forehead and left us alone. I sat on the edge of his bed. "It's me. I'm sorry I bothered you. I was just worried. I'll go."

He grabbed my arm and pulled me down on top of him. "Don't go. I've missed you. I'm sorry I've been so busy. And as Americans say, a real prick."

"*Cazzone*," I nodded. A prick I obviously couldn't stay mad at for long.

"Forgive me," da Vinci said, then in one fell swoop, pulled the sweater off of me and kissed my black lace bra. I felt him stiffen underneath me, and I was instantly aroused. "Kiss me, Mona Lisa," he said, and for the first time in my life, I made love to a frat boy in a frat house and did the walk of shame as the sun peeked over the horizon, yet I wasn't ashamed at all.

Chapter 18

"How's da Vinci?" my sister asked as she stroked green eye shadow on Zoe's little lids the following Saturday. A dozen little girls and their pageant moms filled the brightly lit room a half-hour before the pageant was to begin.

"Da Vinci is …" I rolled the thought around, but wasn't sure what to say. One minute, da Vinci was the best thing that ever happened to me After, and the next … well, I wondered what the hell I was doing with him. I worried he was getting too serious and that I was incapable of being serious with anyone. I worried that my quest for fun had resulted in more than I'd bargained for. I worried my boys liked him even more than I did. I worried most of all that after so many months of not having anyone else in my life, my world was complicated by Cortland, Monica, and da Vinci, and I'd brought it all on myself.

Rachel peered into my eyes. "Earth to Ramona. The boys told me he sleeps in the house now. So this means you're moving on, right?"

I hadn't wanted the boys to know, but keeping it a secret and keeping da Vinci in the backyard like some sort of sex slave—as he'd put it—wasn't what I wanted, either. I'd taken Joel's clothes down from the closet, lovingly folded them, and put them away in a box. I wasn't ready to donate them by any means, but it was a start. Seeing a bare spot in the closet where his clothes had been made me feel strangely calm. I wouldn't have to look at things that he would never wear again.

Next I had cleaned out Joel's bathroom drawer, full of all the products that had kept him so put together: his hair gel, whitening toothpaste, the aftershave that turned me on with one whiff. I placed the aftershave in my own drawer and threw the rest into the trash. I doubted even Judith would want his cleaning products, but I wasn't about to ask, for fear she would reprimand me for tossing them out.

The act was liberating. I wasn't sure if my cleaning binge was because I was truly progressing or if it was a by-product of my nerves.

"Da Vinci is wonderful. I think he's acclimating well to American life."

"*So* not what I meant," Rachel said, shaking her pinpoint straight hair. "I just want to know how you're acclimating *together*. Is this love or what?"

Da Vinci had told me he loved me again, this time as we were falling asleep, my back against his bare chest. (So much for my arm's length policy.) He had kissed my shoulder and said it clearly. In English. I pretended not to hear, and though many days I had wondered if a man would ever tell me he loved me again, I felt no urge to say it back. As a linguist, I am careful with word choice—sometimes *too* careful. I tend to want to correct people when they've said one thing, but really mean another. I had no way of knowing if da Vinci meant what he said, but as a woman with a broken heart, I am even more careful that my words don't come back to haunt me. If pressed, I would feel comfortable with the following:

I really, really, really like you.

I love making love to you.

I am extremely fond of you.

I adore you.

I care for you.

The sum of all of the above *could* equal love, but something didn't add up. I was just shy of being in love, but had no idea why. I knew I needed to tell da Vinci we should slow down, that I wasn't ready for anything serious, but I was afraid he wouldn't understand or that it would hurt his feelings unnecessarily. Just days before, I was certain he would dump me for a sorority girl. He was making such progress, and so was I. Why cause drama? Besides, he made me feel good again. That's what I'd wanted, wasn't it? *La vita allegra.* Joyful living, not drama. Not heartache.

Rachel had opened the door, so I took it. "And you and Cortland? What's the latest there?"

She only shrugged her shoulders and continued to pin Zoe's hair, causing her to flinch. Zoe's face reminded me of the sad blank eyes of a puppy in a dog pound, caged and hopeless.

"Well, *I* really like him," I told her.

"I guess," Rachel said. "What's not to like, right?"

I wanted to tell her that I'd really meant I *like* liked him, but then, I had only just admitted this to myself. I had romantic feelings for my sister's boyfriend. The kiss had been real and made me feel something I hadn't felt with da Vinci. If da Vinci was the fantasy, then Cortland was the reality. Not that I wanted something real. Real was scary. Real was heartbreaking. Real would cause me to become a Normal again, only to get my heart broken again after Cortland moved on to his next socialite. I had to confess about the kiss. Sisters should be honest, and I wanted to beat Cortland to the confession.

"Something happened the other day with Cortland," I said tentatively, but my sister was in pageant zone.

"Zoe, I swear to God," Rachel said, as Zoe dipped her chin down instead of holding it up like a mannequin so her mom could finish sticking, poufing, and spraying her hair.

I was frustrated enough to not give a damn how my sister took it. My anger had been building like a roller coaster charging up a hill, and I'd finally reached the crest. "How come you never listen to me? And aren't you tired of torturing Zoe? Can't you see she hates it?"

Rachel batted her long lashes at me and stared at her daughter, whose hair was now teased eight inches from her tiny head. "What do you mean? Zoe doesn't hate pageants. She just hasn't reached her full potential in them yet."

"Zoe?" I asked. "It's okay to tell the truth. She's your mother. She'll love you no matter what."

Poor Zoe shook her sparkly shoes and took a deep breath. "I hate pageants, Mommy. I hate them more than cleaning my room or picking up Princess's dog poop in the backyard."

"Oh, you don't mean that," Rachel said, shaking a comb at her daughter before turning to address me. "She doesn't mean that. She's just nervous is all."

Zoe stood on her chair so she was face-to-face with her mother. She raised her little arms and screamed so hard, her little face brightened like a stoplight. "*I hate pageants!*" The moms in the rooms stopped coiffing their daughters and stared at Zoe as if she had cursed, but the girls began to giggle.

"Stop that right now," Rachel said, grabbing her daughter. "Don't embarrass Mommy. Do you see what you've done, Ramona?"

"In your motivational speeches, do you not promote girls and women *not* trying to fit into the mold of what society or others think of them?"

"Absolutely! The women eat it up."

"Well, if you mean that, then you wouldn't make Zoe do pageants."

Zoe jumped into my arms and rubbed her face in my neck, smearing makeup all over my white shirt. "Look, if Zoe can't stand up for herself, someone's got to do it for her."

Rachel forced a smile at the other moms and began gathering up her things. "Well, if you meant to humiliate me, congratulations. Pulling Zoe out at this late stage will make me look bad. Is that what you want? Zoe, you don't want to make Mommy look bad, do you? Look at Mommy's sad face."

"Don't manipulate her like that. You're going to give her a worse complex than Mom has given us."

"She hasn't given me a complex."

"Only because you do exactly what she wants you to do."

"Church? Big deal."

"Dating Cortland."

"Completely my decision. He's a doctor. And handsome."

"Remember when you were in third grade and you wanted to play soccer, and Mom said it was only for boys, even though there were two other girls on the team? She made you take baton lessons instead."

Rachel stuffed the curling iron in the bag, burning herself in the process. "Shit. Fine. I remember. Mom wouldn't let me play soccer, I hated baton lessons, I was the fattest girl on the squad and she wouldn't let me eat cookies after practice like the other moms did."

Exasperated, she pulled a Hershey bar out of the bag and ripped into it, splitting it into two. Even my skinny sis needed her chocolate fix. She rolled her eyes back into her head. "Here, Zoe. Mommy's not mad. Let's eat chocolate, and all will be right in the world again."

"Oh, that helps," I said, taking Zoe with me to the restroom while Rachel went to talk to the judges.

Zoe thanked me with a kiss on the cheek. "Think she'll finally let me play soccer?"

"Maybe. We may have cracked her shell."

"Mommy has a shell?"

"We all do, honey. We all do."

"Will you wash my face off so I look normal again?" Underneath all that rouge and lipstick was a regular five-year-old girl. No wonder I identified so much with my niece: we both just wanted to be Normals.

In the car, Rachel's anger at me subsided after a phone call from her manager, telling her she was invited to a party in Los Angeles that weekend where A-list stars were expected to attend—a gala to promote fitness and nutrition for kids, though Zoe was currently eating a Hershey bar her mother had hoarded. "God, why did I eat that Hershey bar? Think you can watch Zoe for me? I'll just be gone from Saturday morning to Sunday afternoon."

"Sure," I said, looking back over the seat at Zoe sleeping in her booster chair. "After all, you're the one with the life, right?"

"Oh, crap," Rachel said as she checked her Blackberry at a red light. "Cortland wanted to go out Saturday night."

My stomach tightened. "Really?"

"Sounded serious, too. Think he'll ask me to move in with him?"

I had to blink back tears. "I don't know. Is that what you think? I didn't think you were that serious."

"He probably likes me more than I like him, you know? But his house is gorgeous, isn't it? And it would be nice for Zoe to have a sister to play with."

"Wait a minute. You'd just move in with him for his house? Are you insane?"

"Chill, sis. God, you make it sound like I'm committing a crime. I wouldn't be the first woman to shack up for prime real estate. Besides, I could grow to love him. Unless I meet Brad Pitt at the party this weekend. Think he and Angelina will stay together long?"

I dug my nails into the leather seat. "Did it ever occur to you that you should let him go so he can find someone that might like him as much as he likes her? That you could be standing in the way?"

"Don't be ridiculous. Who could he possibly like more than me? He has been acting awfully strange the last couple of weeks, though. He didn't even invite me back to his house after dinner at Monica's. Who in their right mind would pick going to bed early to get rested for a surgery over being with me?"

I laughed. Rachel believed it was because she was right, but I was laughing because Cortland was obviously very much in his right mind. What if he was going to break up with her on Saturday night?

"Rachel, there's something you need to know about Cortland."

But she pulled into my driveway and put her index finger up—her sign to make me hold my thought. She began making a phone call. "Guess who's going to party with Leonardo DiCaprio this weekend?" she squealed into the other end.

I rolled my eyes and got out, my sister waving goodbye as she pulled down the drive, obviously not caring what I was about to confess. "I kissed your boyfriend," I shouted in a big wave.

She rolled down her window, obviously not having heard me. "Love you, too, sis. I'll drop Zoe off Saturday. And let me know what I can bring for Thanksgiving dinner next week."

Thanksgiving dinner at my house? I tugged at my coat and opened the garage door where I stared at Joel's tools, bike, and sports equipment cluttering half of the garage, with the other half full of holiday décor. A perfect way to spend my Saturday afternoon while my starlet sister was off to Hollywood.

"I'm home," I sang as I entered the house.

"*Benvenuto*, honey," da Vinci said from Joel's den, which I decided I should refer to from now on as my den.

I found da Vinci bent over a stack of books, clearly tired. "I talked to Panchal," he said. "Promised no more missing English class."

"Good for you," I told him, noticing how much his English had improved since he had joined the frat house. He had picked up slang terms, but he was much more conversational. I felt a pang of jealousy that I hadn't taught him, but then, every bird has to fly on its own eventually. I hadn't instructed him to talk to Panchal. He had taken his own initiative. Maybe he was more responsible than I had given him credit for.

I left him to hang my coat in my closet and slip into more comfortable shoes, when I noticed Joel's side was no longer empty, but cluttered with a pile of clothes and a few hung shirts and jeans. Da Vinci had moved himself in. *Without my permission.*

I held onto the dresser drawer for support, my forehead perspiring. I couldn't blame him. After all, it was the next logical step. Just as Rachel assumed Cortland would ask her to move in with him, da Vinci had assumed he could move a few of his things into my closet. After all, he slept here nearly every night. What kind of a girlfriend would I be to make him traipse back and forth between the studio and the bedroom when he could just as easily keep his things close at hand in the closet?

I went back to the bathroom and opened Joel's drawer to find da Vinci's toothpaste, toothbrush, and cologne sitting inside. I didn't have the heart to tell da Vinci I didn't like his cologne, let alone the idea of him becoming a permanent staple in my bed. Did I?

***

"You can't be sick," I moaned to Monica Friday evening. We had made plans to get a glass of wine, but apparently it doesn't mix well with cough syrup.

"It's these damn depositions," Monica said, her throaty voice even sexier. "I always get sick around the holidays. I should just quarantine myself from November through January."

My mom was already over, playing Scrabble with the boys. "Chicken soup, then?"

"I'm afraid I can't even lift my head off the pillow. It's that aching, stuffy-head, fever thing. I don't want to expose you and the boys."

"Well, if it's that bad," I said. *Dammit. Dammit. Dammit.* "We'll just have to get together after you're better."

Monica coughed into the phone. "Gonna have to be after T-day. We're traveling to Missouri to be with Jonathon's family."

My heart sank. Another week. "Fine. You just get well, then."

I hung up, wondering if da Vinci and I should go on a *date* date but remembered he was going to a frat function—some mandatory pledge thing—and that Anh was on a secret date with Michael, who was upset Rachel hadn't asked him to keep Zoe, because she *was* his child, after all, and I didn't want to spend another Friday night playing Scrabble. I'd had too much Scrabble in my life. It was high time I put some of those words I placed on the board into action.

Next I called Judith with the excuse that I wanted to bring a box of Joel's things over to her house—his great-grandmother's quilt she wanted back and a copy of his high school yearbook—and I'd get her to tell me everything she knew about Monica. She would know if her son ever got over Monica, wouldn't she? He seemed to tell her everything. They'd talked on the phone once or even twice a day. I'd often wondered if his mother was more of his best friend than I'd been. Besides, I couldn't just trust Monica's side of the story, could I?

"I have plans," Judith said a moment later. "We're doing the prep work for the Thanksgiving dinner at the homeless shelter. Why don't you join us?"

"Who'll be there? I mean, besides the homeless." Spending a Friday night helping my mom-in-law peel potatoes was not exactly what I had in mind.

"Oh, just a bunch of Lifers," she said, which made me cringe. Lifers was the nickname she'd given to anyone who attended Life Church, but it came off sounding haughty. I wanted to remind her the term had been used in prisons long before she started using it.

Scrabble began sounding pretty good again, but my curiosity got the best of me. After a quick kiss to my kids, which was promptly wiped off by Bradley, I was out the door.

Chapter 19

A HOMELESS MAN WEARING socks for gloves and a stained Longhorns knit hat greeted me with a toothless smile as I entered the back door of the makeshift homeless shelter that once housed a mid-century clothes manufacturer. I imagined the place had been alive with the buzz of a hundred sewing machines before technology wiped out the need for so many human laborers. I refused to think the same clothes were now being produced in a sweatshop in a third-world country, which was probably the case. I made my way through the maze of cots, which were blocking the route to the kitchen, due to overcrowding from a bout of hurricanes that set the homeless awash in Austin.

A curious Hispanic boy noticed me and followed me to the kitchen. He looked to be about William's age, dirty but happy. I remembered why I didn't like helping in soup kitchens: I always wanted to take the children home with me.

"*Hola, señora*," the boy said, tugging on my jacket.

"*Hola, muchachito.*"

The boy grinned, revealing both his front teeth missing. I asked him if he spoke English. He shook his head. He told me he and his parents had just arrived in a truck, and his mother was going to have a baby.

I had the sinking feeling they were illegal aliens and they would be out of the homeless shelter before INS arrived the next morning. I congratulated him on becoming a big brother and handed him a carrot that Judith had just peeled. I kissed my mom-in-law on the cheek and removed my jacket. The boy crunched the carrot like Bugs Bunny, but didn't take his eyes off of me.

"I think someone has a crush," Judith said. "Poor thing needs a bath like no one's business. Don't tell me. Illegal, right?"

"*Ssh!* Mom," I scolded.

"What? He can't speak English. What difference does it make?"

I asked the boy if he needed anything else and he repeated that his mother was having a baby. A terrible scream rang through the metal warehouse. "Oh, God," I said, looking at the small group of volunteers in the kitchen. "He means his mother is having a baby *right now!*"

Judith threw down her peeling knife. "I'll call the hospital."

The boy's eyes widened. "*Mi mamá dice que el hospital nos llevará a la cárcel.*"

"What did he say?" Judith said, rummaging through her designer bag for her tiny phone.

I thumped my forehead. "He's right. He says they can't go to the hospital because they'll deport them."

"Well, the law's the law," Judith said with a terse smile. I marveled that a woman who believed volunteerism was saintly and would spend hours peeling potatoes for the homeless would so quickly turn against them.

I grabbed the phone from her hand. "No hospital. We can't have a new mom deported. She'll be terrified. And she'll only go kicking and screaming." I'd seen my share of illegal immigrants at the Panchal Center. While you had to have documentation to work for Panchal's temp agency, anyone could learn to speak English, green card or not.

The boy tugged at my arm as his mother's wails continued. "*¡Ven! ¡Ven!*"

"I'm coming," I told him. "We need a doctor."

"Oh, Lord," Judith said. "Unless you have some midwife skills I don't know about …"

"Is there a doctor in the house?" Cortland said, traipsing through the door with a bushel of potatoes.

I caught my breath. "Thank God! A woman is having a baby. Out there."

Cortland plopped the heavy crate onto the counter and rolled his shoulders back. "A baby, huh? Might be a lot more fun than peeling potatoes."

"You can't be serious," Judith said.

"I'll need hot towels, some rubbing alcohol, and clean sheets."

The volunteers rushed to carry out his orders, while I shook my head in amazement. Cortland and I followed the boy, Manuel, out into the main room where his mother's screams were even louder.

"What did she just say?" Cortland asked,

"She said, 'Get this baby out of me,'" I translated, suddenly feeling faint as we came upon the woman lying on her back on the cot, legs bent in delivery position. Her husband asked me if his wife Maria was going to be okay.

"*Sí*," I told him. "He's a doctor."

The couple made the sign of the cross as Cortland spread the sheet over her, then knelt down to check her progress. "I can see the head," he said with a grin.

"Okay, I'm just going to go over there at a safe distance," I said, backing away.

"Oh, no, you're not. I need you to translate for me."

Maria pulled me down by my arm and squeezed my hand until it was white with pain. "Fine. Powerful grip," I said, wincing myself. "Just get her baby out now for all of our sakes."

"I'm glad you came," he said to me, then concentrated on Maria. "Push hard now."

"*Empuje!*" I told her, and she squeezed my hand harder as I held one knee and her husband held the other. Maria bore down, grunting and filling the air with Spanish curse words.

A moment later, Cortland pulled a bright pink baby from under the sheet, turned it over and tapped it three times on the bottom, causing it to wail. "It's a girl!" Gently, he handed off the baby to its mother.

Judith had prepared a makeshift crib out of a box, and another Lifer handed him more hot towels and a suture kit.

Cortland handed me a pair of scissors and nodded toward the umbilical cord. "You want to do the honors?"

"Me? What about the father?" The baby's father shook his head, and I took the scissors. Two snips and the baby was free of its mother.

An hour later, we sat around the kitchen, drinking coffee while the potatoes sat on the counter unpeeled. "Well, it's a little anti-climactic to peel them after what we've been through," I said, putting my feet up on an empty seat.

"Pretty handy to have a doctor around," Judith said proudly, rubbing Cortland's shoulders. "You just never know what life will throw you."

He seemed tired but happy. His chill had worn off.

Judith grabbed her old coat that she always volunteered in and wrapped a red scarf around her neck. "I'm beat. Only so much excitement an old lady can take in one night." She winked. She only joked about being old because she didn't look old at all.

I'd nearly forgotten my purpose for coming there. "Mom G., I wanted to ask you about something."

She swung her purse over her shoulder. "What is it, darling? Is it the boys? I can sit tomorrow if you like."

"No, I'll have Zoe, so she'll want to play with the boys. It's not that. It's about Monica."

Judith rolled her eyes and blew a puff of air. "I have nothing to say about that woman."

Cortland looked at us back and forth, before it seemed to register which Monica we were talking about. I didn't care if he heard. I'd waited long enough.

"I know you don't like her, but I need to know how Joel took the break-up."

Judith jaw fell slack, as if I'd just slapped her. "How do you think he took it? Joel had his entire life planned out. He loved her and she betrayed him."

"But did he forgive her?"

"You mean did he stop loving her?"

"Maybe."

"He loved you, Ramona. With all his heart. That's all that mattered."

"But it *was* different, wasn't it? Just tell me."

Judith's face softened. "Yes, it was different. But honestly, she's not what hurt him the most. He missed Jonathon most of all. Friends since they were three. His mother is still one of my best friends, but she knows not to discuss her daughter-in-law with me."

"You never told me that."

"Why would I? What does it have to do with you?"

"I'm just trying to piece things together. I'm sorry if it upsets you."

Judith stepped forward and lifted my chin with her index finger. "It's *you* I worry about. Why don't you bring all three kids by tomorrow and they can play, and you can go out and have some fun."

She never mentioned da Vinci by name. I knew she disapproved. She wore it on her skin as obviously as her coat. Her code for him was "fun." He was a fling to her. I hoped she didn't find out about his moving in.

"I guess I'll see you at Thanksgiving dinner, Cortland," Judith said as she turned to leave.

"Oh, I don't think I'm coming."

"Of course you are. Don't be ridiculous. Your mother said she'd send you over for some pie."

"Pie. I guess a man needs his pie."

"Ramona makes a delicious pecan pie."

"She does, does she?" He tilted his head my way. "I can't resist her pie, I suppose."

"'Night, Mother."

Judith turned off the main kitchen light, leaving Cortland and me sitting in the near dark, the full moon beaming through the cracked kitchen window. "I guess I should shove off unless you need me."

Cortland stared at me and even when I looked away, I could feel his gaze on my face like a hot blast to my cheek. "I *do* need you, Ramona."

"You know I meant with the baby."

"I know what you meant. And you know what I mean."

"I've told you—"

"I was going to break up with her tomorrow."

Relief washed over me. "Still."

"Da Vinci."

"Yes."

"Well, if you love him, I'll get out of the way. But if there's a chance."

"A chance."

"Possibility, probability, likelihood."

"I know the synonyms, thankyouverymuch."

"I put my house on the market. Will you help me look for a smaller one tomorrow? I don't trust realtors. They just tell you what you want to hear."

"Kind of like men."

"You don't believe that."

"I have the kids tomorrow."

"Nice try. Judith offered to watch the kids so you could have fun."

"And house hunting with you would be fun?"

"Well, if delivering a baby in the middle of a shelter can be fun, then yes, house hunting can be fun."

"I couldn't even pick out a bed, much less a house."

"That's just it. I need your critical eye. Otherwise, I might just buy the first house I see."

"I'm cleaning out my garage. I'm trying to purge the clutter before the new year."

"A pre-new year's resolution?"

"Something like that."

"I'll tell you what. You look for houses with me in the morning, and I'll help you clean your garage in the afternoon."

"You don't take no for an answer, do you?"

"Not where you're concerned."

"It's complicated."

"Maybe. But worth it."

I stood to leave, and Cortland held my pinkie. "You just never know what life's gonna throw you."

"Take a chance?"

"On me."

"On you." My heart sped up. I could hear the baby crying in the other room. The kitchen felt smaller and smaller, until it was only two feet of space between us. Arm's length, yet I could still feel him in my heart. He moved his hand up my arm, his touch sending electrical vibrations throughout my body. Rachel would be gone, history. She was nothing to him, I knew. But it didn't mean she wouldn't hate me for it. It may not register on the Richter scale of betrayal like Jonathon and Joel, but she could see it as betrayal all the same. She was my sister, far from perfect, the most egotistical woman I knew, but she was family.

And what of da Vinci? If I gave Cortland a chance and we didn't work out, I'd lose da Vinci forever.

Chapter 20

ANH HANDED ME THE Flirtini—a martini made of vodka, champagne, and pineapple juice—and tossed her flip-flops off her feet. She wore them all year around, even in the dead of winter. She said Vietnamese were hot-blooded, but I told her in her case, it was more likely her hot-headed nature. She didn't argue.

It was Girls' Night In, something we were used to since I couldn't afford Girls' Night Out anymore. The last of Joel's life insurance money had been used for that bed and some Christmas gifts for the boys I knew their father would want them to have. I would be on my own financially, yet for the first time I knew I could make it.

Anh had become quite a cocktail waitress from our GNI evenings. "She's unbelievable," Anh said, taking a sip of the concoction she'd mixed and rolling her eyes. "This is why a woman should not get in a relationship with a divorced man: you don't just date them, you date their exes. It's a threesome, without the pleasure."

I joined her on the couch, still high from my own unbelievable Saturday, only for a very different reason. My garage was pristine, every inch litter-free, as organized as an After on a home improvement show. And the house hunting with Cortland hadn't been bad, either. That is, until he spotted the house across the street and two doors down that was for sale, a cottage-looking home with a wrap-around front porch, blue shutters and immaculate landscaping. Mrs. Thompson had died six months prior, and her three grown boys were selling it and splitting the profits. I'd watched enough HGTV to know the reason her house wasn't selling wasn't because it wasn't cute, but because it was cutesy cute. Mrs. Thompson had collected ducks. She had duck borders and duck towels and duck rugs and ducks painted on the walls.

Cortland saw beyond the ducks. Besides, he claimed he liked to renovate. "My wife wanted everything brand new," he complained. "I like to fix things with my own hands."

Which got me to thinking about his hands: ones that had lulled people to sleep for surgery, ones that had pulled out a beautiful baby girl the day before, ones that had roamed over my body at the restaurant two weeks prior.

"At least da Vinci has no ex," Anh went on.

"I'm not so sure," I said, tossing her an envelope he'd gotten in the mail that day. It would've been an ordinary air-mail envelope, save for two things: the penmanship was beautiful, carefully scripted by someone who relished writing da Vinci's name, and the return address noted the sender as Chiara, which meant "bright and famous." None of his sisters were named Chiara, I knew, and I doubt they would've spritzed the envelope with perfume, either.

"Smells sexy," Anh said. "I thought he didn't have anyone special back home?"

"Who knows," I downed the Flirtini as Anh poured me another. "He's at another frat party tonight, so I'll ask him tomorrow. I hate feeling jealous."

"Of Chiara or the frat party?"

"Both. When I'm away from him, I start thinking I'd be okay with him leaving, but as soon as I see him, I want him again."

"It's the pheromones. He's a magnet guy. You can't help being drawn to him. Especially with amazing sex. He got chakra two back in action. As long as he doesn't make a habit of peeing in the bed."

I considered the sex, wishing I hadn't gotten used to it. Da Vinci did things to me I'd never let Joel do. I'd been so afraid to explore with Joel, afraid he would think badly of me, especially after we had kids. The sex kept the loneliness at bay. I grabbed a chocolate-covered strawberry from the dish on the table. Anh insisted our Girls' Night In consist of more than Ruffles and ranch dip this time, so she set us up properly: sushi, loads of chocolate and enough Flirtini mix for a party of twelve. "So you were saying … about being in a three-some with my sister?"

"Ugh. This is why I can't date Michael. She calls him nearly every day, and it's not always about Zoe, although she had a mouthful to say about your little stunt at the pageant."

"Well, Zoe gets to play soccer now, so it was worth it."

"Michael thinks she'll flip out when she hears we're dating, and I stopped him and said, 'Excuse me? We're dating? Because I thought we were just sleeping together.'"

"Ouch."

"Yeah. So he goes, 'Fine, then I'll return the tickets to the Bahamas I ordered on Priceline.com today.'"

"You can't resist a guy who knows how to find a good deal."

"Or a beach far, far away from my grandmotherhood."

"Where is Vi tonight?"

"With her mother."

"On a Saturday night?"

"Don't even get me started."

"Fine. I'd rather hear more about you and Michael. And I'd love to see you and my sis in a bitch-slap contest."

"Funny. I don't know who she'd hate worse: me for screwing her ex or you for kissing her current."

"He's dumping her."

"Time will tell."

"No, he wants to buy Mrs. Thompson's house. Probably already made the offer."

"The duck house?"

"He's into home improvement."

"Thrifty with his money, too, huh?"

"If he didn't break up with Rachel, his downsizing alone would cause her to break up with him."

"Crap," she said. "No offense to you, but I wish things would've worked out with her and Cortland just so she'd have a diversion."

"Her diversion is her career. Besides, maybe she'll hook up with Leonardo DiCaprio tonight."

"Her head wouldn't fit on the plane. So does this mean that my widowy friend now has *two* guys in her life?"

"I can feel da Vinci slipping from my grasp. He says he loves me, but I think he's just scared to let go. I've been his lifeline in America up to now, and maybe he's been mine, getting back out there again, but being with him isn't the same as being with an American or someone my own age. He's as lost as I am."

"We all need something or someone to hold onto."

"This coming from someone who swore she'd never love again."

"I'm not loving again. I'm *liking*. And I can like going to the Bahamas, too."

"Well, maybe you should start being a little nicer to him, then. Just because he's a lawyer doesn't mean he doesn't have feelings."

"Nice? What am I, a putz? Maybe I'll just call and see if he needs some company later." Anh grabbed up the phone.

"Oh, my God, you're making a booty call and you've only had two drinks."

"Am not," she said. "Besides, your booty call is on autopilot. Some of us have to work at it."

"Whatever." I poured myself another Flirtini, swearing it would be my last and thankful the boys were staying at Judith's. The doorbell rang. I wondered if da Vinci had changed his mind about the party and wanted to make our own instead. I slunk over to the door and nearly dropped my martini glass when I saw who was staring back at me, as handsome as the photos in his yearbook—older certainly, but distinguished and still All-American.

"Jonathon." I said, trying to shake off the effect of my three drinks. Perhaps he was a mirage.

He wore a jogging suit, and sweat was trickling down his hairline, but he was still gorgeous, perspiration or not. "Ramona? I'm sorry to drop in like this, but I was out jogging and …"

"Not exactly on your jogging path." His and Cortland's neighborhood was at least five miles from mine.

"Monica told me you two were going to meet."

"She did?"

"She's still sick at home, but …"

"Yes, come in, of course." I stepped back to let him pass, as Anh made her way into the foyer. Her mouth dropped open.

"Anh, this is Jonathon. Jonathon Blevins."

She tossed her hair back, a classic flirtation, brought on by his looks and the aptly named drink. "Can I get you a Flirtini?"

"A what?"

Anh and I giggled. How girlish. Men like Jonathon probably didn't drink Flirtinis. "It's good I promise. And we won't tell anyone you drank one."

Jonathon removed his jacket, revealing a Nike shirt clinging to his ripped stomach and biceps even bigger than da Vinci's. "Sure," he said. "After I drink a bucket of water."

We stared at him before Anh broke into a surprised smile. "Not sure about the bucket, but I think we're good on the tall glass."

"Can I get you a T-shirt? I have some of Joel's packed away in the closet. At least Joel liked to wear them big."

Jonathon flinched at the sound of his friend's name. "That'd be great."

An hour later, Jonathon was drunk on Flirtinis and Anh excused herself. "I have a thing I have to do."

"His name is Michael," I said with a laugh.

She playfully slapped me. "Jonathon, it was nice to meet you. I think you and my friend Michael would love to talk shop. I'll call you."

Jonathon kissed her on the cheek, and Anh blushed. Now I got it: I'd thought Monica was a heartless bitch for breaking Joel's heart, but being around Jonathon, even after just an hour, I could see why she was torn between the two for more than a decade. He was everything Joel wasn't and vice versa. I got what Monica meant about the two of them together being the perfect man. Still. It didn't make what she did any less awful. Same goes for Jonathon.

"Nothing helps," Jonathon said, wrapping his large hands around the comparatively small glass. "I've gone to every type of counseling. Marriage counseling, grief counseling. I can't get over losing Joel. Not once. But twice."

"So why did you do it?"

His eyebrows rose. "I was in love. If you look up 'fool in love' in the dictionary, there I am. I was crazy about Monica, since we were ten years old. But Joel was the smart one, the funny one, and he won her heart. It was only after Monica would do something stupid, like flirt with another boy in school, or start nitpicking him, that he'd break up with her and she'd come crying to me."

"But why would he break up with her if he loved her?"

"Well, it got to be a pattern with them. Plus this ping-pong relationship started when we were thirteen, and I guess in some ways, they never really matured beyond that. Monica drove him crazy. She was so beautiful, and all she'd have to say to get his attention was that another man flirted with her. In high school, all the college guys were after her, and in college, all the graduates were after her, and it was all too much for him sometimes. He felt like he'd never be enough for her."

"But you were there waiting in the wings?"

"I can't really explain it. It wasn't a malicious thing. I really was there as a shoulder to cry on, but when you're sixteen and hormones are raging, things just get out of hand. And I knew they weren't meant to be together. They fought all the time. Monica can be hard to handle."

"But you know how to handle her?"

Jonathon crossed his arms, his biceps bulging against his chest. "We're equals. She couldn't throw it in my face that she could have any guy she wanted, because I was that guy. And she knows I could say the same."

"She told me you had a reputation."

"I didn't go through so many women to be a dick. I did it looking for someone I could love as much as I loved Monica. But I never found her."

"So she told Joel about you against your will?"

"No. I threatened to tell Joel if she didn't first. I couldn't stand the thought of them getting married without him knowing that we'd been together before, even though it was over."

"But would it have been? Truly over?"

Jonathon shook his head. "She says so, but I knew better. I knew that I would be friends with Joel until I died. I would've married someone I loved just less than Monica, someone to keep me from being lonely, to have children with, and we'd be together every week, our families. At birthday parties and summer vacations. And Monica would be there in her teeny bikini taunting me, this terrible secret between us. And she and Joel would continue to fight and I wouldn't be able to say no to her. It would've been a miserable life."

"But you're miserable now."

"I'm only miserable when I think about Joel. Just full of regret, though the therapists tell me the life I have now is far superior to the one I described to you. But when Monica told me you two were going to talk, I knew I had to get to you first."

"Why?"

"Because Monica doesn't know that Joel forgave me."

"He *what?*"

"He forgave me. About three months before he died. He was working on the new law firm, and Monica told me she was having meetings with him. So I called him up."

"Because you were scared they would do something?"

"No. Maybe. I don't know. I never really worried about them after he found you. You were the woman I always imagined him with."

"You did? How so?"

"He needed someone to make him feel good about himself. To not belittle his ambitions. Someone who wanted to make family a priority. He needed an equal."

"And *that* was *me?*"

"Of course. You were both attractive and smart and funny. You complemented each other."

"But I was going to ask Monica if he cheated on me before he died."

"He told me you thought that. So he gave up the account and swore he'd never see her again."

"I wonder why he didn't mention the meeting with you?"

"I don't know. I just know I couldn't tell Monica that he forgave me, because he never forgave her. I wanted to be friends with him again. I know I couldn't get back the type of friendship that we had before or the trust, but I was willing to try. But it wouldn't have worked out, my sneaking behind my wife's back to be friends with the man she loved."

"Doesn't that drive you insane that she loved him more?"

"I know my wife: she wants what she can't have. And because they were always two puzzle pieces that never quite fit, she made it her mission to force them to fit. But she didn't love him more, only differently. So stop worrying."

"But he *did* cheat on me, didn't he?"

"I never asked him, but it was me who couldn't say no to Monica, not your husband."

"So then, why do you think she wants to meet with me? To confess?"

"I think she just wants to make sure you're leading a good life. Maybe she feels guilty that she didn't end up with him. Think about it: if Joel would've gone through with marrying her, *she* would've been the widow."

"And then she would've come back to you."

"Exactly. Kids and all, she would've come back to me."

"So you two would've ended up together no matter what."

"No matter what." He stood to leave, and I hugged him good-bye. I thought about destiny and fate, and the possibility that he was right: no matter what, they *would* have ended up together. I hugged him once for me and once for Joel. I could feel Joel's presence around us, and I knew Joel would be happy that Jonathon had come to set things straight.

I wiped away the tears in my eyes. "Thank you, Jonathon. You have no idea how much this helped."

"Thank you for loving him. He may have lived a short life, but it was the one that he deserved, thanks to you."

Chapter 21

"IT'S THE THIRD NIGHT in a row," I whined into the phone, then quickly added, "not that I'm keeping track."

Bellezza licked my feet. I'd been baking and basting and cleaning since sunrise, getting ready for Thanksgiving the following day. In addition to my family, I invited Zoya and Donald and, yes, da Vinci. Then there was the matter of Cortland, possibly arriving for pie, but my first three attempts at the pecan recipe my mom-in-law raved about were disastrous. I couldn't seem to get it together this year.

Da Vinci promised he'd be home before bedtime, and when I'd hung up, William was standing behind me, his arms crossed in front of his chest. "Is *that* what you're wearing tonight?"

I smoothed my outfit: sweatpants and a fitted T-shirt, a slight improvement over my pre-da Vinci attire. At least my sweatpants didn't have holes in them and the Birks had been donated to Goodwill. "Honey, we're not having company until tomorrow."

His face corked into a scowl. "What did da Vinci say? Is he coming home or not?"

I ruffled his hair. "You like him, huh?"

William pushed up his glasses on his nose. "He promised we could play Scrabble later. Can I stay up late?"

I glanced over at the kitchen table with the Scrabble board already neatly arranged. And it wasn't even Friday. I felt the anger rise up to my temples. He could disappoint me all day long, but not my boys. "Yes, he'll be here later, sweetie. But if you want Mommy to play…"

William shook his head. "No can do, Mommy-o. We're playing Italian–English Scrabble tonight. He can only spell words in English and I can only spell them in Italian. That way, he can win, because I don't know much Italian."

"That's awfully nice of you. Just don't be disappointed if you can't play until tomorrow. He may be home late."

"So don't you think you should change clothes, then?"

"For da Vinci?" I considered my undergarments, the funderwear I purposely wore in case of his return. It was the undressing that mattered most.

William shrugged his tiny shoulders. "Suit yourself, Mom. But it wouldn't hurt to wear a little makeup."

I touched my hand to my cheek. Why did William care so much? Was he worried about me losing da Vinci, too? I had dyed my hair, bleached my teeth, microdermed my face, and lost fifteen pounds, but it was much more for me than da Vinci. "Is that so? I guess I could put on a little blush."

He wiggled his loose front tooth with his tongue, obviously proud of himself. "Good plan, Mom."

Every once in a while he slipped up and called me Mommy, but for the most part I was simply referred to as the less endearing "mom." A milestone in the toddler-to-gradeschooler transition. I shrugged it off, remembering I hadn't gotten the mail that day and walked to the mailbox in my bunny slippers when I saw Cortland pull up in the duck house driveway across the street. I tried to duck behind the mailbox (no pun intended) and thought I'd scurry in before he spotted me. Thanks to William, I felt self-conscious about my looks. Perhaps I actually cared *a little*.

"Hey!" Cortland yelled, and I turned around, rolling my shoulders back, as if that would make me suddenly put together.

"Hey, yourself." Another car pulled up next to his.

"Inspection," he yelled back.

I waved my bills at him. "Good for you." I turned around again, simultaneously hoping that they'd find massive termite damage to keep him from moving in and hoping the place's only sin was its tackiness. Cortland sprinted across the street and stopped by my side, so close he could see the lack of rouge on my cheeks.

"Hey, are you still making that pecan pie?"

"I don't know why Judith said that. She compliments me when she shouldn't. It's just an ordinary pie—nothing special."

"They say it's not the food that counts, but the company you keep."

I shrugged. "Suit yourself. I'm sure Rachel will want you to come over."

Cortland put his hands on his hips. "I'm talking to her tomorrow."

I slapped the mail against my thigh. "Please tell me you're not going to be the heartless asshole that breaks up with my sister on Thanksgiving Day."

"She suggested we move in together until I told her I was moving across the street from you."

"I told you she wouldn't like it."

"You called it. But I couldn't stand being in my wife's house one more minute. It was time to start a new chapter of my life. A fresh start."

"That's not easy to do."

"I like a good challenge. Like getting you to give me a chance."

"You don't know anything about me."

"Well, I know enough to know I'd like to know more."

I kicked a rock with my bunny slipper's nose. "I suppose it would be a safe and wise choice to get to know my new neighbor."

"Like favorite food? 35 Across."

I grinned, remembering that morning's crossword. "Twoeggsovereasy."

"I think I speak your language, Rames."

I eyed him suspiciously. "Maybe so, but it just wouldn't be a good idea to date you after my sister. She would never forgive me."

Cortland's smile left his face. "Come on. You really think she'd care?"

"She'd at least pretend to. She's a drama queen."

"This much I know." Cortland glanced back at his duck house. "Well, can I at least get your neighborly opinion on a few things in the house?"

"You need a woman's perspective?"

"Always."

I followed him across the street. The inspector was up on the roof, and we entered the house, the smell of vanilla Plug-Ins washing over us. "Very ducky," I said, noting the feathered creatures everywhere—stenciled, painted, wallpapered.

Cortland shook his head. "Sometimes you have to look beyond how things are now and think about what they could be. You know?"

"Potential? Of course. You should've seen my house before we bought it. The former owner loved pink. Every room, wall and carpet was some shade of pink."

"I knew you could help. C'mere." He took my hand and led me into the kitchen, to the thirty-year-old olive-green appliances, stained linoleum floor, and stark, white-tiled countertops. "I'm going to rip out the kitchen. Install granite instead. Black, you think?"

I shook my head. "Too stark. Go with a beige blend."

"Stainless steel appliances?"

"Why not?"

"And what do you think about stained concrete flooring?"

"Sounds cold."

Cortland inched closer to me and looked down at my feet. "That's what bunny slippers are for."

I cleared my throat, noticing the outdated lighting. "There's a great lighting store, locally owned, just a couple blocks over."

"Maybe you could go with me?"

I stared at my feet, knocking my heels together like Dorothy in *The Wizard of Oz.* "Look, Cortland."

"You won't be able to get rid of me that easily. Especially since I'm right across the street. Here, let me show you something. It's the reason I wanted this house."

I followed him down the narrow hallway to a large bedroom, which I quickly gathered was the master with a large bay window that offered a lovely view into the backyard.

"It's beautiful, isn't it?"

The koi pond was surrounded by stones with a bench and a walking path that winded to another sitting area and fall flowers everywhere in golds, reds, purple and whites. "Perfect for entertaining, being the mover and shaker you are."

"Or just unwinding after a long day. Come on." We walked out the patio door to the pond where two dozen koi swam around, their bright orange scales glistening in the fading sunlight. He led me down the stone path to the seating area with a swing facing a bed of mums, in which stood a statue of a duck and a row of her ducklings. We sat on the swing, me on one end and Cortland on the other. He rocked us gently, his foot tapping on the earthen floor.

"Nice ducks."

"I'm thinking of naming them. Besides, I don't want Mrs. Thompson to haunt me if I remove all of her beloved ducks."

"Oh, yeah?"

He pointed. "That one on the left? He's totally Mr. Quackers. And the one on the end? Yellowbelly. That's all I've got."

I laughed. "So this is why you wanted the house?"

"Think you might slip over at night after you tuck the boys in? We can come back here and rock, and you can tell me all of your troubles."

"Troubles?"

"As in problems, trials, tribulations, woe, grief, heartache."

"I know what it means, thankyouverymuch. What makes you think I have any of those things?"

"Because you're human. And I'm a good listener. And I always have a good bottle of wine to wash it down."

He placed his hand on the back of the swing, his fingers brushing the skin underneath my T-shirt. I wanted to wriggle away, but couldn't. I wondered if he touched me long enough if I could figure out why his touch felt so different than da Vinci's. "I suppose a late-night visit every once in awhile wouldn't be a bad thing."

"And you'll let my daughter play on your cul-de-sac?"

"Well, as long as she can keep up with my boys."

"Deal?" Cortland held out his hand for me to shake.

"Deal." When I stuck out my hand, he turned it and kissed my knuckle. "Okay. I should get back to the boys."

"Does that include da Vinci?"

"He's moved some things in."

Cortland nodded. "I guess I'll be seeing you both tomorrow, then."

I left, feeling lighter and heavier at the same time. I wanted to turn around and tell him I'd like to make him 35 Across and shop at the lighting store and walk on his concrete floor with my bare feet. But I kept it tucked inside, like a secret daydream.

***

I wiped the drool from my mouth and then my dissertation notes when I awoke to the sounds of a man singing, before it registered it wasn't a man singing at all, but *many* men singing. Joel's wall clock read 10:30 p.m. Da Vinci was late. *Again.*

Groggily, I roamed through the house, listening for the source of the singing and my heart sank when I saw the Scrabble board was still on the kitchen table, untouched. Damn da Vinci.

The singing continued. Whatever it was, they were at least in unison if not on key, but I couldn't make out the words. It sounded old-fashioned and muffled, nothing like you heard on the radio in this day and age. TV in the living room? Off. Clock radio by the bedside table? Silent. The singing got louder as I stepped into the foyer when the sight of candles flickering outside caught my attention. The singing was right outside my front door. My heart sped up. What in the world? Isn't it a little early for caroling?

Cautiously, I opened the door to find nearly fifty young men on my lawn surrounding da Vinci. I noticed they'd brought out the whole cul-de-sac: Gabriella and Jesús and Zoya and Donald all watched the scene. Even in the light of their front porches, I could tell they were amused. I waved to them, shrugging my shoulders in embarrassment. Was this some kind of pledge hazing?

In an instant, my boys were down by my side in their pajamas staring out at the serenading frat crowd.

Most girls I've met I'll soon forget,
They could never be true
'Cause for me there is only one
Who could stand for the Gold and Blue.
In my heart is a girl with a smile on her lips
Lovely to see, precious to me
With her eyes like the stars
And our rose in her hair
No one can quite compare.
When shadows try to hide us
Dreams will see us through
Tho' the years come and go,
She'll be loyal, I know,
She's the sweetheart of ATO.

Da Vinci towered above his brothers, handsome and proud, and I wanted to whisk him away from these boys who had taken up all of his time, yet who had welcomed him so openly to America and the mainstream. This wasn't about them, but about me. This wasn't a pledging haze at all, but a sweetheart serenade—something that was only supposed to happen to other girls: cute, young sorority girls, not middle-aged widows. Da Vinci stepped forward and handed me a red rose, kissing me on the lips while his frat brothers cheered him on and chanted, "ATO! ATO! ATO!"

William hugged my leg while da Vinci placed his fraternity pin over my poodle's rear of my flannel PJs. He kissed me again, while I began to cry—not because I was filled with joy, but because I wondered what planet I was on and how I ever landed here. Making love in the frat house had been one thing—a fantasy come true for a part-time linguist and full-time housewife—but *this?*

Da Vinci waved goodbye to his frat brothers as he lifted me into his arms and carried me into the house.

"Neat, huh?" William said. "Was that, like, the coolest thing in the world or what?"

"Put me down," I said, but da Vinci only held me tighter.

"Boys, back to bed," da Vinci said to them, and amazingly, they obeyed.

As they walked down the hall to their room, they high-fived, which was even stranger. "Da Vinci?" I asked as he threw me on the bed he had begun to refer to as "our bed" and began unbuttoning my poodle PJs. "What's going on here?"

He took off his shirt, revealing Adonis abs, and knelt over me as he trailed my abdomen with his tongue. "What does it look like? I'm going to ravage my American bride-to-be."

"Oh, my God." I grabbed for my pajama top, but he had already pulled off my pajama bottoms and began kissing my hips. "Da Vinci, we're *not* getting married. Can you stop that? It's very distracting."

"I know," he said, looking up at me. "That's the whole point."

"Yes, but about the marriage? You know we aren't ready for that."

"We've got time. We're young."

"Well, *you're* young, but that's not the point. Why are you doing this?"

Da Vinci lay his strong body over mine. "Because you're my Mona Lisa. I've been a terrible boyfriend. Spending so much time away for my studies and my fraternity brothers. And I realized something the other day when another woman kissed me."

"What?" I rolled him off of me.

"It was TLC night of pledge week."

My heart began to combust. "What do they do, bring in whores?"

Da Vinci was nonchalant. No big deal, kissing. "Just college girls. I don't want there to be secrets between us, so I must confess. Three girls kissed me and I kissed them back."

"Da Vinci! Was it some kind of orgy?"

"Orgy?"

"Group sex! How could you?"

"Just kissing, *tesoro*."

"Don't call me darling. I'm very angry with you. Mad. Upset. Hurt."

He held my hand. "I admit the pleasure of the body can take over, but I realized they were nothing compared to you. So I wanted to do something to show you how much you mean to me. You're the real thing, Mona Lisa."

We sat side by side in silence until we lay back, his head on my chest. Pleasure versus the real thing. Could it be possible to have both? I knew without a doubt that da Vinci was not the real thing. He was my romance-novel cover model, my sexual fantasy, my key to liberation from loneliness, but he wasn't even close to the real thing. "Leonardo, I don't think we want the same things."

"But I thought this would make you happy."

"I don't think you really love me. And it's not like you need citizenship just yet. You have a student visa."

Da Vinci raised his voice. "It's not about that. I feel safe with you."

"Safe isn't the same thing as love. Love is what you had with Chiara."

He rolled over onto his stomach, his brows furrowed. "Don't speak of Chiara. She is gone."

"She sent you a letter." I resisted adding, *a love letter.*

"I don't care."

"You don't want to read it? It sure smells nice."

"She broke my heart. When I told her I wanted to come to America and I wanted her to come with me, she refused. She is marrying my cousin."

"Why didn't you tell me about her? I would've understood."

"I didn't think the past mattered."

"You're talking to someone who's been living in the past. But you can't stay there, and you can't pretend it didn't happen, either. You learn from it and cherish it and build on it and try again. You're the one that showed me that it's okay to live again. To love again."

"But not love me? I can hope you'll change your mind."

"I love you, but not in the way you want me to. You are a magical, wonderful, beautiful man. You've shown me how to let joy in and be happy. I'll never forget what we've had. And I don't want to lose our friendship, either. And neither will the boys. They love you, too."

He squeezed my hand. "This is classic American break-up, no? The 'let's be friends' speech?"

"I'm sorry. I guess it is. I'm not very good at this. I really don't want to hurt you."

"But I'll miss you and Scrabble and footballing with Bradley. This is American dream."

The American dream. I'd thought you only get one of those, and that mine had died along with Joel. I hadn't thought I'd get a second chance or that I even deserved one, but maybe I did. Maybe I could dream a new dream. "Oh, da Vinci. You've always been a dreamer. Don't lose that, okay?"

Defeated, he got up from the bed, put his T-shirt back on and left to sleep in the studio, his head hung low.

As I watched him leave I thought to myself, what kind of a heartless asshole breaks up with her lover on a holiday?

Chapter 22

"I CAN'T BELIEVE THIS is happening to me! Me of all people," my sister cried as she entered the house with Zoe tagging behind her in an orange-and-brown bow that threatened to capsize her head.

After wiping my hands on my apron, I kissed Zoe and sent her to the boys' room to play. "What's going on? It's not even 10 o'clock yet."

Rachel plopped on the kitchen chair, her face streaked with mascara. "How would I know what time it is? I haven't slept yet."

I pulled up a seat next to her. She must've found out. "I'm so sorry, Rachel. We can get through this."

Rachel blew her nose. "It's not that easy, Ramona. You of all people should know how much it hurts to lose someone that you love."

I curled my chest over the table. "Of course. So you're hurt because …"

"Because he's in love with someone else!"

"Cortland's in love with someone else?"

"Cortland? No! I broke up with him yesterday after I dropped by to see the dump he's moving into! It's not even in a good neighborhood."

"Rachel, this is *my* neighborhood. And it *is* a good neighborhood."

"Oh, I know, sweetie. I don't mean anything by it. It's just, we're obviously so wrong for each other, and he must have something wrong with his *down there* not to want to have sex with me. Who in this day and age waits to be serious to make love?"

I shook my head, confused. "So who are you talking about, then?"

"Michael, of course! He dropped off Zoe last night and said he wanted to tell me that he's been seeing someone."

"Oh, no."

"Oh, yes. And not only that, he's in love with her and is going to propose!" Rachel began wailing again and pounding the table. "How could this be happening to me?"

Trying to suppress a smile, I rubbed her back, comforting her. "But Rach, honey, I thought you hated Michael. The whole world thinks you hate Michael. Isn't he a big part of your seminar? You call him 'Dog Man,' remember?"

"I know what I said. But I just wanted to make him suffer and be miserable without me for awhile, and then I'd take him back and incorporate the power of forgiveness into my speech. Zoe needs to be with her father."

"Got it. Well, life has a funny way of working out for the best."

"You plucked that one straight from Mom's phrase book. It doesn't sound like you talking."

"Well, I'm starting to believe it."

"Who could possibly want to marry that man?"

"Besides you, you mean?"

"She's probably some young tramp legal assistant. Or a bartender. They always go for the young, hot bartenders. Not that they have anything on me."

"You mean, he didn't tell you who he was seeing?"

"I kicked him out. I don't want to know. I'll meet her soon enough, I suppose. Oh, God. Do you think he'll invite me to the wedding?"

"Have you considered that he might be dating a very nice person? Mature, even?"

"Please. I'm not an idiot. I'm going to go take two Tylenol and see if I can sleep for a few hours before dinner. Sorry I can't help."

I had slumped over and considered calling the whole thing off when the doorbell rang. The Evangamoms had arrived early, as usual, and I didn't even feel guilty that the house was still a mess. My mothers would go into turbo-drive and have the whole place in tip-top shape before the dinner bell clanged.

"Aren't you a sight for sore eyes," my mother said as she gave me the up–down, pleased at my selection of a warm gold dress. My father kissed me hello and handed me a bouquet of fall flowers for the table. Judith air-kissed me and breathed, "Oh, my," upon seeing the scattered toys and general clutter in the house. The boys had cleaned up without my even asking, another sign that something strange was going on, but I had to give my mothers *something* to do, so I tossed a few balls and robots and action figures around the place for good measure.

"Barb, it's time to roll up our sleeves."

"When isn't it, dear?"

"What would she ever do without us?"

And I'd actually wondered that myself, but my mothers needed to be needed, so I couldn't get well too quickly.

Two hours later, the house was clean, the table set, and the food ready to be gobbled up, minus a couple of key figures. After a half-hour of trying, my mother coaxed Rachel out of my bed, into the shower, and down to the table, hair wet and sans makeup. A very pregnant Zoya arrived wearing a sexy, red fitted dress with a plunging neckline that revealed most of her swollen bosom, and Donald couldn't keep his eyes off of it. It took all of my dad's strength not to stare, too.

I asked William to fetch da Vinci for dinner, but he returned with a red face wet with tears, fogging up his glasses. The rest of us were already seated at the table, including Joel's framed photo on his plate in his usual seat—Judith's idea. We did it every Thanksgiving, Christmas and Easter. I'm not sure what Joel thought of his symbolic inclusion, but I could feel his energy making a sarcastic remark about it.

"What in Heavens?" my mother said, scooting her chair back.

"Thanksgiving isn't an Italian holiday," Judith said, as if that explained everything.

William glared at me. "It's all *your* fault!" He pointed an accusing finger. "Da Vinci's not coming to dinner because of *you*!"

"This is juicy," Rachel said, taking a gulp of her wine. "Do tell."

Williams' tiny shoulders shook. "All we wanted was for you to be happy again, and you had to go and ruin it! Tell him you're sorry!"

I hugged my son, but he wriggled away. "Honey, I'm sorry. It's a grown-up thing."

"Tell me what we can do to make you love da Vinci." He looked at his older brother, who was slumped in his seat. "It didn't work, Bradley."

"What do you mean, sweetie? Bradley, what's he talking about?"

Bradley mumbled. "It was William's idea. To get da Vinci to fall in love with you."

The dinner guests moaned an "awww," and I could feel my hair stand on end.

"*What?*" I looked at both boys and saw the shame on their faces. "Tell me exactly what you did."

William continued to cry. "I told da Vinci that you liked him and that he should take you to the vineyard. And then I told him he should tell you he loved you, and I moved his things into Daddy's closet."

"You *what?*" Judith asked.

"You *what?*" I asked, gripping his little arm. "Why would you do all that?"

"We could tell that when he was around, you weren't so sad anymore, so we thought if you fell in love and married him that we could have a whole family again."

"Honey, da Vinci and I do care for each other. I still like him, but we're not going to get married."

"But you're pinned now!" He stomped his foot.

"You're *what?*" Rachel asked. "As in, *fraternity* pin?"

"That's absurd," Judith said, with a laugh.

I shot them all a warning glance to stay out of it. "So the pin was your idea, too?"

Bradley pointed to his brother, and William bobbed his head. "I thought you would think it was romantic. A pin is a promise."

Judith and Barbara had tears in their eyes. "Come here, you." I opened my arms, and William walked into them. "And you, too, bud," I said to Bradley, and he joined us. I was too amazed at their compassion to be mad at them. "Even though da Vinci won't be around here as much anymore, he still wants to be your friends, okay?"

"But will you still be happy?" William asked.

"Yes, baby. Mommy is getting happier by the day. Don't I look happy?" I flashed him a big and surprisingly genuine smile. The world was a big, messed-up place, but I was happy. My joy jar was filling up with each passing hour.

William's tiny shoulders lifted. "I guess so. But I can see Oprah's point about the makeup."

My moms laughed. "Well, she is one smart cookie."

Judith took another sip of wine. "I propose a toast, then. To makeup and joy, however we find it," she said.

"I'll toast to the joy part," my father said.

Rachel reluctantly joined in. We toasted and I drank the wine, relishing the plum aftertaste, remembering that da Vinci had picked out the bottle at the vineyard, saying we should drink it on a special occasion. I had so much to be thankful for, including the awakening brought on by his arrival into my classroom and my life.

My father stood to cut the turkey. "Let's eat this bird before he catches a cold."

I kissed my sons on the cheek. After we had begun eating, the clank of silverware and china, a familiar symphony of family togetherness, was when the doorbell rang again. I tried not to think about the ramifications of my son's confession. What did it matter now? If da Vinci had been nudged along by tiny cupids, he hadn't gone kicking and screaming. He was a willing partner. Did I mind that he may have said a few things or done a few things in the name of keeping me on the hook a while longer? It wasn't as if he *used* me, exactly. In fact, I had used him just as much. We had leaned on each other, propped each other up, fledglings now ready to fly on our own.

The doorbell rang again, and I excused myself to answer it. Cortland stood on the porch with a pumpkin pie in his hands. I stepped outside and shut the door behind me.

"It's my mom's. It's not homemade, but don't tell your mother. She's got a rep to keep."

"I'm sure it's delicious. But now's not a good time. Rachel's upset and da Vinci won't come for dinner and William's mad at me."

"What would Thanksgiving be without a little dysfunction? At least your Uncle Louie didn't throw up on the new Persian rug."

Cortland had a way of putting everything in perspective.

"Well, I can just come back later, then."

Barbara came up behind me. "What's taking so long? Cortland! I'm so glad you could make it. Do come in."

"Mom, I was just telling him that we got a late start."

"Oh, we've got room." She led him by the hand, and when Cortland saw Joel's picture on the plate at the only empty seat, he backed away. "I'll just go grab a chair from the kitchen."

I held my breath. The crowd looked at me and then Judith, who stood and plucked the frame from the plate. "It's fine, darling. Joel wouldn't mind. In fact, I'm quite sure he would've liked you. Don't you agree, Ramona?"

Cortland held my gaze. I nodded, and he took Joel's seat. Rachel stuck her nose up in the air. I considered pulling my mother aside to tell her Rachel and Cortland had broken up, but thought it might make an even bigger scene.

While Noble and Cortland talked golf and Judith tried to convince Zoya to visit Life Church that weekend, I noticed a familiar car pulling up in front of the house.

"Daddy!" Zoe squealed.

Rachel peered outside and slammed her fist on the table, rattling the china. "Wait a minute. Is that someone in the car with him? It is! It's a woman." She threw down her napkin and shot up from her chair.

I opened the curtain and saw Anh slinking in the front seat and Michael trying to convince her to get out. This wouldn't end well.

"We'll make room," Noble said cheerfully. "The more the merrier, right, dear?"

"We'll do no such thing," Rachel said, following her daughter out the door.

Anh was resting against the passenger door and Vi was still in her carseat in the back when I reached them.

Zoe rushed to hug her father, and Rachel stopped in her tracks on the sidewalk. "*You!*"

Anh glanced up sheepishly and fingered a wave to Rachel. Michael beamed, oblivious to his ex-wife's reaction. "Great. Everybody's here. But I guess introductions aren't necessary."

Rachel spun on her heel and glared at me. "You knew all along, didn't you? Your best friend was sleeping with my husband and you didn't have the decency to tell me about it. What kind of sister are you?"

Michael took Anh's hand and stared at his ex-wife. "Would it kill you to be happy for me?"

Rachel stuck her nose into the air. "Be nice! Ha! You'll be sorry you ever crossed me! And don't even think about asking me back! I wouldn't take you back if you were the last human on earth!"

Michael smirked. "I don't think that will be a problem. Come on, let's not ruin a perfectly good holiday."

"*Good?* What do *I* have to be thankful for? A jackass husband and a lying, conniving sister who keeps secrets behind my back? Yes, Happy Thanksgiving, indeed! While you're busy ruining my life, is there anything else I should know about?" Rachel stared at me, then Cortland, and back again.

Cortland began to raise his hand, when I slapped it down. "No, I think that will do it for today."

Rachel stomped back into the house. Anh got Vi out of the car seat while Michael began walking up the steps with his daughter. I stayed back and waited for Anh. "For some reason, I thought she'd take the news better."

Anh walked in stride beside me. "Kill me now," she muttered.

Cortland grabbed my fingers, pulling me back so we were the last in line to reach the front porch. "So Rachel broke up with me last night, just before I got the chance."

"So I heard."

"So have you told her you'd like to start seeing me?"

"I don't know if I'd like to start seeing you. Are all doctors this presumptuous, or is it just you?"

He put his hand on my waist, and his forearm next to my head, pushing me back against the brick of the house. "Well, I think you should know our duck house passed inspection. With flying feathers, you might say. I close tomorrow."

"Tomorrow? That's awfully soon, isn't it?"

"When you know what you want, why wait?"

"I suppose I could bake you some cookies as a housewarming gift. To welcome you to the neighborhood and all."

"Cookies? I had something else in mind."

"My father always said patience was a virtue."

"British origin, right? The capacity to accept or tolerate delay, trouble or suffering without getting angry or upset. Yeah, I pretty much suck at that."

"What are you, some kind of walking dictionary?"

"No, but I'm pretty good at defining what I want. Getting it is the tough part."

Our eyes lingered, and I touched his cheek as he leaned in closer. "We better get inside," I said, my hand pressed against his chest.

Cortland stepped back. "I'm going to take off. I've got Lindsey for the weekend. She's going to help me move in."

"Okay, then. I'll see you around."

Cortland began walking down the sidewalk, when he turned back. "You know when you said that I put people to sleep for a living?"

"I recall something of the sort."

"Well, just remember that I wake them up, too."

I walked up the steps and we hugged. "Look out there, Ramona. Take a good, long look."

My eyes moved from one end of the auditorium to the other, empty seats except for one sad sap who hadn't even woken up after class was dismissed. "Don't tell me. You bored him to death?"

"*Muy gracioso, señora.* Very funny."

"What am I looking at?"

Doc inhaled and made a sweeping gesture with his arm. "Your future. When I retire next spring, we'll need a new Word Doc in town. I've already spoken to the dean."

"But I've never taught in a college setting."

He tucked my dissertation in his ratty leather briefcase, the same one he'd had when I was his student seventeen years earlier. "Rubbish. I've spoken to Panchal. We've run the numbers. Did you know that you've taught seven hundred immigrants how to speak English?"

I brushed it off. "Well, that's my job."

Doc led me down the stairs and poked at the sleeping student, who wiped drool from his mouth and scurried off like a mouse running from a cat. Doc slung his worn leather strap over his shoulder. "We both know it's more than a job and you've done more than just teaching them to speak English. You've given them the sword."

I followed Doc down the halls of the English building, recalling the first time I learned Doc's Way of the Sword. "Sword" is an anagram for "words." He liked the swashbuckling analogy of the sword with language; that it is only through effective communication and comprehension that the world can prosper. Doc claims that it is miscommunication that leads to poverty, war, and death.

We stopped in front of a row of photos of the deans of the university. He himself was a dean in the '70s before he went into semi-retirement, but how can one ever retire from words? Words are life. He put his hand next to the photo of the current dean, Dr. Sanford

Theodore Irvin, the first black dean of the college. "What do you see here?" He motioned with his case down the long row of deans.

"A bunch of men with bad hair." I smiled at my power to rankle the old prof.

He pounded his wrinkled hand on the empty space. "No," he bellowed. "You're looking at your future."

I raised my brows. "*I'm* going to be the next dean of the College of Arts and Sciences?"

Doc nodded once. "Well, I'm no psychic, but plan on twelve years from now. God willing, I'll still be alive to see it."

Ten minutes later, I was sitting in my black station wagon in front of the ATO house watching a slew of frats wrap Christmas decorations on the Roman columns of the porch. Da Vinci had been gone for two weeks. I missed him most at night, when he would climb next to me and wrap his warm leg over mine and pat my behind and rub my back, waking me to make love. And in the morning, when he would make the boys and me omelettes and toss the *New York Times* crossword to me with not one square filled in. And after school when he would go with me to cheer on Bradley at soccer practice or play chess with William and lose miserably.

I'd missed his birthday, too. Twenty-six and life to go. Taking a deep breath, I grabbed for my purse in the passenger seat, noticing that one of Anh's da Vinci books I planned to return later that day had fallen to the floorboard. There she was: Mona Lisa, smiling up at me, and I couldn't help smiling back.

The mystery of Mona Lisa's smile was one of the reasons people throughout history had been so fascinated with the painting. Da Vinci himself had been rumored to carry the painting around with him everywhere he went. Five hundred years later, Mona Lisa was still an enigma. Depending on which scholars you believed, she was either the wife of a Florentine tailor, named Monna Lisa, though the painting was named well after da Vinci's death, or the juicier choice was that the woman was Isabella of Aragon, part of the famous Sforza family. The juicy part? That da Vinci was her second husband. If the second rumor was true, then her alluring smile made perfect sense to me. Making love to da Vinci can most definitely put a smile on your face.

And why would da Vinci need to doodle her name in his notebooks if he could carry her painting with him? Always by his side.

I like to think that Mona Lisa could be any woman. Every woman. Whether her veil was to commemorate the recent birth of a child, as was the custom then, or that she was deep into the second phase of mourning the death of a close relative, Mona Lisa was undoubtedly expressing contentment with her place in the universe. Her smile seems to say: *I am who I am and come hell or high water, you can't take that away from me.*

I peered into the rearview and curled my lips into the Mona Lisa smile. The same, exact one. This much I know: when you can feel it, you can smile it.

As I bent to retrieve the Mona Lisa book and return it to the stack, a notebook jutted out from underneath the seat. I caught my breath. *The notebook.* He must be going crazy without it. I plucked it from the floorboard and opened it, half-guilty for peeking at something that could be a man's diary, but after all we'd gone through, I figured I deserved one little look.

I opened it, expecting to find the sketches and musings he'd written there from his journey across land and sea, how he'd tried to love me, only to lose me, but finding a good life despite the odds.

Instead I found pages upon pages of this ...

Brkfst. Omelette w/extra cheese plus dry toast—800 cals
Lunch. Double turkey sandwich. w/chips plus brownie—1,125 cals
And this ...

Monday—
Jog 4 miles
200 crunches

50 push ups

Make love

I laughed out loud. Da Vinci hadn't been keeping a private journal at all, but a diet and exercise journal. He was even more obsessed than my sister. Was making love to me nothing more than a good way to burn more calories at the end of the day? I gathered the nerve to get out of the car, tucked his journal underneath my arm and made my way through the college men, recognizing Pickler and T-Bone.

Figuring I should check in versus sneak in as I'd done before, I stepped in to the small office where a tiny desk and two chairs sat, and a small window through which I could see the guys decorating the front porch. I made my way around the desk, looking at the pile of papers of financials and frat business with notes in the margins. I sat in the swivel chair and saw a picture of me and da Vinci with the boys from Halloween taped to the computer screen. I winced. What were his things doing in the house mom's office?

I opened the middle drawer to find the usual office accoutrements: pens, paper clips, pennies, and a pledge pin like the one da Vinci had pinned on my poodle pajamas just weeks before. Could it be his?

The larger right-hand drawer contained a dozen notebooks just like the one I'd found in the car. How could anyone keep so many notebooks of calories burned and consumed?

Grabbing the one on the top of the stack, I opened it, expecting more of the same chicken scratches of food and fitness. Instead, I found elegant prose written partially in English, partially in Italian.

I flipped several pages, searching for my name. When I found it, my body became very still. *Why do I fear that Ramona does not feel the same for me as I do for her? Why does she look at me like schoolboy who needs teacher? Why do I fear if she knows I know English better than I have let on that she will dump me? How can I make her know how deep my feelings are for her? I wonder most of all if love can be lost in translation.*

"Mona Lisa." His voice was reprimanding, but not cold. He seemed more shocked to be seeing me there than I had been finding the journal.

"Hello, da Vinci. Leonardo." I stood and he hesitated, as if not sure how to approach me. A handshake? A hug?

He air-kissed my cheeks. "It's good to see you. You look well. No, better than that. Ravishing."

I could feel myself blush. "You, too. I found this in the car." I handed him the notebook I'd brought in.

Da Vinci opened it then tossed it on his desk. "You must think I'm shallow to keep a notebook of such things."

I studied his features like one might a favorite painting in a museum. He grew more beautiful every time you laid eyes on him. "I think writing things down for posterity is a very good thing." I gently closed the drawer door with my thigh so he couldn't see I'd found the others.

Crossing one leg over the other, he leaned against the wall. "I am no longer a frat boy. I am, as they say, house dad. You must be twenty-six to apply."

"I hope you had a happy birthday."

"I did. Thank you."

"So you like it here, then?"

"In charge of these crazy Americans. This way I get free room and board and some spending money and can still watch over them. And the work is never tedious."

I stepped out from the desk, proud of his English. Most frat guys wouldn't use the word 'tedious'. "You care about them, don't you?"

"Everybody needs somebody to look out for them. Like you did for me."

I could feel the tears wet my cheeks. "I'm sorry, da Vinci. I'm just crying because I'm so happy for you. I mean, look at you. You made it."

He reached out for my hand. "And look at you. You seem happy. Truly happy."

"I am. I'm glad things worked out for you here. If you need some place to go for Christmas, I'm sure the boys would like to see you."

Da Vinci tucked his longer hair behind his ears. It seemed like ages ago that I had done the very thing for him. Like another life. I resisted telling him he could use a haircut.

"I miss William and Bradley. But Chiara is coming for the holiday. I was wrong to believe that distance would make me love her any less." He pointed to his chest. "Even though I couldn't see her, she was right here all along."

Chapter 24

ANH PLOPPED HER KEYS on the kitchen counter and Vi on my lap. She paced back and forth, and I'd been friends long enough to know not to push her. Finally, she leaned on the kitchen counter and looked me squarely in the eye.

"Who have I become? Really? Because what I'm feeling inside doesn't match who I've always thought I was."

"Am I really supposed to answer that?'

"Vi's mother wants her back."

I held Vi closer. "And you don't want to give her back."

"Is that not the damndest thing? I've been complaining practically since Vi's birth that I don't want to raise her and how I want her parents to be more involved, and when they finally wake up and want her, I can't give her up." Anh's face screwed into a cry. "I *can't*. She's mine. I never wanted to believe it, but she's my baby. She calls me 'Mom,' which is a helluva lot better than 'Grandma,' by the way, and I know I can give her a good life."

"Of course you can. So you'll fight for her. You'll fight for what you want."

"And in the midst of my breakdown, what does my American boyfriend do?"

"Proposes to you."

"How did you know? So much for an anti-climactic moment."

"I've been waiting for you to tell me. He told Rachel before Thanksgiving he was going to."

"And you kept this from me *why*?"

"I wouldn't want to ruin your surprise. It's not often a woman gets proposed to. Wait a minute. I forgot who I'm talking to. So where's the ring?"

"Ring? Ring? I didn't say yes! But saying no felt like lying. Which is why I came here to ask my PhD friend who just did a damn dissertation on love why I wish I would've said yes."

"Because you love him."

Anh made a face and went to the pantry to retrieve food—probably junk food, the stuff that I rarely ate anymore. She turned around, her mouth dropped open. "Ohmigod. You finally got rid of the peanut butter."

"I did. It was time."

"Good for you." She motioned to the Christmas tree in the living room. "And you decorated this year."

"The boys helped."

"Still."

"Still. I know. And as for you …"

"I should say yes."

"Fourth time's a charm."

"I thought it was the third time? That was my most disastrous marriage yet. Where does that saying come from?"

"America. No one knows exactly, but the precursor to it was Elizabeth Barrett Browning, who in a letter in 1839 said, 'The luck of the third adventure' is proverbial. Then it was spotted in 1912 in a snooty newspaper report about a mature woman getting married for the third time."

"Women are such optimists. Talk about your American perseverance."

"We push on. As for love, it's worth the chance, I think."

"Are we talking about me now, or you?"

"You. Of course. Though I might heed some of the advice."

Anh grabbed a fistful of Cheetos. Okay, I hadn't gotten rid of the junk food *completely*. "I'm sure the duck house looks splendid this time of year."

***

The invitation arrived in the mail the next day, a silver envelope with a crisp white card inside with silver foil lettering.

> *You are cordially invited to a Christmas Party at the home*
> *of Cortland Andrews on Friday, December 23rd at 7 p.m.*

I traced my fingers over the lettering. I'd only seen him twice in the last month, our schedules for coming and going out of sync, which was for the best. Every day I thought of him—every hour, though I wouldn't admit it—and I had so much I wanted to tell him but ended up calling up someone else instead to share the news. But instead of feeling satisfied, the things piled up inside of me: that I had accepted the job at UT to teach three days a week in the liberal arts program, that William had won the local chess tournament, that I had now organized every drawer and closet in the entire house and the boys were miraculously keeping their rooms clean.

The little things, too, things that only Cortland might appreciate: that I'd completed the *New York Times* crossword in record time the day before, that I'd seen four ducks walking in front of his house last week on their way to a local pond, and they had stopped and looked at his house as if they knew they were welcome there.

The invitation did not ask for an RSVP, so I decided I would just drop by. He had probably invited all the neighbors, though many would already be out of town visiting relatives, and it would be rude not to wish him happy holidays in his first Christmas in his home.

More than ever, I felt Joel's presence in our home. As I removed the clutter, peace fell over me, the anxiety washed away. I missed him all the same, but as Deacon Friar had suggested, I felt Joel in my heart instead of pushing him out. Thinking of him had transitioned from hurt to comfort.

This would be my first Christmas After with *la vita allegra*. I'd baked Joel's favorite Christmas foods—banana nut bread and peanut butter cookies—and doled them out to the neighbors. I had taken the boys to the ATO house to deliver four dozen cookies to da Vinci to share with his guys, and another three dozen to the Panchal Center. I had saved one loaf back to take to Cortland's party.

Judith and Barbara took the boys to a Christmas party at Life so I could go to Cortland's party alone. I walked across the street at 7:05 p.m., not wanting to be the first one there, but no other cars were in the driveway. As I rang the doorbell, I heard Christmas music coming from the inside—the classics, Frank Sinatra. I wondered if the other neighbors had done as I had and simply walked over, though there were no other footprints on the snowy sidewalk.

Cortland answered the door, wearing a red sweater and pressed slacks, handsomely festive. He took the banana bread I offered him. "You came," he said as if he couldn't believe it.

"Merry Christmas."

"Merry Christmas. Oh, come in. Let me show you around."

"Wow." The place was completely transformed. New tile, new paint, new granite and stainless steel kitchen, just as he'd described. I admired his vision for change. "It's all so different."

"You like it?"

"Like it? I love it. Wait 'til all the other neighbors get here. They'll be jealous."

He took my coat and hung it in the entry closet. I followed him to the kitchen and sat on the black bar stool and noticed two martini glasses on the counter. Two and not ten, twenty?

"Can I pour you a Christmastini?"

"A what-ey?"

"It's pomegranate juice. Nice holiday drink. Pretty tasty, too. And full of antioxidants."

"And vodka, I presume."

"Well, that, too."

"One can't hurt."

He shook the martini mixer and poured me a glass, the rich, red liquid filling it temptingly. "So congratulations on your new post at the university, *Dr.* Griffen."

"How did you know? Wait a minute. Noble, Judith, my mom. You probably know everything that's been going on with me. And I had so much to tell you." I caught myself, too revealing.

"I'd much rather hear it from the horse's mouth. Not that you're a horse, of course."

I drank one, two, three Christmastinis and told him everything that had been bottled up inside of me, beginning with the mundane and getting more and more personal, about how I broke up with da Vinci the night before Thanksgiving and how I'd found his journals and how the boys had wanted to play matchmaker to make me happy again.

We moved from the kitchen to the living room on the plush leather couches and Dean Martin sang to us as we ate the appetizers that seemed like an awful lot of food for two people. I'd been enjoying the party so much I hadn't noticed the time, or that no one else had joined us.

"Where are the people?" I asked.

Cortland looked around. "What people?"

"The party people. Where is everyone you invited to your party?"

"They're all here."

"They're all … wait a minute. You threw a party and invited one person?"

"That's right."

"So it's not a party at all, but more like a date."

Cortland shook his head, playing innocent. "Nope. This has all the ingredients for a party: music, food, drinks. I think even you can't refute that this is a party."

"A party of two."

"Does it really matter what we call it?"

"Of course it matters. Terminology matters very much."

"Well, I, for one, think whatever it is we're doing here is going pretty well." He leaned closer, then noticed the snow falling outside. "Thank you, Jesus." Cortland bounced off the seat.

"Did you just thank the Lord for the snow?"

"Yep. It's the one party ingredient I couldn't pick up at the store. I needed it to snow so I could show you this." He grabbed my hand and led me outside, down the path, the snowflakes tickling our faces as we walked hand in hand to the swing. He'd placed little red scarves on the duck statues in the garden.

"Nice touch," I had to admit.

We held hands and swung back and forth, watching the flakes fall onto the trees, the oak, the evergreen, the tops of the ducks' heads. I rested my head on his shoulder. "You do know how to throw a good party," I said finally.

"If you like this, just wait and see what I'm like on a date."

"Dating is for the birds. I feel too old to date."

"We could probably find a word you liked better. Mating?"

I turned up my nose. "Eww. No."

"I've always liked the word 'rendezvous.' It's fun to say: *ron-daaaaaayvooooo.*"

"I suppose we could rendezvous, though I'll need clarification on your definition."

"Why don't we make it up as we go along?"

He leaned in again to kiss me, and I backed away. "I make it a habit not to kiss on my first party. And I better get back and finish wrapping some gifts for the boys."

Cortland snapped his fingers. "I'm glad you reminded me. I have a gift for you. Nope. Scratch that. It's not a gift at all, but a party favor."

Back inside, he grabbed my present from under the white vintage Christmas tree and handed it to me, wrapped in pages from the *New York Times* crossword. All puzzles he had completed, no less. I may have met my match in more ways than one.

Inside the box lay oversized Scrabble pieces, 8-inch squares, nine pieces total. I lay them out on the carpet: F, R, O, A, D, R, E, K, W. Within a few seconds, I had assembled them in order: WORD FREAK.

"For your new office," he said.

"I love it. It's the nicest party favor I've ever received." I kissed him on the cheek, tempted to kiss him through the night, but it felt good to show restraint, to take things slowly. "Thank you."

"Thanks for coming. It wouldn't have been much of a party without you."

"You can say that again."

"It wouldn't have been much of a party without you."

***

Some traditions remain the same After, and some die along with the deceased. While so many couples and young families struggle to please everyone at Christmas, Joel and I had set the stage early on that Christmas Eve was our private holiday. We would go where we wanted to go and do what we wanted to do. When the boys came along, our parents complained they wanted to see us Christmas Eve, but we insisted Christmas Eve be our day. We tried different things on Christmas Eve, ice skating at a local ice rink (too cold), visiting friends who didn't have relatives in town (too exhausting), until we finally settled into the tradition of attending Jesús and Gabriella's church for holiday mass, followed by Panchal's annual holiday dinner (celebrating multiple religions in one), kettle popcorn, and a game of holiday Scrabble.

As we walked out of the church on Christmas Eve with "Joy to the World" on our lips and in our hearts, I spotted Deacon Friar near the fountain. I had tucked the pennies he'd given me in my pocket and gave the boys each one to make a wish.

"Do you think it's too late to wish for something for Santa to bring you since his elves have probably already loaded up the sleigh?" William asked his big brother.

Bradley no longer believed in Santa Claus, but kept up the charade for his brother. "I'd wish on something else," Bradley said. "Mom, do you think a wish is more powerful if it's at church?"

"I think a wish is as powerful as the intent of the wisher."

Bradley paused, considering it and nodded. "Okay. So wish hard, then."

Deacon Friar saw us and joined us at the fountain. "I see you've put your lucky pennies to good use," he said as we watched the boys close their eyes and toss their coins into the water.

"I didn't need them," I said. "It turns out my wishes had been granted all along."

Deacon Friar folded his arms and motioned to the remaining coin in my hand. "What's that one for, then?"

I shrugged. "Insurance."

The Panchal Center was alive with the sounds of broken English and the warmth of dozens of hearts filled with gratitude. I wondered what had become of Maria and her new baby—if, like Mary and her baby Jesus, they had found a safe haven. Panchal was such a place, and I knew I could never leave this home away from home. I would teach there until I could no longer form words at all. Panchal and Dr. Roberts were both right. It was about more than teaching a language; it was about succeeding in life. I could never abandon the hundreds of immigrants that would need the sword to find their way, the torch of knowledge to guide their path. Three days at UT, one day at Panchal's and three days for home. I would be busy, engaged, plugged in like never before. Happy, even.

Da Vinci found us, his arm wrapped around his Italian beauty with luscious curves Americans would consider plus sized. I was amazed at how much I'd grown. I wasn't jealous of her at all. I was happy for them. They clearly belonged together.

After the dinner, Bradley stood on a chair and popped the kettle corn in the microwave while William set out the Scrabble board. "Too bad we don't have four players," he said, and Bradley looked at his brother and then at me, as if this would hurt my feelings.

"I didn't mean …" William said.

"It's okay, son. You're right. Scrabble is more fun with four players. Maybe we should invite someone to come play with us."

"But who?" The boys asked at the same time.

Fifteen minutes later William explained the rules of the game to Cortland, who had been reading at home when we'd called him. He wouldn't have his daughter until the next morning, and was thrilled at the invitation. "Every word you spell must be a holiday word," William said seriously. "It can be a person, place or thing, but it must have to do with winter or holidays, period. Daddy used to like to bend the rules, but now that Bradley and I are big enough, we don't need to do that, so don't try any funny stuff."

"Gotcha," Cortland said, setting up his Scrabble pieces. "No funny stuff."

I smiled at how at ease Cortland was with the boys, how at home it all seemed, how grown up and real. Like a real thing relationship. I don't know what you called it. Certainly not dating, but certainly more than friends because of the chemistry. Perhaps it was just a relationship, pure and simple, and how that relationship would evolve would depend on us.

The game went on:

William: SLEIGH, 12 points

Bradley: SANTA, 8 points

Me: NOEL, 6 points

Cortland: LOVE, 16 points

"I don't know about that one," Bradley said. "It's borderline."

"Not exactly holiday," William considered. "But God gave us Jesus at Christmas because he so loved the world."

"And you buy gifts for people you love," Bradley added.

"So the verdict is?"

"It's a keeper," I said to him and put my hand over his, feeling compelled to touch him whenever I could, brushing against him in the kitchen as we made hot chocolate, plucking a stray hair off his shoulder, high-fiving him on the twenty-point HANUKKAH.

Cortland stayed after to watch the boys open one gift each: a new science experiment kit for William and a sports Xbox game for Bradley—the gifts I knew Joel would've wanted to give them. They were gone as soon as the wrapping hit the floor.

"Thanks for a fun evening," Cortland said as we walked to the door. "Here I was starting to feel sorry for myself that I had to spend Christmas Eve alone."

"Trust me on this. It's not worth the effort. I spent the last two Christmases feeling sorry for myself, and it didn't do me any good."

"Well, I *was* right in the middle of a very good book. I can't wait to see what happens next."

"I'll let you get back to it then," I said, walking him out the door. I watched him walk down the sidewalk, his feet crunching in the snow, the feeling that my heart was stretching like a rubber band about to snap the farther away he got.

"Cortland!" He turned around, and I ran towards him and stopped inches from him. "I know what happens next."

I reached up and kissed him—a long soul kiss, a Christmas kiss for all seasons, one that I would remember for all time, the first of so many more to come. We stood there in the snow, the North Star blinking above us, children around the world tucked into bed, awaiting their own Christmas wishes to come true. I'd not given up, I'd given in. I'd taken a chance, moved on, opened up, accepted and believed.

My name is Ramona Elise Griffen. I am a 36-year-old widow, a linguist, someone who thought true love could only happen once in a lifetime. One soul mate per soul. How could I possibly define the indefinable? Far better to feel it. I've uncaged it to let it take over, its all-consuming power all around me, within me.

When I set it free, it came back to me.

The End

Acknowledgments

BIG THANKS TO MY family and friends for their love and support, especially my amazing husband and my kids Harrison, Audrey, and Owen for putting up with all of Mommy's computer time.

Much appreciation to my wonderful agent Natasha Kern for her input and belief in me and my writing. To my editor Deb Werksman and the whole team at Sourcebooks, thank you for inviting me into your fold and loving *da Vinci* as much as I do.

Warm regards to Doug Manning, a pre-eminent authority on grief, for his knowledge and passion for helping people during their grief journey.

Special thanks to Sharon Sala, author extraordinaire, and to the members of my OK RWA chapter and Chicklit Writers of the World online chapter, especially Jenny Gardiner. Writing doesn't feel so solitary with friends like you.

To all the da Vinci scholars both in print and online, I couldn't have done it without you.

Lastly I must thank the Renaissance man himself, Leonardo da Vinci. It was his genius and approach to life that inspired me to write this novel. Five hundred years may separate us, but you'll always be my mentor and kindred spirit.

About the Author

Malena Lott lives in Oklahoma with her husband and three children. After a bustling advertising career, Malena transitioned to brand consulting and writing novels, which she could do from home, in her PJs, chase around her toddler, and join the daily minivan parade at the elementary school. Visit www.malenalott.com.

Photo Credit: Rod Lott